I0732356

The Fan Society

Dasha Tryon Wallace

Dasha Writes
LLC

Dasha Writes LLC

Contents

To my sisters and cousins who helped me get this written.

Part I

All the major changes in my life started with a knock on the door. Three knocks, and three points, and if those knocks had never happened, I would not be where I am. Now whether those points were good or bad, I guess we shall see.

Lady Arabella Cooper;
Code name: Cinders
Excerpt from report 170

Chapter One

March 1819, Cooper Manor

The knock rang hollowly against the thick front door of Cooper Manor. In the darkness of the mansion, candlelight flickered in the window, and a very young footman shuffled to the door. With a yawn, he opened it, blinking at whoever would come calling this late. He was startled to find the night watch standing in front of him.

"Boy, go get the master of this household," the gruff watchman said. "There is something that he must hear." He shooed away the lad.

The boy squeaked and hurried to find Lord Cassius. Unnoticed by either of them, a small child slid down the stairs, dragging a blanket behind her and rubbing her eyes. Her curly brown frizz stuck out at odd angles as she came to see what the noise was. Seeing the man at the door, she crouched behind the banister as her father came to greet him.

"Night watch, sir," said the man, taking off his hat and holding it in front of him. "I regret to inform you that we found your carriage on the side of the road."

"My wife?" Lord Cassius inquired, his voice cracking with fear of what the answer might be.

"I'm sorry, sir. We looked everywhere for her, but she was nowhere to be found. If we do find information, we will let you know." The watchman stood silently as tears started flowing from the lord's face. He reached out as if to comfort Lord Cassius, but merely put his hat on and said, "I'm sorry. May God watch over you."

The watchman turned on his heel and left the sobbing man to his grief, the full moon making his form glow like the angel of death after leaving its victims behind.

Lord Cassius collapsed to the floor with his hand clutching his chest as he fought to regain his breathing. The small girl ran out to her father from her hiding place behind the banister.

"Daddy!" she cried, clutching her father, her tiny frame trembling.

Lord Cassius held her fiercely as the tears streaked down his face. With a whisper that only his daughter in his arms could hear, he whispered, "My dear Ella, what am I going to do?"

Chapter Two

May 1826, Cooper Manor

"You missed a spot, Ella."

Ella turned just in time to see her stepsister kick over the mop bucket. A wave of dirty water slid across the hardwood below her, splashing onto the front door.

"This is a big mess. You should hurry and clean it up. We have a guest coming today, and everything must be perfect," Audrey sneered.

Ella resisted the urge to argue with Audrey. Instead, she smiled up at her stepsister and said, "Yes, Sister."

Sniffing, Audrey flicked her fan in front of her face. "Just call me Audrey. I don't like being reminded that we're stepsisters, especially one that's as ugly as you."

Looking at Audrey's day dress, with its long, puffed sleeves and a green floral print, made Ella painfully aware of her own haggard appearance. She looked down at her plain black dress, which was now drenched with water, along with her worn hands stained brown from the work she'd done in the garden that morning. She pushed a lock of curly brown hair away from her face again. It was constantly escaping from the bun she'd tried to wrangle it into. In her fourteen years, she had never managed to get it under control. Her average looks and common blue eyes were vastly different from her stepsisters' delicate features.

"As you say, Audrey. May I get back to work? We have a guest coming shortly, and I wouldn't want them to slip on a puddle of water."

Audrey scoffed, snapped her fan shut, and sauntered off. Ella watched her sashay down the corridor. The dress's cinched waist and thick V neckline emphasized her glamorous figure. Tilting her head just right allowed the light from the morning to hit her silky blonde hair. The same blonde hair as Audrey's mother, Lady Victoria. Ella shuddered at the mere thought of her stepmother and returned to work, knowing that it would only cause more problems if she delayed any longer.

After cleaning up the sodden foyer, Ella stood and stretched. A growing ache had started between her shoulder blades from being hunched over all morning, and it was nice to be able to finally stand up. She placed her hands on her hips and rolled her neck.

"You're lucky it was me and not the housekeeper. She would have sent you to clean chamber pots for being lazy," teased a familiar voice.

Ella relaxed, a smile blooming on her face. "Clementine, what are you doing here? You should be helping in the kitchens. There is a guest to get ready for. And they will be needing your help."

Clementine was wearing the same black dress as Ella. They both wore the same white apron, though Ella's now had a slight brown tinge to it from the dirty water that had soaked through. Ella could only smile at her friend while she picked up the wooden bucket. Clementine made everything she wore beautiful. Clementine had brown hair like Ella, but unlike Ella's, her hair was silky, and her small, round face made her appear innocent and cute. Even though her clothes were as plain as all the rest of the servants, she used her expressions to charm everyone around her. And she also used this to her advantage, many times managing to wrangle out of duties she didn't want to do.

Clementine put on a meek face, her eyes lowering slightly and her hands wringing in front of her, and spoke in a pleading voice. "Cook. I'm so sorry, but I'm scared of breaking the dishes. The last time I pulled them out, I dropped one; the mistress was so mad. Is there any other way I can help? Can I be sent out of the kitchens? I don't mind being placed as a housemaid. Please Cook, can you talk to the housekeeper for me? I have already been trained on how to be a housemaid." Clementine dropped the pleading act and then continued. "Then he spoke to the housekeeper for me, and I was sent to be with the other housemaids."

Ella laughed, shaking her head. "You are so good at acting that maybe you should try theater. With your beautiful singing voice, you could be famous and travel the world."

Her friend tutted. "Then where would you be without me? I've been looking out for you for years, ever since your mother went missing. And who was there for you when your father remarried to that horrid woman? And who was by your side when he passed when you were seven? I could hardly leave you on your own."

"I'm sorry. You even stayed after your mother was sent away. I know you've also tried to get in my stepmother's good graces so that you can stay. And if she found out that you're still friends with me, I don't know what she would do to you."

Clementine placed a hand on Ella's shoulder. "Now, stop that. I don't want to hear any more of that from you. You are the indomitable Lady Arabella Cooper, daughter of Lady Nora and Lord Cassius. You were beating up the house guards since you were a kid and terrifying the maids by climbing trees. What happened to that child?"

Ella sighed. "I thought your name meant mild and merciful."

"That is what my mother wanted me to be, but it's not what I am. Now, go change out of these damp clothes and get ready. The guest should be arriving soon. If Lady Victoria sees you like this, she will torment you."

"She already torments me," Ella huffed, rolling her eyes at the mention of her stepmother's name. "Let's get going. It's best to not keep Stepmother waiting."

They hurried to the cellar where her room was. Lady Victoria had sent her here seven years ago, after the death of her father. From then on, she was treated like a servant in her own home. Her stepmother also changed anyone who was loyal to Ella's father. Only Clementine had managed to escape the purge on account of her being eleven and young enough to be "molded". That, and Clementine's gift for acting. And after everyone was let go, those who were put in wanted to stay on Lady Victoria's good side, which meant that Clementine had to act as if she hated Ella. She had to watch as Ella was given the hardest, dirtiest jobs that no one wanted. The housekeeper made sure of that. Ella shook her head to erase those thoughts and quickly changed into a new uniform while her friend gathered Ella's dirty clothes and dried the puddle where they had dripped on the floor.

Clementine stood and bumped her head on the room's low ceiling. She yelped, rubbing her head, and exclaiming, "I don't know how you can get anything done in here. It's so dark."

Ella finished adjusting her apron and looked around the dim room. After several years, she had gotten used to the small room with only a single candle to light it. Her stepmother did not want to "waste any more resources on her" than what she absolutely had to. The ceiling hung low, and now that she was older, it brushed the top of her head. Even though the tiny space was mostly in shadow, she knew the layout perfectly. In the far corner was a cot that she used for sleeping, a bucket in the opposite corner to relieve herself, and a single drawer that held all her clothes. On top of the drawer was a basin with water and a hairbrush. It was a downgrade from her vast room as a child.

She looked back at Clementine and shrugged. "I'm used to it by now. We should head back up. You also need to finish your chores. If anyone sees you. . ."

Clementine held up the dirty clothes. "I am doing my job."

Ella smiled and said, "You head on up first. It would be better to not remind them that we're friends."

Clementine nodded before disappearing up the stairs. Ella waited for a minute, then followed. She took a deep breath as she braced herself to see her stepmother. The thought of the mind games her stepmother would surely play today weighed heavily upon her. Preoccupied and dreading that thought, she was distracted. When she reached the top of the stairs, she failed to notice a foot that stuck out and tripped her. She landed hard on her knee. She gasped in pain as she struggled up to her feet. A sharp pain stabbed through her knee when she put weight on it, nearly causing her to fall again.

Ella spotted a figure in a muted green dress that turned down the hallway in front of her. The few servants who had witnessed the event that had been gathering laundry at the top of the stairs avoided her gaze. She sighed. *It was going to be one of those days*, she thought when she realized, unsurprised, at who had tripped her.

Euphemia was the youngest daughter of Lady Victoria and was much more intelligent than Audrey about how she bullied Ella. She worked with surprise and always attacked Ella at the worst possible moment. Euphemia, or Effie, as her family called her, looked very little like her mother. She was broader in the shoulders than what was considered becoming for a lady and had straight mouse-brown hair. Though, her cool blue eyes would have been very pretty if it wasn't for the cold and calculating gaze that was perpetually emblazoned across her face. Ella had been on the receiving end of that gaze more often than not.

Ella tried again to put weight on her leg, but decided against it and leaned against the wall. She gently touched her knee against the cool stone until the sharp pain turned to a dull throb. Then, placing most of her weight on her other leg, she hobbled down the hallway.

She slowed and opened a side door that led to the front foyer she had just cleaned. Lady Victoria stood in the center of the room. Complementing her like accessories in a picturesque scene stood her two daughters waiting for their guests to arrive. As soon as Ella stepped into the room, Lady Victoria flashed her eyes in her direction. A slow smile crept across Lady Victoria's face as she watched her limp across the room. Audrey fought a snicker. Ella gritted her teeth as the perpetrator's cold gaze watched not Ella's pain, but her family's reactions. Effie grinned when she saw her mother's proud smile. Ella could only hold her emotions back as she moved closer to the vile woman who had been tormenting her since her father's death.

Ella's stepmother was a stunning woman, with her luscious blonde hair pulled into an updo, two curls framing her heart-shaped face. Her full lips, sapphire blue eyes, and tiny waist had bewitched many men. She would flutter her eyes and pout, creating a picture of innocence. Despite her wiles, Ella had seen how the lady envied those who had a higher rank than she did. She would hide her expressions behind her fan as beautiful words dripped from her lips, but she always said it with a sneer. Ella would always have to walk a careful line when around her stepmother. Even though Ella was being treated as a maid, Ella still had more noble blood than Lady Victoria did. A detail that rankled Lady Victoria to no end.

Ella held her head high and tried to walk as normally as possible. When she approached her stepmother, she tried to curtsy, though her knee refused to bend properly, and it looked more like a stumble than curtsy.

"I see we still need to work on that bow," Lady Victoria commented. "For someone who was raised as a lady, it is always surprising how unladylike you are." Her eyebrows raised as the corner of her mouth curved into a smirk. "It shows that blood is not everything. I'm surprised that your mother allowed you to go untrained for so long. What a horrible mother."

Ella gritted her teeth. She knew Lady Victoria was trying to get a rise out of her, but she was unable to let it pass. "My mother was an amazing woman. She was beautiful and elegant, and was a member of top society. She was known to everyone as a philanthropist. Considering what you think about my blood, I'm surprised you married my father, who is also my blood."

Lady Victoria abruptly raised her hand and struck Ella across the face. Between the force of the blow and the pain in her knee, she fell to the floor. Pain blossomed at her hip where it struck the hardwood floor. Ella gingerly touched her swelling cheek and tasted the coppery blood where her teeth had cut the inside of her mouth. She glowered up at Lady Victoria.

Lady Victoria glared back, her lips flattened from the tightness in her jaw, her nose flaring. "How dare you say such things to me, child? It is obvious that you have yet to learn some decent manners. It seems that I need to train you better. But Madam Briar is arriving today, and I can't have you ruining it. You are banished to your room for a week, and your so-called 'friend' Clementine shall take care of all of your work as well as her own."

"But Stepmother, you can't punish her. She had nothing to do with my outburst!" Ella cried.

"My other methods of teaching you seem to have failed. It was a good thing I kept her. She has some use after all. Keeping you in line. Next time you speak out of turn, she will take your punishment."

Satisfaction shone in Lady Victoria's eyes as she dismissed Ella with a flippant wave. Lady Victoria ordered one of the footmen to drag Ella to her room. She kept her head down, knowing that she wouldn't find any pity on his face. His gloved hands yanked her to her feet and dragged her down to the cellar. As he pulled her along, Ella could only berate herself at the foolishness of antagonizing Lady Victoria. She knew that Lady Victoria would do anything to torment Ella, and she had walked right into her trap. As she limped behind the footman, Ella realized that her fear of Lady Victoria targeting Clementine had come to pass, and she had no one to blame but herself.

After nearly tripping down the stairs, she was shoved into her room. She fell to the floor once again, but instead of getting up, she lay there and watched as the door was shut behind her, and the lock clicked ominously shut.

Chapter Three

After a few hours, Ella's single candle burned out, leaving her in complete darkness. Her only light came once a day when they brought in her one daily meal, a plate of burned bread with cold leftovers, and replaced her chamber bucket. Ella ignored the uncomfortable situation. Instead, sitting in the dark gave Ella time to think. Things must change or else she would hurt the only person she considered family. When the week was over and she was finally released from her room, Ella had made her decision. She was going to keep her friend safe from Lady Victoria's attention the only way she could: by cutting all ties with her.

After her week of incarceration ended, she enacted her plan. Whenever Ella saw that Clementine was trying to find her, she found an excuse to be elsewhere. Pain lanced through her heart when she saw her friend's crestfallen expression, but the determination to not let her friend get caught up in her mess kept her from comforting her friend. The monotony of the job also helped to relieve her stress of avoiding her friend as she dove into her work. Even the taunts and abuse from her stepsisters did not deter her as she did her work at breakneck speed.

That ended one morning when her stepmother called for her.

As Ella stood outside the sitting room waiting to be admitted, she wondered what new torment Lady Victoria had devised for her. Though she was less nervous than usual because Clementine was safe as long as she followed orders. Anything that Lady Victoria could do to Ella would not compare to saving Clementine. A manservant finally opened the door, admitting her. Lady Victoria must have thought that Ella had waited for long enough. Ella entered the room, her head bowed, and curtsied to her stepmother.

"Hello, Stepmother. What can I do for you today?" Ella asked, keeping her voice controlled and calm.

"Look at me, child," Lady Victoria commanded.

Ella didn't need to look around the room to know that her stepmother made sure no one was in attendance. She would want no witnesses. Ella also didn't want to look at what had been done to the room. The room that was once simple yet elegant was now tainted by Victoria's gaudy tastes, just like the rest of the house. Every memory of her parents was erased by Lady Victoria. Rather than peering at the room and being reminded of her loss, she focused on her stepmother. Behind her fan, Ella saw her cheek raise, and she could easily imagine the smirk she hid. Lady Victoria looked Ella up and down, her expression cold. She snapped her fan shut and tutted.

"I guess this will do," Lady Victoria sighed, flipping her fan back open and fluttering it in front of her face. "I have heard that you have been doing your job well. I am not a cruel person, so I am going to give you a chance to show that you have changed."

Ella, suspicious at the proposal yet knowing she could do nothing, bowed her head in acceptance.

"Good. It is nice to see that you aren't talking back to me. I see that my punishment has done its job. I have an errand for you. It must be done perfectly. If not, I'm afraid I'll have to punish dear Clementine, and we wouldn't want that, would we?"

"What is required of me, Stepmother?" Ella asked, her head still down. She knew what was asked would be her last chance given. If Ella acted up again, Lady Victoria's full attention would be on Clementine.

"We have a very important guest coming for afternoon tea. The same guest that you were supposed to attend to two weeks ago when you were . . . 'indisposed'. Madame Briar will be coming, and you need to serve her," Lady Victoria said, looking down her nose at Ella. "I expect perfection. If for any reason you fail to meet my expectations, I will take out my disappointment on your little maid friend. Are we clear?"

Her last words evoked a sense of finality that would only allow for one reply. Ella closed her eyes, knowing her efforts would never meet her stepmother's expectations. Though she knew she would have to try. As Ella curtsied, dread filled her thoughts with every step. Her stepmother's vicious smile emblazoned in her memory.

The rest of the morning was filled with tension as Ella worked through her morning chores. When the appointed time came, she was dressed in her best uniform, nervously straightening it again and again, waiting for Madame Briar to arrive.

Chapter Four

Madame Briar was announced with a solid knock on the heavy front door. Ella's heart pounded in tandem with the knocking, knowing if she failed, it would be Clementine who would be punished. Ella took a deep breath and put on a smile she did not feel as the footman opened the door.

Madame Briar stood tall in the entryway, her wide-brimmed hat festooned with feathers and a large bow. Her floor-length dress was fashionably ruffled with puffed sleeves and was cinched at the waist. She stood, dignified in her posture, her parasol closed in front of her, hands resting on the end. Her solemn face conveyed she would tolerate no nonsense as she waited to be admitted.

Ella wondered with surprise at what such a dignified woman would be doing with her stepmother. Ella's false smile nearly dropped when Madame Briar handed her hat and parasol to another servant in a manner so reminiscent of her mother.

Madame Briar turned towards Ella and looked at her with a raised eyebrow.

Ella took the cue and, with a quick curtsy, responded, "Madame Briar, welcome. Lady Victoria is expecting you. Allow me to take you to the sitting room."

Ella straightened and led the way. When they arrived, Clementine was waiting at the sitting room door to open it. Ella flinched in surprise, but she took a quick breath and recovered. She ignored her friend's presence as her mind thought back to what Victoria had said that morning. Clementine being here was a reminder that she must not disappoint.

Clementine bowed her head and opened the door. Ella went in, curtsied, and announced, "Madame Briar has arrived."

Lady Victoria was seated with her two daughters around a small table next to the window that held small cakes and cookies.

When the door opened, Lady Victoria stood and greeted Madame Briar. "Madame Briar, it is a pleasure to see you again. Please come in and have a seat."

"Welcome," Audrey and Effie chorused as they stood and curtsied. Madame Briar strode to her proffered chair, then sat, daintily signaling for the sisters to also sit.

Ella took her place by the door, waiting to be called. Unable to look directly at them because it would be considered rude, Ella lowered her head just enough so that she could glance at the party. Out of the corner of her eyes, she observed what played out before her, ignoring the few other servants who were standing by the walls. Straining her ears, she listened intently.

Lady Victoria, being the ever-gracious hostess, spoke first. "Madame Briar, thank you for taking the time to travel to our humble home. I know the carriage ride from London can be arduous."

Madam Briar gave a polite smile. "I always come for girls who have promise. Sometimes things need a personal touch. There *is* a reason why my academy is the top in the country."

"We are always glad to welcome you into our home. You must be parched. Ella, bring the tea," Lady Victoria ordered.

Ella bowed and left the room to get the tea cart. Outside the door, Clementine stood next to the cart, waiting for her. As Ella tensed, Clementine moved closer. Unable to move away, Ella froze momentarily when Clementine whispered in her ear. "Why are you doing this?"

Ella flicked a glance at Clementine and then to the servants that were behind her in the hall. Any of them could be reporting to Lady Victoria, Ella thought, and the fear that froze her veins melted. Ella returned her friend's gaze and replied, "Thank you for the cart. I will take it from here."

Ella grabbed the cart swiftly, turned, and returned to the room. The ladies had continued talking while she was in the hall.

"She will be perfect for that class. I am sure she will be at the top of the academy," Lady Victoria said when Ella entered and began to pour.

"My academy is very competitive. There are many ladies who strive to reach for the top. Precious few succeed." Madame Briar stated with a small smile, allowing the tea leaves to steep in front of her.

As Ella moved around the table, Effie stuck out her foot. Unable to see her stepsister's foot, Ella stumbled into the cart. The cart jerked forward, causing cups of hot water to slosh out, spilling out from the cart to the floor. Hot droplets burned Ella's hands as she reached out to grab the falling teapot before it crashed onto the floor. Pain flared, and she quickly dropped the pot back on the cart. She wrapped her hands in her skirt as her scalded skin began to turn red.

Ella turned back at the horrified looks that now occupied everyone's faces around the table. Lady Victoria's face was livid as she clenched her fan in her fist so tightly that her hands turned white.

Effie discreetly flipped open her fan to hide the growing grin on her face. Ella turned to Audrey, who was looking down at her dress, and saw traces of tea sliding down her skirt. Ella could see Effie's triumphant gaze, as she saw Ella watching Audrey's horrified look.

"I am so sorry, Madame Briar," Effie crooned. "I am so sorry you have to see this unseemly display. It's terrible to say, but my stepsister is tragically clumsy. It is hard to believe that she even has any noble blood. I guess blood doesn't mean everything."

Lady Victoria smiled at her daughter before hiding her face behind her fan. "It has been rather difficult raising her. Her mother let her run wild. I was hoping that learning to serve others would help to teach her finesse. I was sure that seeing how my own two daughters acted would help her. As you can see, it hasn't helped."

Victoria's sad expression was masterful. She looked like she was genuinely sorry that she couldn't "help" her poor stepchild. It made Ella sick. She clenched her fists in her skirts, the pain in her burned hands echoing the pain her stepmother was inflicting. This conversation of her stepmother "helping" her and the overt jab at her mother nauseated her. Combined with the fear that, even though it was not her fault, Lady Victoria would blame this incident on her and punish Clementine. With trepidation, she turned to Madame Briar to gauge if she agreed with her stepmother.

Madame Briar sat calmly, sipping her tea, seemingly unconcerned about what had just transpired. She took another sip of her tea, looked at Ella, then looked at the cart.

"I am sorry you had to see such a display, Madame. I will get this cleaned up right away," Ella promised, resetting the cups that had tipped over on the cart and rolling it out of the room.

She had nearly made it to the door when Madame Briar called out, "wait." Her tone was not loud nor sharp, but it was a command.

Ella stopped instantly and turned back towards them, her escape halted. She offered a curtsy. "Yes, Madame?"

Madame Briar was not looking at Ella. Rather, she was looking at Lady Victoria. "I would like to ask something of you, Lady Victoria. I would like to take that girl to my academy as well. I have an interest in taking . . . difficult cases."

"To be a lady?" Victoria exclaimed, covering a horrified look with her fan.

"I think that might be a bit above my skill level. No, I was referring to our courses for servants. Servants who are rebellious need to be broken so that they serve only the will of the household and are loyal to them. Anything other than loyalty will not be tolerated. Even if they work to exhaustion, they are not allowed to pass out until their master gives them leave. That is how a servant should be," Madame Briar stated, taking another sip of tea.

Lady Victoria smiled, and Ella had a horrible sinking feeling that she knew what Victoria was going to say.

"That would be wonderful. It has been so heart-wrenching to see her this way. Such a troublesome child."

"No!"

The door burst open and there stood Clementine. She turned to Madame Briar and got on her knees. "Please, don't send her way," she pleaded. "Take me instead. I beg of you!"

"No, Clementine, stop. Don't do this," Ella cried, trying to pull Clementine away.

"I'm so sorry, Madame. She is one of the previous servants who refuses to believe that I am the new Mistress of this house. She must have been corrupted by this troublemaker," Lady Victoria hissed as she motioned with her fan towards Ella. "It seems I must teach them both a lesson."

"I have an idea, if I may," Madame Briar interjected.

"Yes?"

"Why don't you send them both with me? They seem to have gotten too comfortable here and their insolence may poison the rest of your servants. It is better to cut out the bad now before it's too late. They are young, which means they can take more . . . *training*. This sort of problem will need a more personal touch. I can keep them from influencing your daughters' before it's too late."

"Will this interfere with Audrey's training?" Lady Victoria asked.

"No, they will be enrolled in very different courses. I doubt they will ever see each other over the next four years."

Lady Victoria's eyes narrowed at them, a malicious smile growing on her lips. "Take them."

A reciprocal smile graced Madame Briar's lips as she said, "My pleasure."

And those two knocks were the start of the change. The first was when news of my mother's disappearance arrived, and it was the start of the end of my life as I knew it. Then, when I felt like I was at my lowest, Madame Briar knocked and changed my life once more.

Lady Arabella Cooper;
Code name: Cinders
Excerpt from report 170

Chapter Five

May 1826

The carriage ride to London was oppressive. It had been decided that they would take two carriages. One would take Lady Victoria and her daughters at a later date, once they had a chance to properly pack. As soon as the arrangements were made, Madame Briar would take Ella and Clementine with her on the way back to the academy, so as not to let them taint her other servants any longer. That meant a long carriage ride with Madame Briar, who neither Ella nor Clementine knew and who had sentenced them to hard labor. The only other occupant was Clementine, who she had not spoken to for a week. It had also been decided that they would be traveling nonstop to the academy and not stop to sleep, and would have to eat in the hard, jostling carriage for hours.

The nauseating ride finally ended late at night. Getting out of the carriage was a nightmare on the lower back as well as on the legs. After creaking her way out of the carriage and stretching her aching body, Ella looked about. After the light from the city, the academy was dark except for a few lights from the streets, though she could tell the building was massive. Madame Briar, who acted more like she had taken a stroll in the park rather than an exhaustive carriage ride, led the drooping girls around the building. They followed along a path around back until they reached what Ella assumed to be the servants' quarters. Madame Briar knocked on the door and a matronly woman holding a candle opened it.

The woman looked at both Ella and Clementine, who were struggling to move, and stepped aside to let them in. She looked to Madame Briar and asked, "Special course, Madame?"

"Yes. Make sure they get initiated as soon as possible. I have high hopes for the both of them," Madame Briar said as she left them and disappeared into the darkness.

The gray-haired woman turned to the girls. "Follow me." With a swish of her black dress, she led them down a narrow hallway.

Ignoring how weary her charges were, the matron headed down the hallway at a brisk pace. "My name is Matron Sophia. You may call me Matron or Matron Sophia. Do not call me Sophia or Sophie. I am not your friend, nanny, or family member. I am the dormitory keeper. While you are here, you will follow my orders. You will wake at five each morning and begin your daily chores maintaining this building. This is to help pay for your classes. After your chores, you will eat breakfast and then head to class. After class, you will have lunch after you have finished serving the other students. Finally, you will help make dinner as well as prep the food for the morning. You may *then* help yourself to the leftovers for dinner. Saturdays are laundry days and you will have no classes. Sundays will be light chores and church. Lights out at nine.

Here we are." She stopped in front of one of the many doors along the hallway. "You two will share a room. Your nightclothes are in the drawers. They should fit. In your downtime, you should make any needed adjustments to your uniform. We do not want any disheveled servants. A well-kept appearance is a must."

The quarters were a small, rectangular room holding two beds and a single dresser at the far end. It was a little cramped, but it was serviceable. The stern woman herded them into the room and used her candle to light another candle that sat on the dresser. She paused at the door. "I am warning you that this is an elite academy, and there are quite a few girls here who have ambitions. If you want to get anywhere in this academy, you must earn your place."

Then, before either girl could reply, she exited and shut the door behind her, leaving Ella and Clementine alone together for the first time since the ordeal began.

Clementine turned towards Ella and spoke. "Ella, it's going to—"

"*What do you think you are doing?*" Ella cried, interrupting her friend and grabbing Clementine by the shoulders. "I did everything to protect you! Why did you throw it away? I worked so hard so that you would not get punished as well. Why did you barge into the sitting room? If you had just stayed out, then you would have been fine."

Clementine's face turned a darker shade of red with each word that Ella said. "Fine? It would have been *fine*?" Clementine yelled. "I have been looking after you since you were a child. The last thing my mother told me was to stick with you. How can I stick with you if you were sent off to the academy without me? And do you really think I would be better off left behind with Lady Victoria? Do you really think she wouldn't do anything to me? I don't think so! You better deal with the fact that I am here with you."

Clementine breathed heavily after finishing her tirade. She looked down at the floor and whispered, "I would stay with you even though you hate me."

"Hate you? How could I hate you?" Ella demanded, her anger instantly dissipating. "How could you think that?"

Clementine placed her hands on her hips and raised an eyebrow at her. "Well, because you haven't spoken to me for a week. That may have something to do with it."

"Well, that was because of ... that was the only way to . . ." Ella stammered.

"To what?

"It was the only way I could protect you, alright?"

Clementine stared at Ella. "I'm eighteen years old and you're only fourteen. I'm the adult here. Do you really think I couldn't handle Lady Victoria? Ignoring me isn't the answer. Never do that again."

Clementine smiled at Ella and gave her a hug. She pulled away and placed her hands on Ella's shoulders, staring directly into her eyes. "You're smart, but you mustn't let your emotions take you too far doing the right thing. You weren't thinking far enough ahead. It's like that time when you jumped from the balcony into the tree to save a cat, but you could not get down after. Even when you were found it took you hours to get down and you missed dinner. You had wanted to get down yourself. Remember what your mother said to you afterward? That if you had asked for help earlier, then you could have gotten down and had time to get ready for dinner. If you ask for help, you could accomplish amazing things."

Ella closed her eyes and took a deep breath. When she opened them again, her calm gaze reflected in Clementine's eyes. Clementine smiled and said, "That's the Ella I know. Now, what are we going to do?"

Ella smiled back. She was glad that they were back together again, but now was time to plan on how they were going to get out of this situation. Ella looked into Clementine's ready eyes as Ella spoke. "We should take a look around this place and see what's going on. For now, we do what needs to get done. After, we shall see. But this time I'm not going to stay as a servant. We will get out of here and regain my family home."

"That's my girl," Clementine whispered.

Warmth flooded through her at that thought. Ella let it fill her until its warmth made her eyes droop. "For now, let's head to bed. It's going to be an early morning." Ella yawned.

They settled into their chemises, and after being thoroughly exhausted, mentally and physically, they quickly fell asleep.

Morning came rather abruptly. After only a few short hours of sleep, a servant strode into their room. She rang a bell and informed them they had five minutes to get dressed. Stunned by the unexpected awakening, they rubbed their sleep-crusted eyes and hurriedly changed. As soon as they opened the door, another maid had them follow her on a quick tour of the quarters before setting them to work.

Ella and Clementine were assigned to different areas of the academy to clean. Ella quickly noticed oddities happening around them. Even as exhausted as she was, Ella could not help but notice some of the maids that were cleaning with her changed to different people. After spending years trying to avoid her stepsister's traps, she had grown ever aware of her surroundings. Being used to doing all the odd jobs, she allowed her body to fall into the rhythm of working as she observed. The serious brown-haired girl who had been sweeping down the hall was now replaced with a redhead with freckles who was cleaning the windows on the other end of the hallway. It wasn't that she had moved to a different location. It was that within moments of her bending down to rinse out her rag, the girl that was with her was no longer the same person. The only reason she remembered the girl before was because of the glare the servant gave her when

Ella greeted her. Ella wondered when the change happened; it was difficult to tell since she could barely keep her eyes open and the day had just started. Driven by another maid to hurry up, she lost her train of thought and went back to work, making sure to keep her eyes open.

When she finished cleaning the many windows of the massive hallways, she was then directed towards the kitchen where some bread and cheese were provided for a quick breakfast. Then, it was off to her classes. It was in those classes she was finally able to catch a glance of Clementine. Clementine looked as haggard as Ella felt. They took their seats in a classroom consisting of twenty-five wooden desks, all full of other women and a few men dressed in servant's uniforms. Ella and Clementine barely had any time to take this in as Matron Sophia strode in and promptly began to teach the proper ways of cleaning the hallways. After her lecture, she then went to each person who was assigned to clean the halls and described to the class exactly what they had done wrong.

Ella watched as Matron slowly made her way toward her. When the matron arrived at her desk, she smiled and said, "You are the only one here who did the job correctly. You also are one of the youngest here. Well done. I have high expectations of you."

Twenty-three pairs of eyes turned towards her, each filled with jealously at her getting praised. Matron Sophia had just made her the enemy of everyone in that room. The only one who wasn't displaying jealousy was Clementine. Ella's instincts pricked at her. As Matron Sophia moved on, Ella had a fleeting thought. *Where is the serious girl from the hallway, and why isn't she here now?*

After classes, everyone was ushered into the kitchen and given a task to prepare for lunch. The duties were noted so that as school went on, they would be on a rotation. This was so each of the students would learn all positions within a household, and they even had to learn some of the men's roles. By accomplishing each task, they were taught the understanding of whose roles were whose for a specific reason. And when they were ever elevated to the station of housekeeper, they would know with expert knowledge how to delegate duties. This was only allowed because of the prestige and history of the academy.

Ella was assigned to bring the food from the kitchens to the footmen, who in turn served the food to the noble students. As expected from the praise the matron had said, the bullying started. Most of it consisted of knocking Ella on the shoulder or bumping her hip as people passed. Several even stuck their foot out in an attempt to trip her. They were not as sneaky as her stepsister was and she easily evaded each attempt and was able to keep hold of the tray she was carrying. She also made sure that the servant she was passing the tray to had a good grip on the tray before letting go. She knew that dropping it would earn her the ire of the cook, who cared little for the petty squabbles of servants.

The failed attempts only made her classmates angrier, so Ella made sure some of the attacks hit and did just enough damage to ease their anger, but not enough to draw any real attention. The beefy chef kept an eagle-eyed watch over his domain, and Ella did her best to keep from earning a glare from him. She did manage to see Clementine once or twice when she passed off the dirty dishes to her. But since it was so busy, they didn't have time to talk. Even when she was finally given time to eat some lunch, it was barely enough time to scarf down a sandwich, let alone speak to anyone. Lunch for the servants was served two at a time, and the servants made sure Ella was last with what little time was left over. And since she was on their bad side, they made sure there wasn't much left.

After hurriedly eating her skimpy lunch, Ella was put to work slicing tomatoes for dinner. After that, she was then sent off to mop up a spill from another maid who dropped a bowl of soup and was currently being berated by the cook. Her day continued to be much the same, and by the time the day was over, she felt like she had been dragged through the mud by a horse after it had thrown her and stomped on her a few times. Exhausted from the previous day's travels, the emotional late night, and then the early morning, she barely had enough strength to eat the soup that was for dinner.

Ella met up with Clementine as they headed toward their dorm. As they were about to head inside, a flicker of cloth drew her attention. The stern maid with a glower on her face was heading outside when it was almost lights out.

Ella felt that something odd was going on. Ella's thoughts bursted with questions. First, it was the servant with a glare as she disappeared and reappeared. And why was the headmistress making it so that she was singled out? If she was going to survive here, Ella needed to find out. After entering their room, she discussed what her plans were to gain information on how to get out of their situation, then collapsed into an exhausted sleep.

After that first day, Ella and Clementine settled into a schedule. An exhaustive, demanding schedule. The day started out with a cleaning job. Ella kept an eye out for disappearing servants, scrutinizing each of their faces. She noticed it was not just the brown-haired maid. There were five others who seemed to disappear and reappear throughout the day.

After cleaning, the trial of meal times commenced. Clementine cozied her way to the other students' good sides by saying how horrible it was to be bunked with Ella. She used her charm to become the girl most liked by everyone. Much like how Ella was now the most hated, but she was used to that. Ella knew everyone was out to get her and she was prepared. Ella was able to foil the worst of the bullying. Their trivial attempts couldn't compare to her stepsister's attempts when it came to cleverness or her sneaky nature.

One thing that she could not affect, however, was how long she had for her meals; the others made sure she had very little time to eat. Clementine tried to help, but if she didn't take as long eating, then the others would just take longer. The best thing Clementine could do was to subtly question the servants, and sneak an extra roll to her from lunch.

After a grueling week of finding nothing, Ella flopped onto her bed and groaned. "Are you sure you haven't found anything?"

Clementine sat primly on the edge of her bed, cleaning the dirt from under her nails. "Sure. Those servants don't pay attention to anything, and I didn't see any of those servants you mentioned in class. Mary said that she's heard of ghosts in the hallways at night, which could be the people you are seeing, but I haven't really seen them either."

"Maybe they really are ghosts," Ella said, staring at the ceiling. An idea blossomed in her mind. "Or what if they're thieves? They pretend to be servants to sneak in, and then, while both servants and nobles are in classes, they steal stuff from their rooms."

Clementine tilted her head. "Why keep coming back?"

"That's because . . ." Ella started to say, but faltered. "I don't know. It was a good idea, though."

Clementine laughed. "I'm sure you'll find out soon enough. You are not one to leave a mystery unsolved. You are like a kitten; your curiosity knows no bounds."

Ella rolled her eyes. "Anyway, this is still a good chance. If we find out something bad is going on, then we may be promoted, and may find a way to get back my family's manor from Lady Victoria. Or find out what happened to my mother."

"You're never going to give up on that, are you?"

Ella looked down at her hands. "The manor is the only thing I have left of my family. And no one knows what happened to my mother. Whatever the case may be, we still need to be in a higher position. Can you get me on collection duty?"

Clementine feigned offense. "Of course. Watch me work my magic. Roy, the assistant, finds me cute." She said, fluttering her baby blue eyes and pouting.

Ella laughed, "I can't believe people still don't know your real personality."

"I was born to be an actress," Clementine said with a dramatic flair.

Ella threw a pillow at her.

"Hey!" Clementine complained, throwing it back at Ella.

"Aren't you supposed to be respectful to your master?"

Clementine looked at Ella and raised one eyebrow. "I only see a young girl who smacks herself with sticks, trying to copy the guards."

"That was *one* time."

Clementine smiled. "I haven't seen you act like this in a long time. It is good to see."

"Thank you for being here."

"Always. Now go to sleep."

Ella huffed, exasperated at Clementine, but exhausted as she was, she didn't complain and did as she was told.

The next morning started with laundry day. The day that was most dreaded by the servants. With such a massive academy, and considering the vanity of the noble students, there was a lot to wash. Laundry day was also physically demanding. Masses of bedsheets needed to be scrubbed, stirred, and beaten. Not to mention the hot boilers. Being near them was sweltering, but if you were away from them, the frigid morning air froze you. Then the wringing out and drying before finally folding and returning laundry.

Ella sighed as she looked at the academy building. It appeared no less imposing in the light than it did in the dark. It was several stories tall, with many windows dotting its geometric structure, its white stone walls turned gray from age. Its heritage oozed off it like the expensive perfume of a noblewoman.

Ella took a deep breath, steeling herself for the difficult job she was about to undertake. She released her breath and trudged up the steps into the building. She grabbed a waiting cart and began knocking on each door to gather the ladies dirty laundry. She dreaded each step that took her toward the stairwell that led to the next floor, which meant lugging everything up by hand. At each room, she took a good look inside each of the student's rooms, seeing if any of the occupants matched the five people she had seen go missing.

As she approached the stairs, she heard something strange ahead. The rasp of stone against stone.

Ella quickened her steps until she arrived at the stairs and peeked around the corner. No one was there. She looked at the walls for anything that could have caused the noise, but it was just an empty stairwell. Sighing once again, she grabbed the basket and started hauling it up the narrow steps. As she climbed, Ella again heard something. She paused, and looked both up and down the stairs, but still, no one was there. She listened intently and was shocked to find the noise next to her. Ella jumped, nearly dumping the hamper down the stairs.

Ella waited quietly. She put her ear against the stones; now she could hear voices. The thick stone muffled the voices so they were unrecognizable. There was no door in the stairwell. There might have been one above where she heard the voices, so she took her hamper and, with renewed energy finished climbing the steps. Ella turned to her left, the direction where the voices came from, and knocked on the door.

The door opened and framed a pretty young maid with blonde hair. "Yes? What do you need?" She inquired.

Ella motioned to the basket full of laundry. The girl nodded and turned to grab the sheets. Through the partly opened door, Ella could see a young noble lady sipping tea, her brown hair up in a bun with ringlets framing her face. The maid returned, and the noble lady turned fully toward Ella and glared at her.

Ella's eyes widened in surprise. She remembered that glare. That was the same glare the servant in the hallway gave her. The same one she saw sneaking outside the first night. Ella recovered quickly as her view was blocked by the maid. She shoved the laundry into Ella's hands and shut the door with a wordless thud.

Ella stood staring back at the door, still stunned by that revelation. *What was a noble lady doing dressed as a servant?* Ella wondered. She dumped the laundry into the basket and wandered toward the next door. Another thought struck her, *Or perhaps it was a servant dressed as a noble?* Ella continued collecting down the hallway, her mind racing with every step.

Chapter Seven

The day ended without any more conclusions. "What is going on? I know that was the servant I saw. I know it! She was the one that just appeared." Ella said, lying on her bed.

Clementine interrupted her musings. "You need to stretch or else you're going to be sore in the morning."

Ella grumbled and started stretching her already aching arms. "The question is, if she is a born noble, then why would she need to dress as a servant? But if she is a servant, then how is she pretending to be noble in this school without anyone knowing about it? And are the other five I saw the same? Or are they from another group?"

"I'm sure you will figure it out. Good night," Clementine said, blowing out the candle.

"But what if they are thieves? Or maybe spies?"

"Go to sleep," Clementine scolded. "Or at least question it in your head. I need my beauty sleep. You need it too, considering what tomorrow has in store."

"What about tomorrow? It's supposed to be our light work day."

"Never mind. You keep thinking about disappearing servants who reappear as nobles and I'll go to sleep."

Ella tried to egg Clementine into telling her what was going to happen tomorrow, but she refused to answer. Finally, Ella gave up and tried to get some sleep.

The next morning, she awoke without aching muscles, and she easily got out of bed. Clementine gave her a smug grin, knowing that it was because of her that Ella wasn't sore that morning. Ignoring her friend's annoying self-satisfied grin, Ella stood up and stretched some more, then got dressed in her black uniform before they headed out for the day.

The "light" cleaning expected today may have been not as deep a cleaning as the previous days. Instead, it had to be done more quickly because it had to be finished before early morning church services. By the time they finished cleaning, they had to change uniforms once more, which made it just as exhausting as normal workdays, only in a different way. When they finally made their way across the grounds to the small standalone chapel, they found all the pews filled. Seated in the front section were the nobility, and in the back few rows were the high-ranking servants. The rest of the servants were expected to stand along the edges of the room. Ella and Clementine stood on opposite sides of the room so they could see one another, but not close enough that they would be considered friends.

The church was beautiful with its high, arched ceilings, and stained-glassed windows which let in the morning light. The morning light allowed her to see all the nobles, many for the first time. Now, Ella had a chance to see if any of those other five people were in sitting with the nobles or if they dressed as servants like she had seen them before. She scrutinized the crowd, trying to pick out the other disappearing servants, as the preacher droned out his sermon in a monotonous voice. She had to look very closely and double-check to make sure. It was difficult, but Ella spotted three of the mysterious servants seated with the high-ranking servants in the back and the other two seated with the nobles. All five were here. But were the ones dressed as servants really servants? Or were they nobles?

That train of thought halted when she saw Lady Victoria and her two daughters in the front row. They must have finally arrived at the school. She had forgotten they were scheduled to arrive the evening before, allowing their mother to stay the night and join them for church the next day. Ella glared at Clementine from across the room, glanced at her stepmother, and then back at Clementine.

Clementine shrugged, as if to say, "I tried to warn you."

Ella gave Clementine one last glare, then returned to looking at the profile of her dreaded stepmother. Ella could imagine her stepmother's eyes as if they were looking at her now, a hint of malicious glee as she peered over her fan.

Ella shuddered at the thought and took a deep breath. There was nothing she could do about it now. She turned her attention back to the noble girl who was constantly glaring at her. The girl sat near the front, her dark brown hair pulled into a bun and face covered with a sheer white veil. As she sat, every now and again, she would tap her face with her fan as if in concentration. The motion looked natural except, since Ella was concentrating on her, she could see it was a repetitive tick, done with purpose.

Ella shifted her gaze to one of the other servants, who was also now dressed as a noble. Her curly, light honey locks bounced as she leaned next to her neighbor and whispered something. The girl next to her tried unsuccessfully to hide a giggle. Ella watched in fascination as the curly-haired girl tapped her face as well. This was after the girl with the glare did, as if in reply. This happened several times. One girl would tap her face, then the other one would soon follow. All was done under everyone's noses. If she wasn't looking closely at the two of them, she wouldn't have thought anything of it. Curiosity bloomed within her as she tried to decipher what they were signaling about, only wilting slightly when her gaze slid past Lady Victoria's graceful neck.

When church had ended, Ella hadn't heard a single word from the preacher, though the service had passed faster than expected. The servants were then directed to the kitchens where they would serve a light lunch to the nobles. As Ella was herded inside, the head server instructed her that her assignment was to be a footman for lunch. He gave a vague explanation of what she was supposed to do and pointed to her assigned area to serve. Ella was growing uneasy at being called out. It was starting to feel like someone was setting her up. It was odd that she would be chosen to be a server so early in her training. Considering seniority and scheduling, she shouldn't be practicing until next year.

Ella's eyes studied the area she was assigned, and the uneasy feeling turned to worry. Her eyes had gravitated towards one table in particular. The table where her stepfamily was seated.

"May I please be assigned to a different area?" Ella asked, trying to keep her voice calm.

The head server glared down at her. "You were specifically requested for this assignment. I would never have put a new servant on this job, but since it was requested, I can't do anything different. Don't mess up."

The head server dismissed her with a condescending sniff of his nose.

With a feeling reminiscent of the fateful incident that led her to this school, she did as she was told. The dining area was filled with medium-sized round tables. Even though she wasn't familiar with many nobles, she could already see different factions based on how they seated themselves. You could almost see those of old high-ranking noble blood gathered together, identified by the tilt of their heads and how they looked down their noses at everyone around them, which spoke volumes about what they thought of everyone else.

These were seated on one side of the room, and on the other side were those who had no nobility but could buy their way into the school. The *nouveau riche* had been growing with the new Industrial Age. Those ladies who were wealthy enough to buy their way into this school were gathered facing in the opposite direction, though they occasionally glanced at the nobility with envy. In between were some of those that had a title but weren't a high enough rank to be seated close to those with more money and higher status. Ella's stepmother and stepsisters were a part of that group, the group that she was to serve.

The first platters were handed to Ella, and envy glinted in the servant's eyes at the higher position Ella had received. Just one more thing for them to hate her for. Ella sighed and then walked step by dreaded step towards her stepfamily.

They were chatting amongst themselves as she came to set the dishes in front of them, all of them dressed in more muted clothes that were more appropriate for church.

"That was so tedious. I can't believe that we had to arrive on a Sunday," Audrey complained, as she adjusted the curls that were framing her face just so.

"We did that so we could be more comfortably adjusted when classes started and so we don't make a fool of ourselves on the first day because of sleep deprivation," Effie retorted. She sipped the tea that had already been served and continued. "Better for one day to be monotonous so we can have an amazing entrance."

Effie's eyes flicked to her mother as she smiled at her sister; only a slight tremble of her fingers showed her nervousness.

Lady Victoria raised her eyebrow at her brown-haired daughter, "Yes, that is correct, dear. We must make sure that Audrey shines when she is presented."

"Yes, we must make sure that Audrey shines," Effie repeated, her smile only falling slightly until she regained composure.

Audrey smiled back at her sister. "I heard that Crown Prince William always comes to the graduation ceremony. And he plans on bringing his son as well. Just imagine if the other nobles were to talk about me to him. Who knows, I may even marry into royalty."

"For now, we need to make sure that the nobility sees Audrey in a positive light, right, Effie?" Lady Victoria asked, but the tone said it was an order.

"Of course, Mother. All for Audrey," Effie said with a polite smile, which changed into a mischievous grin when she saw Ella approach. "Look who we have here: our poisonous stepsister. How do you find your life as a servant here?"

Ella smiled politely and moved towards the table, speaking and acting politely to get her revenge, as her mother would have. "I like it very much. It is nice sometimes to get away from a parent's prying eyes."

Effie's smile twitched angrily at Ella's reply.

Lady Victoria grinned savagely. "It seems that you haven't worked hard enough. Maybe I should have kept you at home. Maybe this place is too good for you. I know that this place has odd teaching habits for servants, but how could they put you as a footman? It's disgraceful."

"I'm sure that the only reason you have not been punished severely is because they haven't yet seen your incompetence," Effie added snidely.

Ella clenched her teeth and set the platter in front of Audrey, who sniffed at Ella and turned away. Ella gripped the plate tighter.

It had been a week since she had last seen them, but they were far worse than anything this school had done to her.

Setting the next plate in front of her stepmother, Ella tried to restrain herself from dropping it on the table in a rage. Now that Clementine wasn't in danger, it was a lot harder to control her temper.

"I thought that the headmistress was going to keep an eye on you. I guess you were considered far less than she thought. Perhaps she thought of you as manly, and put you to work doing a man's job," Effie said, glancing at her mother's whitening fingers that griped the fan. Lady Victoria was watching the other ladies in the school, some who had turned towards them with interest.

"That must be it," Lady Victoria said, her jaw clenching as she refrained from spitting out her words.

Ella continued around the table, pointedly ignoring her stepmother's comments and focusing on Effie. Ella, wary of Effie causing trouble, set the last plate in front of her. Once that was done, she relaxed and breathed a sigh of relief, and headed back toward the kitchen. As she moved away from the table, she felt a tug on her apron strap and heard shattering plates. Ella turned quickly and saw that someone had tied the tablecloth to her apron tie. She looked at Effie, whose face was now hidden behind her fan, but her blue eyes glittered with malicious glee from above its edges.

Audrey screamed, "Look what you have done!" She stood and food fell from her lap and onto the floor. "How dare you! Look at my dress!"

Ella turned from Effie to Audrey and opened her mouth as if to speak, but snapped it shut when the headmistress strode in. She advanced with grace and a commanding presence that only age and authority could grant. She held a fan in front of her that she snapped shut.

"We are ladies. Calm yourselves." The room was instantly quieted by those words. She looked from Ella, to the food on the ground, and then to Audrey's red face.

Madam Briar turned to Lady Victoria. "I apologize. It seems that I did not pay as much attention to Ella as I should have. I will rectify this mistake."

Ella opened her mouth to explain it wasn't her fault, but she was silenced by a stern look from the headmistress.

"You, follow me to my office. It is time we had a chat," Madame Briar ordered, raising her eyebrow at Ella. She turned to Audrey. "I will have your lunch sent to your room so you can change. I will inform you of the punishment I will administer to Ell after I determine what is appropriate. Good day, Lady Victoria. I will see you soon."

And with that, madame Briar strode off, leaving Ella to follow in her wake.

A fire burned in Ella during that walk to the office as she thought about all the injustices that had been inflicted on her by her own "family". All the pain that had been inflicted on her since her mother's disappearance and the treatment of her stepfamily stoked the fire. Everything that she had pushed down started bubbling to the surface. Yet again she would be punished for something that was not her fault. Her indignation burned so hot that once she stepped through the door, she spouted what anger had been brewing over. "This is not my fault. Neither was it the last time. There is something wrong here, and you know it. This whole school is strange. Why did you want to take me? Why are there students who are pretending to be students one moment, then nobles the next? There is no way they could have done that without the headmistress knowing about it. Who are you, and why am I here?"

Madame Briar walked around her desk and sat in the large chair. She sat silently, waiting until Ella got her breathing under control. Ella finally calmed down and looked around the office. There were two large windows on either side of the wall behind Madame Briar that framed the large cherry oak desk. The chair where Madame Briar sat was imposing but not overly ornate. On the side walls were two massive paintings, one a portrait of King George IV and on the other a very old painting of a queen Ella didn't recognize.

"She is Queen Jane, the founder of this academy. Marvelous woman," Madam Briar said. Her arms were folded on the desk, fan lightly clutched in front of her.

Ella looked back to Madame Briar. "That is not what you want to speak to me about."

"No."

"You knew that it was Effie who tied the tablecloth, didn't you?" Ella accused, feeling the fire of anger building again.

"You are correct. I do know that it was Effie both times, here and at your estate, but it gave me a good excuse to bring you here. You've followed your ques quite nicely, by the way. You show promise."

"Why did you want me here? What is going on?" Ella demanded, confused by this turn of events.

"Dear girl, I made a promise. Your stepmother, the vicious woman that she is, would have never allowed you to leave the household otherwise. Though it was good fortune that Clementine caused troubles. That gave an excuse to bring her, too. I hadn't expected that she would be able to come as well. You will need the support."

"And when I left the house that way, it made it seem like it was all her idea," Ella said, starting to put things together. "Then why me? Does it have something to do with the other five people?"

Madame Briar lifted her eyebrow. "It seems you figured out more than I gave you credit for. Yes, those five are involved with why I had you come join us."

"Join? What are you, some secret society?" Ella scoffed, staring back at Madame Briar's unblinking expression. "You can't be serious."

"Yes, I am. Now come, child, we shouldn't be speaking of such things here. Follow me and I will explain everything."

Madame Briar stood and walked to Queen Jane's portrait before the portrait swung open. Ella gaped in awe as the headmistress motioned to a hallway hidden behind the painting. "Shall we?"

She followed behind the headmistress into the secret passage, curiosity filling her mind. It was pitch black once the portrait closed behind them. "It will be a little dark, but follow closely and you'll be fine."

Despite the darkness, Ella could follow without much trouble. The floor was even, and the hall was narrow, so there wasn't anywhere else to go. Ella placed her hands on the cool stone walls and used them as a guide as she followed the sound of the headmistress's footsteps.

After a short walk, Ella could see light ahead. Eventually, they arrived and looked down into a huge, well-lit space. It was chilly, but that was to be expected of a room this size. It opened to stairs that led down to a wooden floor, one half covered in mats, the other designed to look like a parlor. There were a few ladies scattered about, dressed in anything ranging from servants' uniforms to elaborate ball gowns.

It was bizarre, but Ella couldn't pull her eyes away from the oddity that lay before her. A clash of metal on metal captured her attention to the side with the mats. A pair of girls seemed to be fighting, one dressed in clothes for exercise, the other in a frilly white dress. What instruments they fought with she couldn't tell from this distance, but they both fought with grace, even the one in the elegant dress.

"What is this place?" Ella asked, unable to pull her eyes from the scene below.

Madame Briar smiled and said, "Welcome to the Fan Society.

Chapter Eight

Ella tore her eyes away from the scene below to look at the headmistress. "Fan Society? I thought secret societies were just fables. I didn't think any actually existed."

"Here at the Fan Society, we train young ladies, such as yourself, to become spies. Our only goal is to protect England by protecting the royal line."

The look in Madame Briar's eyes showed how serious she was. "Then why haven't I heard of anything like this before?"

Madame Briar laughed. "Even the royal family hasn't heard of us. Anyway it wouldn't really be a secret if you had heard of us."

"Now I'm confused. You train ladies to protect the royal line, but the royal line has never heard of you?"

Madame Briar shrugged. "Follow me and I'll explain." She led Ella down the stairs. Ella watched as the girls in the parlor-style setting did actions benefiting of them being ladies. Some poured tea and a few others chatted amongst themselves. Near the back of the room, almost like the backstage to a play, there was an area for changing, a large rack of clothes, and an area for hair and make-up. She studied this area as Madame Briar began speaking.

"Around the year 1550, a fifteen-year-old girl married into the royal family. As was the norm, she gave birth soon after. Not long after that, her husband, the king, passed away, leaving behind a young queen and her infant son with no one to protect them from the jackals of society. It was during this time that Europe still had good relations with Japan. The queen had made friends with some of the Shogun ambassadors. They saw England as rather primitive and found it amusing to entertain the barbaric Englishman."

"They thought us barbaric?" Ella asked, turning from the ladies to Madame Briar.

"Yes, and from what I heard, rightly so. Though, as Englishman we would never say that out loud. It was through the ambassador that she befriended one of his wives. When she learned of the young queen's predicament, she helped her train in the art of ninjutsu, or the art of unconventional warfare, and tessenjutsu, the art of the war fan. Because of this training, she was able to protect her son until he came of age and assumed power. Eventually, she founded this academy as a way to continue to protect the throne. Though some things have changed to match how our society works, it is still fundamentally the same."

Madam Briar pointed her fan at the ladies in the parlor area. "This is where we train girls to be ladies. They learn to gather information, to pass information, to gain connections, to properly dress and attire themselves for whatever disguise is needed."

"Why women? We have very little power in society. Most of society only sees us as pretty dolls to be sold off for marriage," Ella said, vague memories of sneaking down to watch her mother's parties filtered through her mind.

"That is what we want people to think. Why do you think we call ourselves the fan society?"

"Because the queen was taught tessen-something, the war fan?"

"Tessenjustsu. Yes, and no." Madame Briar held out her fan flicked it open, and then snapped it shut again. "Have you ever seen a lady do this before?"

Ella nodded, remembering some of the ladies in the parlor area doing the same thing.

"To our agents, it means no or is a negative response." The headmistress flicked it open and made a small fanning motion in front of her face. "And this is a positive or open for negotiations. The fan is our power and our weapon. Most ladies in society know some of the language of the fan and can talk about certain things without their husbands knowing. The fan society takes this one step further. Think of it as a second language that uses the fan. And of course, for us in the fan society, it *is* an actual weapon."

The headmistress passed the fan to Ella, who nearly dropped it in surprise. It was far heavier than she expected. She felt the ribbing of the fan, and noticed they were made of metal, all hidden by delicate lace. It reminded her of her mother's fans.

"What is this?" Ella asked, passing the fan back to the headmistress.

Madame Briar pointed to the two girls who were fighting. Now that they were closer, Ella could see the one in the exercise clothes held a dagger and the girl in the frilly dress was holding a fan. The sound of metal on metal made Ella notice that the fan she fought with was the same as the headmistress's fan. The girl who held the fan closed would knock the blade aside whenever the other girl struck. She watched as the girl with the dagger overextended herself and the girl with the fan took the initiative. She smashed the girl's wrist with the butt end of the fan, causing the dagger to drop from her now slack fingers. The white-dressed girl then stepped forward, flicked the fan open and held it to dagger-girl's neck.

"Come," Madame Briar said, prying Ella's eyes from the fight and moving to the back of the room. "We also use fashion as defense," as she pointed to a stack of corsets.

"What's so defensive about them compared to a normal corset?" Ella questioned, glancing curiously at them.

"They are ribbed with steel, much like how our fans are ribbed with iron. Whalebone and goose-feather spines are not as strong. We once tried leather instead of the normal cotton, but it made it more difficult to move. And in the summer, it made the ladies overheat. We have tested their defensive capabilities, and they have proven to be successful.

"Over there is some more of our weaponry."

Ella's eyes followed where her fan was pointing and looked at a row of parasols, necklaces, purses, hair pins, hat pins, and other accessories most ladies wore. There were other more conventional weapons such as staffs and knives, as well as unconventional ones such as chains, straps, and nets.

"What are all of these used for?"

The headmistress laughed. "I'll get to that later. For now, this is our last stop."

Curiously, Ella followed Madame Briar into a room she had not noticed at the back of the large training room. It was a long, narrow space filled with portraits, each of a different lady through various periods of time. Judging by the styles of clothing, these portraits dated back to the 1550's. Underneath each portrait was a brass plaque that had a single word. The words seemed to be random with names such as Hawk, Observer, Seeker, and so forth. In each portrait, the ladies wore the same golden ring.

"Who are they?" Ella asked, fascinated by the different ladies, as well as how many of them there were. "Were they all part of the society?"

A polite smile graced Madame Briar's face as she pointed to the ladies around her. "These are our legacies. Each of these ladies has sacrificed much for the royal family. The lady I made a promise to was one of our best."

"Who was she?"

"She was one of the elites and one of my best students. She was a very curious girl, much like yourself. One day she disappeared. She was supposed to be at a meeting with us but never showed. We never found out why." Madame Briar stopped and looked at Ella with a sad smile. "You remind me very much of her when she was your age." Madame Briar reflected, then continued walking forward.

"What's her name?"

Madame Briar came to a stop in front of a hauntingly familiar face, and Ella reached out her hand to touch the painting. This woman was young and was wearing something that was in style a few years ago, along with the gold ring. Ella felt as if she could remember her from her childhood, but as she reached for the memory, it faded from view. She looked at the plaque, but all it said was *Cinders.*

"What is her name? Her real name," Ella asked.

Madame Briar grinned wider. "Lady Nora Cooper. Your mother."

Part II

The Legacies were the best of the best. They were
the children of members of the Fan Society and were
trained to be the elite. They were the ones who
underwent lifelong missions so they could be in places
of the most influence. They were accompanied by
assistants who helped them to maintain their cover as
well as the maintenance of their specialized clothing
and of other necessities of being a lady.

Lady Luella Jones, Codename:
Warrior
Excerpt from essay 5

The start of my academy life was harsh. My stepmother wanted me punished, so I was sent to work in the stables shoveling manure as well as to spend the mornings with the headmistress as she "personally" took care of me. This was all a cover so that I could be trained. Clementine joined me in training a short time later, after "accidentally" breaking an entire cart of clean plates. She began her punishment and was introduced to the Fan Society, and took her place in training as my assistant. Those four years of training were some of the most difficult and most fulfilling years of my life, considering the information I found about my mother during that time.

Lady Arabella Cooper Code
name: Cinders
Excerpt from report 10

Chapter Nine

3 July 1830, Academy

It was time to see Madame Briar. Ella had become close to her after all the training she received, though it was nerve-wracking to finally be learning what her lifelong mission was to be. This was what Ella had trained for.

Ella walked through the now familiar passageways to the headmistress's secret office. Ella had to hide in the walls in preparation for this mission. Three years ago, Madame Briar told Lady Victoria that she'd caused injury to a noble, and as punishment was shipped to the Americas as a slave. Believing this her family wouldn't expect to see her again, and when Ella was reintroduced to society as a lady, they would not recognize her.

Clementine bumped into her shoulder. "Nervous?"

"No, I'm only getting the mission that I will be spending the rest of my life doing. The mission that will prove whether I'm worthy to become a full member of the society. It's not that big of a deal," Ella retorted, rolling her eyes.

Clementine smiled with a mischievous glint. "Oh, if it's like that, then maybe Luella should do the mission instead. She wouldn't mind taking it off your hands."

Ella glared at her friend in the dimly lit passage.

"I thought you were getting along better. The last time you talked, it looked like you were friends. " Clementine teased, her voice laced with sarcasm.

Ella sighed, "She has always had animosity toward me because I am a Legacy. And getting along? More like healthy rivalry."

"Ahh, rivalry at first glare."

Ella laughed, remembering the first glare that started her on the trail to the mystery of the Fan Society and all the clashes that happened during her academy training.

Clementine nudged her with her elbow. "Feeling better now?"

Ella smiled warmly at her in return. "Yeah, thank you for that."

"Always. Now let's show the madame what we've learned."

Ella took a deep breath, stood up straight, and strode the final steps to the office. Clementine rapped lightly on the door.

"Come in," Madame Briar called.

Clementine opened the door, allowing Ella through, and followed closely behind her as they entered the office. The room was narrow, as most of the hidden rooms were, and made of the same stone that lined the outside walls. There was little adornment in the room, only a serviceable desk with several stacks of reports. Behind the desk was the symbol of the Fan Society engraved into the stonework: an open fan in a circle. Along the border of the circle was a pattern of ovals with dots in the center reminiscent of eyes. Above the circle, as if perched there, was a crown, and at the base was another eye set with some curlicues. Pride flushed through Ella as she realized she was going to be part of the same organization her mother had been in. And if she did well, she may be able to find her. The headmistress was seated at her desk, looking through reports. Ella looked at the headmistress's gray hair and stern features that softened whenever she gazed upon her girls.

Madame Briar glanced up as they entered the room and motioned to the chairs in front of her. "Have a seat." Clementine pulled out the chair for Ella and stood behind her. Madame Briar gave a small nod of acknowledgment. "It seems I have trained you well."

"Yes, Madame." Ella gave a genuine smile of affection to her teacher. Madame Briar had gray streaks throughout her hair and wrinkles on her face, but her demeanor also held a sense of reserved strength. Even if she were to wear dirty servants' clothes, you could feel the authority she held. Not that dirt would ever dare sully her skirts. On her finger was a gold ring that had an imprinted symbol of the Fan Society, proof that she was a full member. The same one that Ella's mother wore in her portrait.

Ella saw a smile tug at her mentor's lips, and then she started talking. "We have decided on your mission. This is a very important task, and it is vital to the goals of our society. But first, tell me what you know about the current situation of the royal family?"

Ella paused, surprised, as she tried to organize her thoughts. She recalled what she had learned from her growing network of sources. "King George IV died not long ago. His son, William, was crowned on the twenty-fifth of June after the death of his older brother. King William Henry IV is the third son of eight, and he married Princess Adelaide of Saxe-Meiningen.

"Princess Adelaide had several children prematurely, and they didn't survive. In her final pregnancy, she had twins, prematurely again. It had been a rough pregnancy and delivery, and she died in childbirth. One of the twins was a stillbirth, but the other managed to live. Prince Adrian is the first son of King William. Though, because of King William's advanced age and Prince Adrian's poor health, many wonder if he will outlive his father. Most believe that Alexandria Victoria, King William's niece, will be next in line, despite King William's hatred of his niece's mother."

Madame Briar nodded. "What personal information do you know about Prince Adrian?"

Ella felt Clementine twitch at that question behind her. Confused, Ella replied, "There really isn't much known about his preferences. After nearly dying when he was born and being constantly sick, he doesn't really leave the house much. He only comes out on a few occasions, and he is known to not stay long when he does."

"After the death of the queen, we have been unable to get any members of the society close enough to protect the royal family. Your mission will be to marry the prince," Madame Briar explained, her demeanor the picture of calm as if she had not said life-changing information.

Dumfounded, Ella blinked, opened her mouth as if to speak, then closed it.

Madame Briar smiled. "Do try not to show so much surprise, my dear. This is an important mission, and you are the only one who had the qualifications for it."

"But what about my stepfamily? If I am working to become his wife, I will have to be at the same parties as they are. What if they recognize me?"

"Then you must not be recognized," the headmistress stated. "This is what we've trained you for. You go by Arabella very rarely, and your family has only heard you called by your nickname, Ella. Arabella is not an uncommon name. We can even shorten it to Ari to make it sound different."

"Why keep my name at all? Wouldn't it be easier to just pretend I am a different person?" Ella asked. She felt the tension rising as she realized just how daunting the task that had been set before her was.

"There are several reasons for doing it this way. First, because we're dealing with royalty. You should stay as truthful as possible or you could be tried and executed for treason. Second, your mother's family actually has connections to the royal family. We can only use these connections if we use your real identity. Third, it is a beautiful name that your mother gave you, and I didn't think you would want to be rid of it that easily."

Madame Briar gave her a sad smile, one that she got whenever she thought of Ella's mother.

The headmistress sighed and handed Ella a small stack of papers. "Here is the plan on how we are going to play this, along with all the information you need to know about your cover. You must memorize its contents before graduation, when you will be introduced as Lady Arabella, the granddaughter of the Prince of Wales."

"I thought we were going to keep it truthful," Ella said, looking at the stack of papers in her hands.

"It is the truth. Your mother was the fourth daughter of the Prince of Wales, and he had so many grandchildren that he doesn't remember them all. We can keep to the truth without bringing attention to your parentage." Madame Briar held Ella's gaze. "You are capable of doing this."

Ella swallowed, then took a deep breath. Could she do it? She had to. This was her chance.

"Now, about a code name. What do you think of the name Protector?"

Then, before Ella could even think about what she was saying, she blurted out, "What about the mission of finding my mother?"

The headmistress froze. "I thought I already told you. It is far too late to save her. Most likely, she is already dead." Madame Briar's tone indicated this was not up for debate.

Ella continued despite Madame Briar's tone. "But with the information that I found, maybe we can find where she was sold to. There are only a few places that slave traders sell to, and . . ."

"Not another word." Madame Briar's voice was cold enough to freeze the room. "I miss your mother too, but we cannot spend more resources than we already have to find someone who was sold ten years ago. Even if that person was one of ours. No new information has been found. It is too late to find her. We already have people watching the viscount. There is not much more we can do. There is not enough information."

Ella bit her tongue to refrain from saying something she might regret and held back her emotions. She gripped the fan that she held in her lap as if to keep back her anger and sorrow.

Madame Briar sighed, her lips tightening. "Again, I miss her too, but searching for her will only bring you more sorrow. And it will put both you and the Society in danger. Your mother wouldn't want that for you. We will still keep a lookout if we find more information."

Ella nodded, looking down at the fan clasped in her hand. It was a beautiful lacquered paper fan, the kind that her mother favored. She would not give up on her mother, nor her family home. Even though everyone had given up. She would get them back, even if she had to go against her teacher's wishes.

"Madame Briar?" Ella asked, letting some of the unshed tears fall. "May I take the codename Cinders?"

The headmistress relaxed and let the warmth back into her eyes. She thought for a moment, then responded. "Yes, dear, I think that name will suit you well. Now, begone with you. You have a ball to get ready for and your mission plans to memorize."

Ella stood, gave a deep curtsy, then left with Clementine in tow to get prepared for what would be the beginning of the rest of her life.

There are many different positions within the Fan Society. They each serve a specific function. The most interesting group is called the Whisperers. It is a very important support group for other agents. They are the ones that gossip, gather information from the society ladies, and plant information. This is very important in helping agents with their identities as well as getting others to change their attitudes toward another idea. They can help in many ways such as . . .

Lady Nora Codename: Cinders
Except from a note written to an
unknown person

Chapter Ten

Preparations for the graduation ball consumed most of the time Ella had. As her hair was being washed, brushed, and put into an elegant style, Ella spent her time reading through the papers out loud to Clementine.

"What type of mission is this?" Ella asked, rubbing her head.

"Don't move," Clementine muttered with a mouth full of pins. Clementine tugged Ella's hair until Ella's head was back in position. "If you mess up my curls, don't blame me." She looked at the papers in Ella's lap. "Who are we going to stay with?" she asked as she pulled another pin from her mouth and stabbed it into Ella's hair.

"Seems like we will be staying with Eleanor."

"What about her family? What do they know?"

Ella looked through the sheets. "They are friends of the society and are willing to keep my identity secret. They don't know what my mission is, only that I need to marry someone of high station."

"Well, this is going to be interesting," Clementine said, whirling another piece of hair around the locks that were already piled high on her head. "Eleanor is quite the character."

"Indeed she is," Ella replied, thinking about her academy days with Eleanor. She was a perky person who got on easily with everyone. Looking at her, it was hard to believe she had a such conniving mind. Eleanor had pulled many pranks and was quite skilled at getting away with them. Clementine was talented at getting information, but Eleanor was made to be a Whisper.

"I like her," Clementine added.

Ella rolled her eyes. "Of course you do. Another thing we need to do is choose a name for you. Calling you Clementine may be too much of a coincidence with my given name."

Clementine placed a feather in Ella's hair and paused, thinking. "Minnie. It's a common enough name and can be considered a nickname for Clementine. And I like the name. I think it suits me far better, don't you think?"

Ella looked at her friend in the mirror. She was even more stunning now that they were away from Lady Victoria. Clementine's light brown hair was in a simple bun, and her blue eyes glinted with mischievousness. Her skin had a soft glow, and even wearing a simple maid's uniform, a long-sleeved black dress and white apron, did not detract from the fact that Clementine was very pretty.

"Perfectly."

Clementine beamed. "Now, let me burn these papers and finish getting you ready."

Ella passed her the mission papers, and Clementine threw them in the fire. She used the poker to make sure that they completely burned before turning back to Ella.

"Let's make sure you are the belle of the ball so the prince will marry you."

Giving a small laugh, Ella replied, "I leave myself in your capable hands. Though, if you take too long, I will be late."

Clementine sniffed. "It's fashionable to be late." She glanced over Ella's appearance. "Don't move while I powder your face."

With practiced ease, Clementine put on Ella's petticoats and dress, all the while never messing up the hair. After dressing, Ella sat while she applied the talcum powder to her face and tried not to sneeze. After a light brush of rouge to the cheeks, charcoal to the eyebrows, and lip salve, she was finished.

"Done." Clementine grinned as she surveyed her work. "You look like your mother. Though, that hair is definitely your father's." With a happy sigh, she helped Ella stand and let her take a proper look at herself in the mirror.

She had on a beautiful pale pink dress set off her shoulders, with a thick neckline that came to a V. Her short sleeves were properly puffed, and encircling her waist was a peach sash. The skirt of the dress had a ruffle and peach embroidery. The differences between the Ella who had come into the academy as a servant had now transformed into a lady. Ella now looked fair skinned from her years hiding away in the secret tunnels and her rough hands had smoothed during her lessons to be a lady. Her hair, which used to constantly escape whatever bun she tried to contain it in, was now behaving itself, sleeked back into a braided bun. Into it were beautiful white feathers that contrasted beautifully against her dark brown hair. Her wispy strands now elegantly curled, framing her face. The minimal makeup gave her a rosy glow that was perfect for a young lady in society.

"Now, I can't leave you unarmed." Clementine helped Ella slip on long, elbow-length gloves and don a string of pearls with a matching pair of earrings. Finally, a ring was placed over the gloves, and a pearl and pink bracelet were added to her wrist.

Ella grabbed her shawl and draped it over her shoulders. When she turned back around, Clementine was holding a small white box.

"Madame Briar asked me to give this to you as a graduation present. She said it was your mother's."

Reverently, Ella opened the box. Inside was a beautiful fan, its metal spines covered with cream fabric and draped in lace.

"It's beautiful," Ella gasped.

Clementine pointed to the pattern near the base of the fan. Ella looked closer and could see there was an emblem weaved into the lace. It was difficult to see because both the lace and the fabric beneath it were cream, but as she looked closer, she could tell that it was an open fan in a circle. The symbol of the Fan Society. Just touching it made her feel a connection to her mother.

Ella smiled as she traced the pattern with her gloved hand. "Mom, I miss you."

Clementine elbowed her in the arm. "Don't cry or I'll have to redo all the makeup and you really will be late."

Ella laughed, blinking away her tears until she composed herself. She looked at Clementine, her face serious. "I'm going to find my mother, even if it is against orders. I won't ask you to go against orders. I'll do it on the side, but I have to find out what happened to her. It is —"

Clementine grabbed her arms. "Stop. You don't need to say anymore."

Ella sighed. "I understand. I won't ask you to break protocol."

"Silly, that is not what I meant. Of course, I will help you. I was just wondering why you even had to ask." Placing her hands on her hips, she added, "Honestly, do you really think I didn't know you would go against orders? How long have we been together?"

"For a long time."

"Did you really think that I wouldn't help you now? After all the times I have before?" Clementine asked. A smile graced Ella's lips as she remembered all the times Clementine had helped her get out of trouble. Sometimes even being punished in her place.

But then icy fear laced through her veins at the thought. "But it could really be dangerous this time. You could get sold as a slave or even die. We are dealing with illegal slave traders against orders. We won't have any support, and we may never even find her."

Clementine wrapped her arms around Ella's shoulders. "That is why we have a genius Legacy running the show. I trust you."

"I could make a mistake."

Clementine was already shaking her head. "You've grown a lot these past few years. You're ready."

With a determined humph, Clementine stood straight, brushing Ella's skirts so they fell just right. She looked Ella in the eye. "No more fussing. You can do this. Go show them what you can do, Lady Arabella."

Ella snorted, and took a deep breath, holding tightly to her mother's fan. "Lead on Minnie."

Clementine smiled and opened the door.

The patient was born early and his lungs were not developed properly. He is prone to wheezing, and other lung related sicknesses. Make sure the patient stays out of wet weather. Constant childhood illnesses have made his body to be weak; help the patient gain strength through horsemanship. Stress may cause his lung condition to be exacerbated. Make sure he is kept from stressful situations.

D octor Thomas: Royal Physician
    Medical records for Prince Adrian

Chapter Eleven

Clarence House

Adrian, his ear pressed against the door, listened to his father loudly proclaim his annoyances. "Those idiots in the House of Commons! How dare they bring up the Reform? It is a noble's duty and right to rule the people. Bah, those imbeciles. It must be the Whig Party, those bleeding hearts. And that Earl Charles Gray is the worst of that lot. Why is it that nobility is supposed to be part of the Whig Party? Bah."

Adrian jumped when he heard a voice behind him. "Your Highness, it is highly improper for a prince to be listening to a private conversation. Aren't you getting a little old for games like this? Especially when His Majesty made it explicitly clear that no one was to be in this wing. Anyway, it is time to get ready for the academy's graduation party."

He turned to face Phillip, his father's valet, standing beside him. Adrian sighed and straightened. He began walking slowly down the hallway. He turned over his shoulder and saw Phillip still standing stoically in the hallway, his hands folded behind his back, his expression never changing. Growling in frustration, and realizing that he wasn't going to hear any more of the conversation, he stomped away.

Adrian knew he was acting childish, and he slowed his pace. It was so frustrating when his father shut him out. His father was so worried Adrian would get sick from stress that he refused to allow him anywhere near politics. If his own father thought he couldn't handle being king, then how would any of Parliament believe in him?

He gripped his hair in frustration, then stopped himself. Letting out an exasperated sigh, he finished the trek back to his room.

Abigail and Mathew were waiting for him. His manservant opened the door as he approached, allowing both him and Abigail to enter. Abigail was his personal nurse. She checked on him every day, making sure he didn't get sick. Because of his condition, if Adrian caught a cold, it could spell death for him. While his health was not as poor as had been before, his father still insisted the nurse check on him every day.

"I'm fine, Abigail."

She entered and motioned for Adrian to sit, then set her bag down. "I still have to check. And since you will be going to a crowded place, it would be good to make sure everything is actually fine before you leave."

"Fine." Adrian spewed, sitting down in a huff and holding his arm out.

Abigail raised an eyebrow. "What has gotten you all riled up?"

He sighed and ran his fingers through his hair. "I'm sorry, Abigail. It's just so frustrating how my father treats me like a porcelain doll. That if I were to trip, I'm going shatter into a million pieces. How am I supposed to do my duties as a noble, let alone have others believe I can do my duties, if he refuses to allow me anywhere near politics?"

"I can see that you are breathing well. No wheezing; that's good. Now hold still while I check your pulse," Abigail murmured, holding his wrist lightly.

"Abigail, what am I supposed to do?"

"First off, whining to me does not prove that you are ready to do anything. You are already eighteen years old, and you're considered an adult, so act like it. Second, why don't you find some way to prove yourself to him, like actually attending your lessons?" She finished with a pointed look. Mathew snickered by the door.

Adrian glared at him. "Don't you start." He looked back to Abigail, his gray eyes looking into her blue ones. "I don't go to lessons because I've already learned everything on my own. And my teachers always stay away from topics my father doesn't like."

Abigail patted him on the knee. "Today, you are leaving the house. Maybe something will present itself."

"Yeah, for a girls' college graduation." Adrian rolled his eyes in disgust. "And all those available girls will be fawning over me so they can marry into nobility."

"You are a smart boy. You'll figure it out." She patted his knee one last time and then headed for the door. She stopped by Mathew. "Do keep an eye on him."

"Yes, Madam," He smiled at her as she left.

"Boot licker." Adrian snorted. "She is much older than you."

"Hey, I resent that," Mathew retorted, coming to help him get ready. "She is very refined and not *that* much older."

Adrian rolled his eyes. "She's old enough to be my mother."

"*Almost.* Almost old enough to be your mother, though she's only two years older than me." Mathew said, laying out Adrian's clothes. "Besides, she's still beautiful. Her auburn hair is luscious and her rosy cheeks are divine."

Laughing, Adrian watched as his freckled friend gave an elegant twirl with his jacket. Mathew had been with Adrian since they were both young. Mathew was assigned to Adrian as both a playmate and servant to help him with the day-to-day tasks. He was technically Adrian's valet, but he was more than that to Adrian. He was closer to a friend than a servant. Mathew was usually a mature person, but he always acted childish whenever Abigail left the room.

"Calm down, lover-boy. Someone would think you want to marry her."

"No, it's not like that," Mathew insisted a little too quickly.

Adrian could see his friend's ears turn red. "Sure."

Mathew turned to face Adrian and was back to his normal calm demeanor. "Of course it is, Your Highness. Now let's get you changed."

A grin crept onto Adrian's face, and he left himself to Mathew's ministrations. Then he went through getting his hair done, though luckily his hair had a slight wave to it and it didn't take long. Adrian was eager to be done getting ready.

"You're like a two-year-old. Why can't you sit still?" Mathew complained as he gave up on fixing Adrian's hair and released him.

"I have been stuck in bed for most of my life. I am finally healthy enough to get out and about that I would rather not spend it stuck in a chair."

Helping with his jacket, Mathew sighed. "It makes it seem like you *want* to go to the ball. Maybe to meet a girl?"

"I could have you fired for that," Adrian scoffed, adjusting his shirt and cuff.

"You could do that if you wanted," Mathew said, brushing Adrian's shoulders so the jacket sat properly.

Annoyed that he didn't get a raise out of Mathew, Adrian rolled his eyes. "You know, most nobles don't have put up with this kind of treatment from their servants."

Mathew smiled and opened the door. "Most nobles have more than a single servant for a friend."

"I have Abigail too." Adrian shot back. Then realizing that Mathew had just made his point, he glowered at him. "Fine, you win."

As Adrian passed through the door, Mathew stopped him with a hand on his shoulder. "Abigail is right, you know."

"About?"

"That this is your chance. You'll be out of the house. Try listening and conversing with people. You might find some way that you could prove yourself to your father. Stay and try it instead of escaping as soon as possible." Mathew released his shoulder, then fell instep behind him at a proper distance.

"What am I supposed to do? It's just giggling girls who care only about getting married. They aren't even involved in politics." Adrian turned to face Mathew. "What sort of opportunities will arise from that? Other than me getting mobbed by marriage-hungry women."

Mathew shrugged. "Who knows? But if you listen and observe, you might find one. You certainly won't if you bolt at the first opportunity"

Adrian turned on his heel. "Whatever you say."

Mathew smiled behind Adrian and they made their way toward the carriage that waited to take them to the academy.

The language of the fan should be known by all members of aristocracy. This is instrumental in how ladies play their role in the family. This allows them to display to the outside world that they are pure and virtuous while also allowing them to be as aggressive as need be when dealing with others. Though there are claims that other languages have been used with the fan, those have never been verified.

Written by Lady Mary Taylor
A Ladies Guide to Society

Chapter Twelve

3 July 1830, Academy

Each of the graduates were called one by one and presented to the guests. Ella was presented near the end, not the last one, as the last person would be remembered more easily than lady number twenty-four. She smoothed her skirts one last time, more nervous now since Clementine was not with her. This graduation was to be when she would meet her future husband, assuming that the mission went well and he would become her husband. Tonight would be the battle against every unmarried lady in this room. Horror struck when she realized she would have to do all of this while trying to avoid her stepfamily. As those terrifying thoughts raced through her mind, her name was called.

"Lady Arabella, Grand Daughter of Eugène de Beauharnais, who was the Grand Duke of Frankfort. She was one of the best students in tea brewing."

The mission had officially begun, and there was no more time to prepare. With her thumb, she rubbed the emblem on her fan, calming her nerves. She took a deep breath and stepped forward through the double doors. She entered a balcony in the large ballroom. The room was well lit and beautifully decorated, with chairs lining the outside edges. The center of the room was open with enough space to dance, though it was currently full of bejeweled guests that watched the graduates as they entered.

Ella had entered from the balcony at the back of the room, which had a staircase that led down to the dance floor. The entrance the girls were using was specifically used once a year for the graduation ceremony. The familiar space normally felt far more open when the room was used as a practice room for dancing, but now was full of obstacles.

Ella looked down at the crowd and could see front and center two chairs that could only be for King William and his son, Adrian. She tried to get a clearer view of the two, but she couldn't get a good look at them from this distance. She knew she would have to wait a little longer. Gliding through the door at the top of the staircase, she gave a beautiful curtsy to the guests. Lightly lifting her skirt, she descended slowly down the stairs, hoping with each step she wouldn't trip. Relief flooded through her as she arrived safely on the first floor. She curtsied again and moved towards the lineup of graduates, waiting while the last few girls were presented. Ella looked to where the king and his son were, but she still could not see their faces owing to other graduates blocking her view. She tried not to fidget while she waited for the graduation to continue.

Once the last girl had taken her place in the lineup, Madame Briar gave a final announcement. "Our graduates!"

Light applause followed that announcement and the headmistress gave the girls a moment to shine. After several seconds, she signaled for the musicians to begin playing.

Ella hoped to catch a glimpse of the man who was to become her husband, but was stopped short as several gentlemen came forward to sign her dance card. By the time the gentlemen had finished, the two chairs had been moved and the dancing had already begun. Realizing she had lost her chance, she ignored her dance card as she surveyed the dance floor.

To untrained eyes, it would look like an ordinary ball with gentlemen and ladies dancing the quadrille with complicated steps, across the middle of the room. On the sides of the room, a few people watched, and some parents spoke amongst themselves. Other hopeful men who wanted to marry a lady who graduated from the academy were asking ladies to dance. Though, in Ella's eyes, it seemed like a war zone. This was a battle of tactics, and it was one she had been trained to win. She calmed her nerves as she observed the flicking of the fans and the tapping of the fingers that told a much different story.

Ella observed as an intense bidding war was being made. With the polite face of proper society, the ladies spoke out with a passive voice. What they communicated in the fan language, however, was different. Parents would ask various ladies about their talents and what they could bring to the family, and aggressive negotiations would commence. Some young ladies were asked to show their various talents and others were asked questions that would indicate their compatibility with their children. Some of those involved dancing, how to speak to others, and embroidery. If the young ladies' talent showed promise, a mother would point their son in the right direction or speak to her husband. This was done all without any of the men knowing the fierce competition taking place right under their noses.

Ella took a deep breath and was about to head into the crowd when her eyes landed on her stepsister, Audrey. Audrey's blonde hair contrasted with the red dress that fit her like a glove. It was a little more risqué than was proper for a graduation, but that was Audrey. She was talking with her mother and stepsister on the edge of the floor.

Ella could see Lady Victoria was deep in debate with a countess about whose child should dance with the prince.

Audrey sighed at her mother, then eyed the available gentlemen who were watching her with appreciation. One gentleman finally gathered the courage to ask her to dance and led her to the dance floor.

Ella wandered to the opposite side of the room and saw Luella dancing in the center of the floor. Luella, her not-so-friendly rival in the Fan Society. As another member, she would be able to help her avoid her stepfamily, even though they don't really clash well with each other. Wanting to make sure that her first meeting with the prince went well, she flashed her ring in Lucilla's direction. When she looked Ella's way, Ella flicked her fan in a sequence that asked Luella to help as a warning system. In the chaos of the bidding war, the motions Ella made would seem like the normal fan language, and no one took notice.

Luella responded with a small nod. Luella would never want to be responsible for a failed mission. Satisfied that for the moment she would be safe from her stepfamily, Ella began searching for the prince.

Watching each of the many conversations being flung across the room, Ella caught a glimpse of the conversation she was looking for. There was a passionate debate about who would be the first to ask Prince Adrian to dance. The women were using their fans to discuss who had the highest status to go up to him to entice him to a dance, all the while gossiping about the ladies who had forgotten their training and approached him already. They flitted about him, hoping his attention would fall on them and ask to dance.

As Ella watched, the weight of her mission slowed her steps. With each step, she hoped to see the man who was to be her lifelong mission. Fear and excitement flooded her veins when she finally saw the one who could only be the prince.

He was sulking as he leaned against the wall, trying unsuccessfully to avoid the other ladies who approached him, wanting him to ask them to dance. They flitted around him, and he deftly avoided their longing looks. His dark brown hair, which was almost black, was curly and slicked to frame his fine features. His small sideburns stopped at the base of his earlobe. She could tell that he was rather small for his age and was thin, most likely due to his ill health. Though he wouldn't be considered masculine, he had elegant features that would make most women swoon, even if he didn't have a title.

The longer she watched, the more her irritation rose toward those ladies who flitted closer to the prince. With each step of a woman that got closer, the prince pushed himself further back against the wall. His nauseated expression made him appear as if he might try to leave the ball, and soon. Ella glanced around and spied King William, who, while speaking to the marquess and marchioness at the head of the room, was sneaking glances at his son. Worry creased his features every time he peeked in his son's direction. If Ella was going to have a chance to speak to him, she would have to do it soon, before the King sent Adrian home.

Knowing she had to do something, her training ran through her head, and her fear melted away. Taking a quick assessment of her surroundings, she quickly thought about what she needed to do.

She caught the eye of Eleanor and made a small gesture with her fan. Eleanor gave a bob of her head, her conversation never stopping, and Ella continued searching.

By the time the first song ended, she found her quarry. One of the young earls who had signed her dance card. He was standing awkwardly to the side and was one of the unlucky few attendees who did not have a mother in attendance directing his every move. Ella began moving in his direction, making sure to indicate to him that she was available for the next dance. When his gaze finally landed on her, she could see relief flash through his expression.

The earl approached her and bowed. "May I escort the young lady to the dance floor?"

Ella gave a small nod of her head and accepted his hand, letting herself be led away. They headed to a group of three couples that were too near where the prince was being accosted. Using a light touch, Ella guided him in their direction until the earl was closer. They joined the circle as a bouncy tune started to play. Ella curtsied, and her plan was in motion.

Chapter Thirteen

Adrian was having difficulty breathing as the ladies continued to surround him. His lungs clenched as sweat dripped down his neck from so many people crowding in on him. What was Mathew thinking? Observing these ladies only proved they were greedy raptors, hiding beneath beautiful dresses. Unable to take it anymore, he begged for their forgiveness as he tried to edge himself away from their greedy claws.

He sighed in relief as the next dance started and a few of the ladies were taken to the dance floor. Adrian took a deep breath and relaxed his tense shoulders when a flash of light caught his eye. Blinking, he turned his attention toward a dancer on the floor. It was a lady in a pale pink dress.

During the dance, whenever her partner lifted her hand, the ring on her finger would catch the light just right to shine in his eyes. She danced beautifully with kicks and hops. He could see that she kicked just a little higher and with more energy than the others as she twirled about the floor. He couldn't help but watch as she danced with the other couples in the group. As the music came to an end, the dance finished with a flourish. They flung their hands in the air. Adrian watched as a bracelet sailed through the air until it landed at his feet. Instantly, he reached down and picked it up.

The lady in pink noticed her bracelet was missing and started a fervent search around the room. When her eyes finally rested on what was in his hand, she turned to her partner, gave him a small bow, and headed his way.

She curtsied. "Good sir, I am so sorry, but I believe that bracelet is mine."

For once not hearing his title of prince, he smiled. "How do I know that this is your bracelet? It could be any number of ladies who own it."

The corner of her mouth turned up, and she hid it behind her fan. She leaned forward conspiratorially and whispered, "Because you were watching me the whole dance."

Adrian's face reddened a little, but having a lady speak so bluntly to him made him excited. "And how did you know that?"

"I believe it is proper for a gentleman to give his name," she said, sidestepping the question with ease.

Adrian opened his mouth to speak, then stopped, realizing this was his chance to talk to a girl without his royal blood interfering. "Lord Adrian," he said with a small bow, then holding out his hand, he asked, "And may I have the pleasure of knowing your name, lovely lady?"

She giggled, placed her hand in his, and he gave it a small kiss. "Ari . . . I mean Lady Arabella, honorable sir."

"You certainly are an answered prayer," Adrian grinned, recognizing the meaning of the name. "You have saved me from being snatched away by ladies who wish for my attention."

A smile peeked from behind her fan as she tried with little success to hide her expression. "And how do you know that I am not one of them?"

Adrian looked at her, thinking. He could see an unusual intelligence in her eyes. It seemed that Mathew and Abigail were right. Something interesting had appeared before him. "You knew that I was the prince."

Adrian enjoyed the sound of her gentle laughter. She brought it under control and replied, "It is not that hard to tell you are the prince. You have the pin of the royal line there on your jacket."

He glanced down at his jacket. "That is very true." He blushed and laughed at himself. "I see you've had a joke at my expense."

"No harm intended, your highness. Anyway, you look much more relaxed now. Don't forget that the ladies who are trying for your attention have a reason for what they are doing." Her dance partner finally approached her, and she curtsied one last time to Adrian. "Your Highness."

The earl bowed a proper greeting to Adrian. "Your Highness." He turned back to Lady Arabella and held out his arm.

She turned from Adrian, instead facing the earl, and held his proffered arm. The earl led her away, and she smiled at something clever he said. Adrian was surprised that he felt irritation as he watched them leave. For some reason, it bothered him that she hadn't tried to get him to dance with her. He decided he would ask her why she hadn't tried.

He had just made his decision and was about to go after her when a cheerful lady stopped in front of him. He tried to step around her, but she stepped in front of him. Adrian tried again to step around her and yet again found her directly in his path.

"Would you move, please?" Haste caused his words to come out harsher than he meant.

He could tell that she was grinning behind her fan as she curtsied. "Of course, Your Highness."

As she curtsied, he looked around her, seeking in vain to find the lady he was speaking to. "Where did she go?" He asked under his breath, his eyes searching fruitlessly.

"My cousin, Your Highness?" the girl asked, still in her curtsy, eyes tilted up at him.

Adrian stopped searching and finally scrutinized the lady in front of him. She was petite and had honey brown hair piled on top of her head. She wore a dark green dress that matched her glimmering green eyes.

Realizing that this young lady might be of help to him, he bowed, remembering his manners. "May I have the pleasure of knowing your name, lovely lady?"

She smiled an infectious smile. "I am Lady Eleanor Taylor. I am honored by this chance to speak to a gentleman such as yourself."

"May I ask for your help? Do you know where your lovely cousin has gone?"

Mischief glinted in her eyes as she asked, "The lady who just left with Earl Brown?"

"Yes, that one," he answered, annoyance growing but not knowing how to extract the information in any other way. "It would be my pleasure to speak with your cousin."

Adrian could tell as he watched her that she was purposely taking longer to think. "Humm, I don't believe I know where she is going, Your Highness." Adrian sighed, irritated that this conversation was going nowhere, and he was about to excuse himself when she continued. "But, I may know where she is going to be in a few weeks."

"You do? Where?" he asked excitedly.

Lady Eleanor flicked her fan shut and tapped her chin. "Do you really wish to know?"

"Beautiful Lady Eleanor Taylor, please tell me your wisdom," Adrian spouted, hoping she would relinquish what she knew without making him wait any longer.

Eleanor gave a polite smile, green eyes flashing. "There is a summer boating event soon that I know she will be attending. I hope to see you there."

She gave a curtsy and wandered toward a gaggle of girls that had been watching the exchange. Adrian sighed and went back to his wall, pondering about the intelligent woman dancing in his thoughts. He wondered why she didn't act like she wanted something from him like all the others, and felt excited about the prospect of seeing her again. Lost in thought, he did not notice Eleanor signal Ella from across the room with a few flicks of her fan.

Rumors regarding agent Cinders will be sent out.
Set the Whispers to spread information to the effect
of her being an illegitimate child. Make efforts to
obscure her background. Add that she is a cousin to
Codename: Poltergeist.

Chapter Fourteen

That evening, Eleanor's house

Ella landed on her bed with a squeal of excitement.

"I take it things went well?" Clementine asked, moving over to help Ella undress. Clementine had arrived at Eleanor's house after helping Ella get ready for graduation, so when Ella returned from the ball, she could immediately begin her duties as Lady Arabella's personal maid.

Ella rolled over and stood back up. "It was like all of my training came together." She turned, allowing Clementine to help her out of the complicated laces. "When it seemed as if things would all go wrong, I was at my calmest."

Clementine stopped fiddling with the laces and leaned around to face Ella. "See? I knew you could do it. I am never wrong about these things."

Rolling her eyes, Ella said, "Yes, yes. You know better."

Clementine nodded, a smile on her face as she finished helping Ella out of the fancy dress. "So, how was it seeing your step-siblings and Lady Victoria?"

"I avoided them the entire night. It wasn't hard. It's not like they were looking for me. I wanted my first meeting with the prince to happen perfectly," Ella explained, walking to the vanity and sitting so Clementine could undo her hair. "I thought it went rather well."

Ella could see a mischievous grin on her friend's face as she started plucking feathers from her hair. "What?"

"Nothing," Clementine replied, and smiled wider.

Ella turned in her chair, glancing briefly at the feathers in her friend's hands. "What are you smiling about?"

Still grinning widely, she turned Ella's head back to face the mirror. "I'm glad your meeting with your future husband went well."

"That is . . ." Ella tried to turn back to her, but was promptly shifted towards the mirror by Clementine.

In the mirror, Clementine's eyes gleamed with mischievousness. "What was he like, the prince?"

With a sigh, Ella folded her arms. "He seems rather naive about how society works. I don't know how he is going to be king like that. He avoids people like they are trying to eat him. He also doesn't know anything about the norms of talking politely to people. Though, he does know how to take a joke at his own expense, but that is not how a king should act. He is rather easy on the eyes. But he needs to eat more. He is way too small."

"Seems you like him a lot." Clementine laughed, pulling out the braid and hairpins.

Irritation bubbled through Ella. "In anything that I said, what makes you think I like him?"

Brushing her hair, Clementine raised an eyebrow. "And what is so wrong with you falling in love? Isn't that good? You are supposed to marry this man."

Ella sat, lost in thought as Clementine continued to rake through her hair, then put her hair into a loose braid. Once she was finished Clementine came around the chair and knelt in front of Ella, holding her hands in her own. "Do not just view this as a mission. A lifelong mission is just life. Your mother certainly loved your father even though he was her mission. If do not, you will just be hurt and resent the choice you made."

"But I am using my mission as motivation to marry him."

"All I'm saying is if you truly fall in love with him, your mission and your motivations will align. You will want your mission because you love him. Now off to bed. A girl needs her beauty sleep."

Ella smiled at her lifelong friend and headed to bed.

Adrian ambled into his room with a lightness in his steps and a grin on his face. Mathew smiled at him, picking up the jacket that Adrian had dropped on the floor.

"You were right, Mathew. I just needed to observe and things became different."

Following after the prince, Mathew picked up the cravat that had been dropped on the floor. "Very good. What did you learn?"

Adrian turned around with a sudden stop, nearly knocking his friend over. "I met someone who may have changed my views on these dreadfully tedious balls."

Mathew snorted, picking up a sash and vest from the floor as well. "I had hoped it would change how you view the floor as the laundry basket."

"Then what would you do?" He smiled as Mathew made a pile of his clothes on the chair and went to help him prepare for bed. "No, there was this girl who had the gall to tease me."

"So, she realized that you listen through doors, then?"

Adrian frowned at him. "I could have you fired."

Mathew raised an eyebrow. "Then who would be your laundry basket, sir?"

He laughed as he finished getting dressed. "That would be a problem then, wouldn't it? I guess you can stay."

"Thank you, sir." Mathew gave a bow. "Though I did tell you to listen in on your father next door, and not in the hallway. If you had done as I told you, then Philip wouldn't have found you. Now, who is this girl that has changed your views?"

Sitting on the edge of the bed, Adrian sighed. "Have you ever heard the name Lady Arabella?"

"No last name?"

Adrian shook his head.

Brow furrowed, Mathew slowly finished gathering the clothes. "I may have heard that name before."

Adrian eyed him curiously. "Out with it"

Mathew hesitated and turned to face him. "It's not very flattering."

"Speak."

He paused before continuing, "There have been . . . rumors. . . that she is the illegitimate daughter of a baron. She probably hasn't been acknowledged by her family. I heard that the baron's wife hated her and sent her to live elsewhere. It is quite the scandal."

"Oh," Adrian sighed. "That must be why she avoided speaking of it. She must be living with her cousin. It must also be the reason why her cousin knows where she is going to be."

"I suspect so."

"It must also be why she didn't want to dance with me. She must not have enough social status to dance to with me, let alone speak to me. And why she spoke so bluntly might just be because she has never had the proper training." Adrian suddenly felt as if his eyes had been opened. He stood up and grabbed Mathew by the arms.

"That also must be why she said that people had their reasons for trying to get married. She might see people wanting to escape their own families by marrying. Or that she wishes she could marry and get out of that situation."

Mathew grunted as he eased Adrian's grip from his arms. Rubbing them, he retorted, "That may be the case, or it may not. It was just rumors that I heard. It could be nothing. I would advise taking rumors with a grain of salt."

Eyes clear and full of determination Adrian looked at Mathew, holding his gaze with his own. "No, I will go to the party and help her, like she helped me at the ball. She was kind enough to help me with my awkwardness. I will see what I can do to help her. Now, what do you know of a summer boating event?"

I don't know how many times the Friends of the Society have saved a mission. Many of them are relatives or children of the society and know how important our objectives are. Very few become Friends unless they are related, but those who do are very, very trusted. Eleanor's parents were these. They helped save the life of one of the members of the society. They helped in so many ways. I don't know that I will ever be able to repay them.

Lady Arabella Cooper;
Codename Cinders
Excerpt from unknown book
Page 120

Chapter Fifteen

15 July 1830 London, England

The sun was shining when guests began arriving for afternoon tea. This would be the first time Ella would be interacting with her stepfamily after starting her mission as Lady Arabella. The earl and his wife set up a tea party to specifically help set her identity for when she might first encounter someone from her old life.

Ella curtsied to the countess when she came to the foyer. "Thank you for the help today, Countess."

Looking over at the countess, Ella could see where Eleanor got much of her personality and looks. The countess had the same bubbly personality that her daughter portrayed, as well as the same hair. Her green eyes held the same mischievous gleam that her daughter displayed whenever Eleanor was on a mission. With their sharp wits and easygoing manners, it was no wonder everyone adored both the mother and daughter.

Ella was enveloped in a warm hug. "Call me Margret. There is no need to be so formal since you will be living here for the foreseeable future. If you need anything at all, don't be afraid to ask for it."

Still in her embrace, Ella pulled away slightly. "Then call me Ari."

"That is an easy request." The countess relinquished her embrace, then held Ella's hands. "Ari, I hope this tea party goes well for you."

That final sentiment held considerable weight as both of them understood the party's true purpose. Eleanor came in and greeted her mother with an embrace. The countess whispered something to Eleanor and then ushered them both in to greet the guests.

As they made their way to the sitting room, Ella asked, "What did your mom whisper to you?"

Eleanor sighed, rolling her eyes. "She asked me to keep an eye on you. Such a worrier. You were the best at the academy. It's not like you need my eyes on you."

Laughing, Ella elbowed her. "I will always need someone as talented as you by my side."

A giggle bubbled from Eleanor and she gave a radiant smile. "Why, thank you. I know you appreciate my talents."

"Can I count on you to help me validate my identity?"

Another laugh bubbled from Eleanor as she beamed. "Will do, Ari."

"Then I'll take my cues from you." Ella was happy to follow Eleanor's lead since she was the best Whisper in their class. Eleanor was a master at making gossip the truth. With her cheerful demeanor and speaking with utter sincerity, many would believe the sky was green if Eleanor said it was so.

They reached the sitting room, and Clementine opened the door for them. Eleanor smiled, letting her happy aura fill the room. As host, she bounced forward to eagerly greet everyone. Ella trailed behind so that Eleanor could introduce her as Lady Arabella, her cousin.

Eleanor's family, the Taylors, had many friends throughout the different ranks of society. In this household, a baroness could sit near a marchioness and it was acceptable because of the Taylors. This made it the perfect way for Lady Arabella's identity to be introduced into all walks of the social circles. Although this also meant her stepfamily would be there.

Ella's heart thudded when she realized who they were going to greet first. Her nerves tingled through her as she saw noticed a very familiar face seated next to the lady they needed to greet. Taking a deep breath, she folded her hands in front of her and strode forward, a smile plastered on her face.

Eleanor greeted the lady she didn't know first, but had read much about her due to her relation to the prince. "Duchess Victoria of Kent, I would like for you to meet my cousin, Lady Arabella."

Ella had to refrain from grimacing at her stepmother, who bore the same name as the prince's aunt. Ella quickly curtsied, as she needed to get on the good side of Prince Adrian's aunt, and said, "Duchess of Kent, I am pleased to meet a lady as noble as yourself."

The duchess looked Ella up and down, noting how Ella was standing near Eleanor, and gave a polite smile. "Charmed."

"I see you have met Countess Victoria of Cooper and her daughters," Eleanor said, introducing Ella's stepmother, whom Ella had been trying to ignore. Ella pressed down on her flutter of irritation as she focused on the Duchess instead.

The duchess smiled. "Yes, I have been charmed by her. It seems we have much in common besides our names," the duchess replied, motioning to Ella's stepmother.

Even though the duchess was spouting polite words, Ella could see that her smile didn't quite reach her eyes. She had been looking at Ella's stepsisters like a puzzle and wasn't quite sure where to stick the pieces. It seemed her stepmother and the duchess have more in common beyond just their names.

"Yes, having both lost your husbands at such a young age and leaving women such as yourselves all alone to raise your daughters. That must have been very hard," Eleanor said, spouting out information at the drop of a hat. Ella was a little jealous of how Eleanor always was able to dredge up facts on everyone with such ease. She quickly stomped out the feeling; now was not the time to be thinking such things.

Instead, Ella refocused on the duchess. The duchess was regal even as she sat, conveying that she knew full well that she was the highest ranking at the party. Her dark hair had roses in it. Her brown eyes pierced through Ella as she calculated just how much attention she needed to put towards her.

Eleanor continued with the greetings and introduced Ella to Ella's own stepmother. Feeling a sliver of worry, Ella kept a polite smile on as Eleanor went through the greeting, "Countess Victoria Cooper, this is my cousin, Lady Arabella. She is staying with us until she marries into a good family."

Ella didn't need to be worried. Her stepmother eyed Ella with speculation, her fan flicking in front of her face as she hid what Ella knew to be a look of repugnance. "Pleasure to meet you."

Relief spread through Ella when she realized her stepmother hadn't recognized Ella. It was amazing what a new demeanor and a growth spurt could do. Ella gave her a bright smile, hiding her disgust at having to speak with her stepmother. "Baroness Cooper, it is wonderful to meet you."

With a flick of her fan, Lady Victoria pointed to her daughters. "Lady Audrey and Lady Effie."

Ella curtsied to them. She watched to see if any recognition flickered through their eyes. Contempt filled Audrey's demeanor as she nodded, then flicked her fan in front of her face, as if it were to fan away a horrible smell. Effie, however, looked at Ella with curiosity and confusion. "Have we met before?"

Fear froze Ella's polite smile on her face. Ella's mind tumbled through what would happen if she couldn't keep her composure and if her sister discovered her identity. Eleanor, sensing her hesitation, jumped to the rescue.

"I doubt you have had the chance to ever meet her. She has had some. . . special circumstances. Due to these circumstances, she will be staying with us. And I apologize for her manners; she is still learning. She didn't have an opportunity to learn them until recently." Eleanor gasped and covered her mouth. "I'm sorry, Ari. I didn't mean to say that."

Regaining control of herself, Ella smiled at Eleanor, thankful for the save. "It's alright, dear Cousin. I do still have a lot to learn." Ella turned back to her stepsisters and fawned over them. "It is wonderful to meet such fine ladies such as yourselves. I hope I can learn to be just as elegant as you are. I would love to get to know you better, and learn from you."

The interest that Effie showed in Ella died as she said those words, something she never would have said to them if she didn't have a role to play. She forced down her hatred for them as she and Eleanor moved on, introducing her to the rest of the gathering, and ignoring the final glance from Effie.

Ghosts are anyone who gives information. They could be men, women, and children. Nobles, servants, and coachmen are all considered when choosing the best people to become your Ghosts. They are generally motivated by money, kindness, or loyalty. Those motivated by kindness and loyalty will best serve you. Never choose someone who is motivated by fear. You cannot trust the information given. Choose someone who can work without you having to spell out every detail of what needs to be done. Some training should be given, especially if they are young so they won't be caught and will know how to deal with other offers to gather information. Make sure. . .

Unknown author
Untitled book, page 24

Chapter Sixteen

After the tea party, Ella spoke to Clementine as Ella sharpened her blades. Ella kept an eye on the door in front while Clementine kept an eye on the one behind Ella and listened for anyone coming. "Did my stepfamily notice you?"

Clementine sniffed as she dumped the water bowl out the window. "As if. The only one that would have recognized me is Effie, she always was the smarter one."

Ella replaced the blade and pulled another blade from its hiding place. She began to sharpen it. "She almost caught me. It's going to be difficult to be around her."

Wiping the blade clean, Ella went to work on another, keeping an eye on the door. It would not be good if any of the servants saw their new lady sharpening knives. Ella let her thoughts wander as she tucked another knife away. Effie was always trying to win her mother's approval, but Ella knew that she never would. She didn't know why, but at times when Effie wasn't looking, Victoria would look at her daughter with disgust. Maybe Ella could use this to her advantage. "What new information have you learned?"

"The duchess is promoting her daughter to the next in line for the throne. She was also eyeing all the other ladies to see if they were eligible to marry the prince."

"I wonder what my stepmother thought of that."

Clementine laughed. "They clashed, though of course with all propriety. Still, I doubt the duchess thought anything of a countess."

Ella smiled. "Her daughter is third in line for the throne, the king is old, and the prince is sickly. By the time her daughter comes of age, she will have her daughter already placed on the throne. My stepmother would hate that idea and wants her daughter to marry the prince instead. That way, their child would be next in line instead of the duchess's daughter."

"That could be a problem," Clementine replied, concern evident on her face.

Pulling out her last dagger, Ella thought about it. "Depends on how far the duchess is willing to go to put her daughter on the throne. We will have to keep an eye on her. Though right now it seems as if the duchess is just trying to keep him from getting married. We will —"

Ella stopped speaking as Clementine made a quick motion with her hands to warn Ella of someone coming. With quick hands, Ella slid her dagger under her skirts and opened a book from the nearby table. Clementine bowed her head when a maid came in.

The young girl carried a bucket of water and was startled when she looked up and saw Ella. With a sudden jerk, she bowed, water sloshing over her bucket at her nervous bow. "I am so sorry, my lady. I forgot you were staying in this room. Please forgive me."

With a quick flick of her fan to cover her face, Ella tried to suppress a laugh. It was horrible to laugh, but with the tense moment and the servant bobbing nervously like a buoy, it was hard not to. Taking pity on the poor maid, Ella gave a polite cough and raised her hand in a soothing gesture. "It's alright. You can stop now."

The maid stopped bobbing, but that didn't stop the shaking of her hands. The maid was young. She seemed to be close to twelve years old, and had a black smudge across her cheek. She was tall and lanky for her age. Her dirty blonde hair was drawn up into a cap, and her hands were visibly rough from scouring floors. Her face was tanned from working outside, but she possessed intelligent brown eyes. Ella felt a kinship with this girl, who was new and facing someone who had the power to ruin her livelihood.

"What is your name?" inquired Ella.

Switching hands with the bucket and wiping her damp hand on her apron, she answered in a quiet voice. "Harriette, my lady."

Ella eyed Clementine and tapped her fan, letting her know what she was planning. She smiled at the skittish servant. "Harriette, are you new?"

The girl bobbed. "Yes, my lady. The countess just let my mother allow me to work here. I'm sorry for interrupting you."

With a soft laugh, Ella replied, "It's nice to learn that I am not the only one who is new. Do you live around here?"

Harriette gave a small nod.

"I'm wondering if you would be willing to guide me around the town." Ella gestured towards Clementine. Clementine opened her hand, revealing a crown. "Of course, we would be willing to pay for your time."

Henrietta's eyes went wide as she stepped closer to Clementine. She stopped and turned to Ella. "Do you really mean it, my lady?"

With a small chuckle, Ella nodded.

A whoop of delight sprang from the girl's lips, and she slid the crown into her apron pocket. Dropping into a perfect curtsy to Ella, she said, "Lady Arabella, anything you need, just ring for me."

Bounding away, Harriette bowed her head as she passed Ella into the room beyond. Ella watched and listened until the footsteps disappeared. Tension eased from her shoulders when the girl was gone.

Ella turned to Clementine. "What do you think?"

"She is perfect to be a Ghost. She seemed to be quite happy with how you treat her. Though, I worry about her barging in without knocking."

Ella gasped, grasping her heart with one hand, as she threw her other arm over her head in feigned surprise. "Clementine, I'm shocked. Did you not realize she was faking it?"

Raising her eyebrow, and looking down her nose at Ella, Clementine retorted, "Of course I realized she was faking it. Who do you think I am? No, what I meant is that she didn't listen at the door to see if we were here. Or if we were to eavesdrop. I don't know why she came here."

Ella shrugged. "My guess is that Eleanor sent her to get information on us, to test and train her, while giving us help. Eleanor is sneaky like that."

"That sounds like something she would do." Glancing at the door, Clementine added, "She could have at least come back to listen. Eleanor is going berate her for that."

"It looks as though she is new at gathering information and wants to get in Eleanor's good graces. She is just over eager. As Eleanor trains her, she will get better. Eleanor is good at training Ghosts. She did do well with the girl's acting," Ella allowed, thinking about the actions of the girl. "Though, a little over exaggerated."

Clementine smiled. "She reminds me of you. Mind you, not like you are now. Back when you were cute and listened to adults better."

Laughter erupted from Ella, and she wiped a tear that leaked from her eye. "I never listened to adults."

She sighed. "Guess that was only in my dreams. You listen much better in them."

Ella threw a pillow from a nearby chair at her.

"Hey!" Clementine complained. "Aren't we supposed to be planning things right now?"

"Harriette will be a good Ghost. Eleanor trains them well. I'm sure that Harriette will tell Eleanor what we told her, and I'm certain Eleanor will speak on our behalf. We can ask for help when she heads out and can find out more information about the citizens. If they are angry with the royal family, it doesn't matter what other nobility are planning in the end. Remember what happened to the French. We don't want another revolution on our hands."

Chapter Seventeen

Red Lion Hotel

The boating event took place on the banks of the Thames River. Providing a beautiful backdrop was the Red Lion Hotel, which lived up to its name. Its red brick was vibrant and full of wisteria that climbed the front of the building. At the top of the entryway was a red lion statue, its namesake. Behind the hotel was the tower of St. Mary's Church, peeking over the rooftop. Dotting the banks were ladies dressed in white, shading themselves with parasols, sitting on blankets. The ladies watched the river as couples and others glided out over the water. Several of the gentlemen had started a rowing match with each other. Other gentlemen, who were escorts, called bets on who would win and asked for a kiss from the lady's hand if their rower won.

Clementine spread a blanket out on the lawn and leaned towards Ella, eyeing the men who were rowing. Clementine fanned her face as she said, "It seems we have a great view."

"Focus. We have things we need to do." Ella nudged her.

With an exasperated sigh, Eleanor retorted, "We can have fun while we are doing it. Though, I guess you already have a man you should be looking for. Do you think he's coming?"

Twisting her hands on the handle of her parasol, she looked over the people on the banks. "Eleanor said that he would, based on how he reacted, but who knows?"

Ella glanced through the crowd one last time, then returned her gaze to Clementine. "You know what you need to do?"

"Yes."

"Then I guess we each need to get to it," Ella said, giving Clementine a nod for luck before heading towards the assembled crowd for a more thorough search.

Ella still didn't see who she was looking for. She looked out over the water, her eyes roving over the boats until they caught a familiar face. Her stepmother. Sitting across from her stepmother was the lady she had been debating with at the ball. They were seated in a boat a little way out near the bridge. They were far enough away from most of the other boats that their conversation would not be overheard. As Ella watched, Eleanor appeared beside her. "Who are you looking at?"

Ella, who was used to Eleanor's mystifying ability to appear precisely when she was needed, nodded her head towards her stepmother.

Following Ella's line of sight, Eleanor looked closely at the lady. "That's interesting."

"Why is that? Who is she?" Ella whispered, taking a closer look at the lady. She was dressed in white with a large floral hat. Her features were sharp, like a knife. She had a regal bearing and looked like a lady of status, but Ella felt like she was dangerous.

"Ever hear of a man named Viscount Edmund?"

Hatred instantly pierced through Ella's heart. She took deep breaths, trying to calm her anger. During her school years, when she had looked for any information on her mother. She had found this name. This man was connected to the disappearance of her mother. And why was her stepmother talking to this woman? And how was this woman connected to the Viscount?

Through gritted teeth, Ella spoke. "Viscount Edmund is known to have ties to the underworld, though most don't know how deep. While he may play the part of a gentleman, he has a reputation for being able to obtain anything, for a price. He also is known for making people who poke their noses into his business disappear."

Eleanor nodded. "That woman is Countess Matilda. She is an associate of Viscount Edmund."

"*What?*" Ella exclaimed. Then realizing she had spoken too loudly, she whispered, "How is she connected to him?"

Pointing her chin at Countess Matilda, Eleanor replied, "We don't know much about their connection. All we know is that she mingles with the ladies of society and if they have a need, she is the person who puts them in touch with Viscount Edmund."

Ella looked over the countess, trying to glean everything she could from her, the way she looked, what she was wearing, and most of all, how she was reacting to her stepmother.

Turning to Eleanor, she said, "I need to get closer."

Eleanor raised an eyebrow at her and twirled her parasol. With a small tilt, she pointed a little way down the bank. Ella turned to see Earl Brown peeking glances at her. Then gave a small signal to Eleanor, who had turned towards her. With a small nod, they started their act. Ella giggled loudly and made pointed glances at the earl. Eleanor giggled back, looking at him as well. Ella could see a flush grace his cheeks as he mustered up the courage to approach her.

He gave a bow and offered her his hand. Ella placed her hand in his, and he gave it a short kiss. "Lady Arabella, it is a pleasure to see you again."

"And you as well." Ella let a flush fall across her face and offered a smile that could turn into a giggle.

"Would you like to accompany me to the boats?"

"Well," Ella hesitated.

Eleanor chimed in, "Of course my cousin would." She gave Ella a nudge towards the water. "Go have some fun.

Giving Eleanor a fake glare, she turned back towards the earl.

"It seems like I will be happy to accompany you to the river. Lead on," she said as he held out his arm. With a smile, she laced her arm through his, and lifting her white skirts so they wouldn't get dirty, they approached the water. A servant was standing on a small dock lined with rowboats. As they neared, the servant knelt on the dock and held the boat steady. The earl stepped into the boat first, then held out his hand to help Ella in. Ella managed to keep her balance as she stepped over the side and sat. Rearranging her skirts, she waited while the boat was untied and Earl Brown pulled the oars out. With a soft push from the servant, they were sent off from the dock to the deeper waters.

"Where do you want to go, my lady?" he asked as he began rowing to the center of the river.

Ella smiled and made a show of taking her time to think. All the while an annoyance grew at how long it was taking to get to her target. "Humm, how about near the bridge?"

"As you wish," he said, and he turned the boat towards the bridge, ever closer to Countess Matilda.

While he rowed, the earl made proper small talk as a gentleman gives. Ella nodded and smiled at appropriate times, even throwing in a girlish giggle occasionally to keep him happy. Her attention was divided, though, as she strained her ears to hear the conversation her stepmother was having.

Ella caught a few words that rose above the noise. Her stepmother said, ". . . after all that he must help me again . . . Duchess. . . heir to the throne."

Ella could only hear a few words of the Countess' reply. "No . . . You got your help too. . . worry about . . . daughter. . . Prince . . . dead soon. Just like . . . husband. . . Edmund will help only . . ."

Leaning towards the conversation as the distance narrowed, Ella nodded distractedly at a question from her rowing partner. She strained to catch any information that could be evidence of someone's death when there was a jarring thud and the boat flipped over, dumping them both into the water.

Chapter Eighteen

5 mins earlier

Prince Adrian watched from the carriage as people began to arrive at the Red Lion Hotel.

"You will need to leave the carriage if you want to find her." Mathew reminded him, standing by the open door. The footman kept a straight face as he did his best to ignore the exchange between the prince and his valet. Mathew shifted a large heavy picnic basket and tried not to drop it.

"Remind me, why am I doing this again?" Adrian sighed, careful to not mess up his carefully arranged hair by dragging his finger through it. Instead, he gripped his top hat that was sitting in his lap.

Mathew, with his endless patience, replied, "Because you want to have lunch with a young lady that you are falling in love with?"

"I am not in love with her," he spouted instantly. "I am just intrigued by her, that's all."

"As you say, Your Royal Highness," Mathew replied, not budging from his position by the open door.

Adrian waited, watching the unmoving Mathew. He threw his hands up. "Fine, you win. Let's get this over with before I die from being outside for too long."

Mathew stepped in front of him, which was unusual, and gave him a stern glare. "Don't you ever say that Your Highness. You are not going to die on me, do you understand?"

Looking into Mathew's unflinching eyes with anger still burning in them, Adrian realized his mistake. Mathew had been watching over him since they both were young and had seen all of Adrian's sicknesses. There were more than a few times that Adrian just barely managed to escape death's grip. Realizing he had gone too far, he apologized. "I'm sorry, Mathew. I will never again refer to my death until I'm old and gray. Happy?"

Mathew nodded and stepped back to his normal position. Relieved that Mathew was once again happy, Adrian took a deep breath and gathered his nerves. He strode to the bridge to get a better view of the gathering, shying away from the crowded banks. It still made him sick when he was stuck in a crowd, and he would never be able to find her if he was constantly trying not to throw up.

As he stood on the bridge next to the hotel, he watched those who had arrived for the boating event. There were many people, and it was difficult to single out a specific person. Some guests were on the water and others were along a wide area in front of the riverbank. As he stood there observing, a giggle drifted in the breeze towards him, one that had danced through his head a million times after the ball.

Standing near the banks was the girl from the dance. She was smiling and laughing with her silver-tongued cousin. She was beautiful in her frilly white dress and hat festooned with flowers. She reminded him of the fey in fairy tales, stealing away men's hearts with their beauty and lively nature. Planning pranks on humans and men's hearts. A smile grew on Adrian's face until he noticed who she was looking at. Making his way towards them was a familiar man. The dance partner who carried her away from him the first time.

"Mathew, who is that man?" he asked, pointing. A scowl etched his face as he watched them chatting by the river.

Mathew moved closer, setting the lunch basket on the railing, and looked. "I believe that is Earl Brown. He is the eldest of the estate, well known for having good manners, good looks, and being plenty wealthy."

"He is not that good-looking," Adrian muttered under his breath, still watching them from the bridge. He could see that they had decided to go on a boat ride. They were launched into the river and Earl Brown began rowing the boat in Adrian's direction. Quickly Adrian crouched down, hiding behind the gray stone rail.

"Is this how you are planning to get the girl?"

Adrian startled in surprise when Mathew spoke next to him. He looked up at Mathew, who was standing with his hands by his side, ever the proper servant.

"No, uh, I just dropped something," Adrian spluttered, feigning a search. "I found it, see?"

Mathew raised an eyebrow as Adrian held out nothing to him. Wiping his sweaty hand on his pants, Adrian turned back to the water to see where they were. The boat continued to approach the bridge, and he watched the girl smile and laugh as the Earl spoke again. Adrian leaned forward, trying to hear what Earl Brown was saying that would make her so enthralled.

As Adrian strained over the railing, his elbow knocked the picnic basket, dumping it over the ledge. The basket tumbled over, knocking the boat and forcing it to turn into one of the support pillars. The boat capsized, sending its occupants flying into the water. All the while, his basket bobbed innocently on the surface.

Chapter Nineteen

Ella swam up, spluttering as she reached the surface. Ella tried to swim for the banks, but her wet skirts dragged her down, pulling her under. Floundering, she reached towards the surface. Ella could hear voices yelling, calling for help.

As she was about to be pulled back down, her flailing hand felt something hard. Gathering her strength, she kicked as hard as she could and managed to get a solid hold on the boat. Now that she had a secure position, she took a moment to look around. Several boats paddled towards her to help. Her stepmother and Countess Matilda were disappearing in the mass of boats that were now starting to crowd around her. Remembering a voice shouting her name from above her, she looked up, but she could only see a quick movement. She looked in the opposite direction and saw, bobbing down the river, a large picnic basket. It was only spotted for a moment until it filled with water and submerged.

Several hands worked to pull Ella from the water into a boat. She let herself be wrapped in a jacket and handed off at the bank. Several servants led her a little farther up the bank, away from the shade of the bridge. They had her sit on a blanket that had been set out a little way from the others. They replaced the now soaked jacket with a dry blanket. Feeling removed from the world, she let it all happen. The fear from nearly drowning had made her heart pound so hard, she didn't notice someone had been talking to her.

She finally turned to the speaker. It was Earl Brown spouting apologies that he couldn't find her sooner and wondering how the boat tipped over.

Daring to test her voice, she waved his apologies away. "It is alright, Earl, you should get yourself dry. It would do neither of us any good if both of us get a cold."

He hesitated, looking at her for a moment before a servant approached and led him away. Ella took several breaths to calm her frayed nerves, but people kept crowding her, making it difficult. Then Eleanor arrived.

"Oh, my poor cousin. Ari, I am so glad you're alright." Eleanor pushed through the crowd and gave Ella a hug around her shoulders. She then looked at the people surrounding them, and with a small tear in her eye, asked them, "Would you please give me a moment to speak with my cousin? It has been a rather horrifying experience, and I think she would appreciate some privacy."

The crowd began to disperse. When they were finally alone, Eleanor whispered in Ella's ear. "That was cutting it close. Why did you tip the boat?"

Ella had gathered her senses and was now wringing out her dress. "I didn't. I don't know what happened. Something tipped the boat over, and I doubt it was the poor earl's fault."

"Oh. Then it must have been that person on the bridge then. He was acting rather strange. That is why I made note of him."

Ella dropped her sodden skirts. "Who was on the bridge?"

Eleanor shrugged. "I couldn't see. I'm working on my own mission."

Ella's thoughts raced as she tried to piece together the event. "There was a noise and then the boat hit something. I could only tell because I was trying to listen. If not, I might not have heard it."

"Do you want me to go poking around?" Eleanor asked.

Ella shook her head. "It would be better if I did it."

She nodded back to Ella and then looked at her sodden dress. "Although, you can't go around looking like that. It is highly improper. And if you're trying to pass as a lady of society, you're going to have to change."

Though Ella wanted to continue searching for information, she knew things would fall apart if she was considered a pariah in society. She looked one last time at the guests to see if she could catch a glimpse of her stepmother. Figuring her stepmother had probably been spooked, Ella stood up, brushed off her skirts, and motioned for a nearby servant.

A young maidservant, who had been waiting just out of earshot, quickly responded, "Yes, my lady?"

"Are there any dry clothes that would be of benefit to me?" Ella asked, making sure the blanket was tightly wrapped around herself.

The woman bowed. "As soon as your boat overturned, I sent for a maid to find you something to wear. If you follow me, I can lead you to an appropriate place to get changed, Madame."

Ella motioned her forward and followed behind her. A serene smile was plastered on Ella's face, though her heart was racing as they walked. She was led past a red brick archway to the west side of the structure to a white outbuilding attached to the main building. This was where guests were housed during their stay. Moving quickly so she wouldn't be seen, Ella didn't have much of an opportunity to see the building. The maid led her to a private room and showed her in, and closed the door behind her.

As the door shut, Clementine asked, "Are you alright?"

Relief washed over Ella as Clementine came over. Ella allowed herself to be tended to by her friend and replied, "Yes, I'm alright, just a little startled."

Clementine sighed. "What am I going to do with you? I know you will always get yourself in dangerous situations, but I never expected it to happen on a boat. Well, let's start by changing you out of those wet clothes."

Clementine immediately went to work undoing the laces, having a difficult time since they were still wet.

As she worked on the dress, she leaned over and whispered to Ella, "It has been done."

Chapter Twenty

The prince paced back and forth in front of the carriage. His hair that had been so neatly styled was now completely undone by the many times he ran his fingers through it in frustration. He ignored the muggy air that caused his curls to drip with sweat.

Mathew stood unmoving, his eyes following the prince's path. He had sent the footman and carriage driver to eat at the inn so Adrian could have some space. Luckily, they hadn't seen what had happened at the bridge.

Stopping mid-pace, Adrian turned to look at Mathew. "Why did you stick the basket there? She could have been killed."

He bowed his head. "I am sorry for that. It was fortunate she was rescued and seems to be doing fine, Your Highness. It was a lucky thing you were not seen as the culprit."

Face turning red, he stepped closer to Mathew. "Who cares if I was seen as the culprit? She nearly drowned. I am just glad she is alive."

Mathew took a deep breath, waiting for Adrian's breathing to stop wheezing and return to a more normal sound. His eyebrows raised as Adrian continued to wheeze. Adrian knew that Mathew had infinite amounts of patience and wouldn't say a word until he got his breathing under control. Trying to calm his anger, Adrian took deep breaths until the wheeze turned into an airier sound.

"Happy now?" Adrian questioned.

With a small bow, Mathew replied, "Much better, Your Royal Highness. And to answer your question, it matters a great deal. You have yet to play a role in politics, but you want to. What do you think something like this would do to your reputation?"

"Well, I suppose. . ."

"And what do you think would happen to the young lady you have set your sights on, if it is rumored that the crown prince nearly killed her?"

"I-I don't know. It was just an accident," Adrian stammered as Mathew continued.

"With her already poor reputation, it would be societal doom, Your Highness. You could push the blame on me, and get away with it, but her? She would be ruined. Right now it is just an unfortunate accident that she could use to her advantage. Do not do anything for an unnecessary attempt at guilt, Your Highness."

He blinked as Mathew finished his tirade. His usually calm, unruffled companion now had an angry flush to his cheeks. There were a lot of things Mathew had done today that were unusual for him. Then again, it had been a rather unusual day.

Adrian sighed and ran his finger through his hair once again. "Thank you for saving both of us from a scandal. I was very upset. And I know you worried just as much about her safety as me. Let's just make sure she is okay before heading home. Does that work?" He paused. "Mathew, are you even listening to me?"

As he spoke, he noticed that Mathew's attention was somewhere behind him. More than a little peeved, Adrian turned to see what Mathew was looking at. Walking towards the bridge was Lady Ari. Still as beautiful as ever, even though her hair was still damp and her new clothes were a little rumpled. She was striding purposefully towards the bridge. As she approached the bridge, she slowed, taking everything in until she came to where the basket had been sitting, and stopped.

Unable to stand still, Adrian walked over to her. As he approached, he thought about calling to her, but he didn't know what to say. The questions that Mathew had posed ran through Adrian's mind, slowing his steps. By the time he had reached the bridge, he had come to a stop. His mind warred within him, one part wanting to ask how she was doing and the other wanting to go back and forget the incident had ever taken place. Hesitation made the choice for him.

"Your Highness, I did not know you were there. I apologize for not greeting you sooner." Lady Ari curtsied. The sound of a carriage came, and she hurried off the bridge, nearly tripping over him as she got out of the carriage's way. He caught her hand before she fell. Ella looked up into his eyes. Warmth spread across his face as he cleared his throat.

She jumped back, quickly pulling her hand from his, and brushing out her skirts. "I am so sorry for that, Your Highness."

"Adrian," he murmured, clearing his throat, then speaking louder. "My name is Adrian, my lady."

A barely visible blush washed across her cheeks. She curtsied once again, her glorious smile gracing her face. "Prince Adrian. It is a pleasure to see you again."

"And you as well."

"Did you come for the boating event, Prince Adrian?" she asked, tucking a loose strand of hair behind her ear. "I don't remember seeing you here earlier."

Guilt thundered through him. He had completely forgotten in that moment that he was the cause of her distress earlier that day.

Shifting from side to side, he ran his fingers through his hair and looked down. "Yes, but I don't really like crowds."

She raised an eyebrow. "And yet you came."

He shifted again. "I was going to try to find you, but then your mishap occurred. I was going to leave, but I wanted to make sure you were doing well."

Lady Ari smiled once again. "I am doing just fine. Thank you for asking. Though, if that carriage had hit me, I may have given you a different answer."

Chuckling, Adrian couldn't help but smile back at her. "Yes, it would be a terrible shame to have been saved from drowning just to end up as a horse's stomping ground. I don't know whether to say you're lucky since you survived or unlucky since you've had so many near misses."

"What do you think?" She laughed.

Ella's blue eyes stared into his. It felt as if she knew many secrets. This young lady was nothing like those who had spoken to him at parties before. Strength permeated her gaze, and yet it was softened by a lady's grace. Polar opposites, but it seemed as natural as breathing to her. Yet again, he was reminded of a nymph, full of beauty, mischievousness, and strength.

"I think that you make your own luck, my lady."

She smiled and started walking by the banks, away from the Red Lion Hotel. The air was cooler as a soft breeze picked up the cool air from the water and blew it across the banks. The stirring air funneled through the small tendrils of her hair that had escaped from her bun, and she once again brushed them back behind her ear.

Ella turned back to Adrian, a tendril escaping again. "What if I had managed to avoid the lunch basket that nearly caused my death? How would I make it my own luck then? Should I ask the perpetrator for an apology?"

His breath caught as she said those words. Those eyes, clearly seeing what had happened, and yet no anger could be seen in them. She turned away from him and started walking back along the banks.

Adrian opened his mouth and stuttered out an apology. He was about to finish when she whirled back toward him. "Do you think I should ask for compensation for my ruined dress?"

Like a fish out of water, Adrian opened his mouth and closed it, yet again being thrown off by this lady. "Compensation. For the dress. Not for nearly killing you?"

She nodded. "Of course. Obviously, it was an accident, and I was unharmed. But my dress, on the other hand. Do you have any idea what losing one dress can do to a lady during the Season? I had planned on wearing this dress to the garden party with the countess, but now it is no longer feasible. I had planned everything I would wear so that I can be a proper lady in society. Every dress was for a specific event; the only outfit that I don't have planned for is for my riding dress. Unless you can know of a place for me to wear it?"

Following what she was saying kept him off balanced. When she asked about riding, he managed to pick up on what she was implying. "I happen to know that the duchess is putting on a riding event to show off her daughter's riding skills. Would you be my partner for this event?"

She smiled. "That would be wonderful."

Ella noticed the sun getting lower in the sky. "Would you be so kind as to escort me back to the hotel? I wouldn't want to be hit by flying lunch baskets on the way back."

Her polite smile turned to a wide, teasing grin. Adrian knew full well that she was leading him around by the nose, but he held out his arm anyway. "As you wish, my lady."

A smile rose on his face as he led her back to the hotel. The smile stayed there for the entire ride home.

Many important buildings have hidden passageways.
Buildings have hidden passageways and also secret
peepholes for a variety of reasons. These passages
could have been used for hiding criminals or victims,
eavesdropping in on important conversations, and
escaping from authorities or from enemies. Some
have been used for nefarious dealings, and some were
put into place for more benign reasons.

The Households for Nobles
Author Unknown
Chapter 5, Page 23

Chapter Twenty-One

Ella quelled the excitement in her steps as she was led back to her room. The prince definitely liked her and he had invited her to an event. One that would allow her to get closer to the duchess and maybe see what she was planning. They arrived at the door, and Ella calmly thanked Adrian and entered.

It took only a few moments after the door closed to do a happy dance, twirling around and falling on the bed.

"It went that well? Considering Adrian escorted you to your room." Clementine stood by the bed, looking over at her, a mischievous smile clearly visible.

Sitting up, still unable to completely wipe the grin from her face, Ella replied, "Yes, it went well. I even managed to get an invitation from him."

Clementine sat on the bed next to her.

"I thought you were going to go find out who had tried to drown you? I guess you found something more interesting. Such as a young, handsome prince." Clementine had placed her hands under her chin and was batting her eyes at Ella.

Ella shoved her, nearly dumping Clementine off the bed. "Turns out they were one and the same. The prince was the one who caused the boat to tip over."

Surprise dropped all playfulness from Clementine's features. "He did *what?*"

With a calming gesture, Ella held her finger to her lips. "Keep your voice down. The walls have ears."

With a knowing look at the walls, she whispered to Ella, "Why would he do that? I thought you said he invited you to an event. Is he really a scoundrel?"

Ella laughed. "No, he is not really a schemer. If anything, he is a naive boy who caused an accident. He felt very guilty for doing something so horrible to someone he likes that he wanted to give an apology. As an apology, he invited me to the duchess's event."

"Well, I'm glad he didn't do it intentionally. I suppose any gentlemen might get clumsy around a girl he is trying to win the attention of." Clementine swooned into Ella's lap with a dramatic sigh.

Ella stood, dropping Clementine to the floor. "That is the whole point of the mission. To get his attention and marry him."

Rubbing her wrist, Clementine pouted. "You didn't have to dump me on the floor."

Ella raised her eyebrow. "It's not like you're hurt. You know how to break your fall. And why do you keep bringing up love into every conversation we have? It isn't needed for this mission."

Clementine stopped rubbing her wrist and stood to look Ella in the eyes. "If you don't start seeing him as the man you are going to spend the rest of your life with, you won't be happy. What do you actually think of him?"

With a sigh, Ella turned to glance at Clementine. "He is like a child. Kind, inquisitive, and knows nothing about how the world works. That is going to cause him trouble if we do not find out what the duchess is planning. You said you got it done. Where are they?"

Clementine pointed to the chest at the foot of the bed. Rolling her eyes at her friend, she went to the chest and opened it. Inside were the servants' uniform from the hotel. She passed one to Clementine, and they started suiting up for tonight's escapade.

The two girls lumbered up the servant's corridor, holding baskets brimming with laundry. They ignored all others as they progressed through the passageway. Nobility doesn't always like to see an overabundance of servants all about the place, so hidden staircases and hallways were often built to keep them out of sight while they went about their business. One of the hotel's previous owners must have found it rather intriguing to eavesdrop on conversations in the rooms. And though that owner was no longer around, many members of the society had often used the many peepholes hidden throughout the hotel.

The girls ducked into one of the passageways that led to the blue room. With a nod to Ella, Clementine stationed herself near the front of the narrow corridor, thus hiding Ella from view. It would give Clementine ample time to warn Ella if anyone approached. Ella did not want to find out what would happen if they got caught.

Ella felt along the wall, finding a divot. She lifted the small metal disk and peered through the opening.

Much of what was inside was obscured by the tiny opening, but she could see two people in the room. She pressed her ear against the wall. As she listened, she heard a familiar voice.

This was the voice who had been speaking to her stepmother in the boat. Countess Matilda was speaking to the other person in the room. Based on the lower vocal tones, the other person in the room was a man, but it wasn't someone that Ella had met before.

"Is this it?" the man asked.

"Yes, all that you asked for. And the payment?" Countess Matilda replied, her voice sounding as if she was bored with the proceedings. Maybe she was, considering this woman probably made many secret trade-offs.

Suspicion crept into the man's voice. "You will keep all of this confidential. No one must know who asked for this."

A laugh erupted from the countess. "Who do you think we are? Nothing will happen as long as payment has been made. If you keep your end of the deal, you have nothing to worry about."

He answered curtly, "It will be done." Footstep made a retreat, and a door opened and closed. Ella waited to see if the countess would say or do anything else. After nearly a minute of silence, Ella once again heard footsteps. Coming from the opposite side of the room from where she had last heard the countess and another person entered the room. She had not heard any doors open.

"What do you think?" Countess Matilda asked the unknown presence.

"It's always good to place another person in my debt." Chills spread down Ella's spine when she heard the voice. If she thought this woman was dangerous, he sounded as though he would be a class unto himself. All of Ella's training screamed at her that this man was a man to be very wary of. Though to others, his voice would seem pleasant and charismatic. Ella could tell it was all just a mask. This man felt of death.

Snapping her out of her dark thoughts, Countess Matilda spoke again. "Having those nobles run around like scared mice is rather amusing. Though, why did you ask for that specifically in exchange? Do you really think that the nobility would allow it?"

Something was going on, something big. Ella just didn't know what that could be. Straining to hear everything, she listened as the man said, "I did not get this far without being careful. We should not speak of this here. This is not a safe place to talk. There are some rats in the wall."

The room went silent. No door opening, just some soft footsteps. The thought struck Ella that they must know of the passageways. She dropped the peephole cover, grabbed her basket, and hurried back to Clementine.

Clementine didn't ask any questions and followed Ella back to the room as they had previously discussed. As they returned to Eleanor's home, her mind raced as she wondered if the mystery man was Viscount Edmund. And what were the secret deals between Countess Matilda and the man, and also what connection they have with her stepmother?

Chapter Twenty-Two

Clarence House

Adrian was so happy at the prospect of helping Arabella. His excitement was tempered, though, by the fact that not having already told his father about the riding event may yet cause him some problems. His father was rather overprotective of him and insisted on knowing where Adrian was at all times. Adrian could only imagine his father's anger if he found out that he had gone to the boating event without permission.

He sighed; he would have to ask for his father's permission to go to the duchess's event. Two excursions without telling his father would be too much. As they rode home, Mathew gave him a very judgmental stare. The same stare he gave when he thought Adrian had done something stupid, but he was too good a manservant to actually comment about it.

Adrian refused to speak on the matter and ignored his stare. Instead, he gazed out the windows. The sky was starting to darken, and he wondered if Ari was safe.

They arrived at their new home. Even though it was overcast, it was still easy to see the white rectangular building as the carriage drove forward. When they stopped in front of the house, Adrian immediately went upstairs to speak to his father. Outside the door to his father's study was Phillip the steward, standing and waiting in case *some* young prince decided to listen through the door again.

"Phillip, I need to speak to my father. It's important."

The imposing valet looked down at him, faint surprise on his face.

"Your Highness? What matter do you need to speak to your father about? He is about ready to leave to a ball that he cannot be late to."

Adrian stood firm. It seemed his father always had some place he needed to go or some place he had to be. He was the king, after all. "Since he is about ready to leave, I must speak to him now."

With a sigh, Phillip knocked on the door. "Your Majesty, Prince Adrian would like to speak to you."

Adrian was pleased to hear his father's voice boom through the door. "Let him in, Phillip."

Happy that he had finally pulled one over on the stuffy valet, Adrian gave Phillip a smug grin as he was admitted. The room was spacious and was lined with bookshelves on either side of the room. Only a few of the books showed any signs of wear. Mounted in the center of the wall was his father's naval sword and flag. Below them, behind a rather messy desk, sat his father. His hair had turned mostly white and his military body was now softer and pudgier than his younger days. Adrian would never say that to his father. He still had more strength than his form would suggest.

When Adrian entered, his father looked up from his papers and boomed, "Welcome, my boy, come in. We haven't talked for ages."

With trepidation, Adrian walked into the room as his father waved the servants away, leaving them alone. Adrian drew closer as his father blew on a paper until the ink dried. He motioned

Adrian to come closer. "It's good to see you. It's been a hassle dealing with this reform bill these days. It is good to see you instead of those doo-gooder Whig Party members. It would be better if the Duke of Wellington stayed Prime Minister, but the public is in outrage."

Adrian was happy to hear anything about politics and eager to hear more. "Why is the duke not going to be Prime Minister?"

King William looked up from his papers, realization crossing his face, and stopped what he was saying. "You don't need to worry about that. I wouldn't want to stress you. It would do you no good if you fell ill again."

With a deep sigh, he muttered, "Yes, Father."

Looking at his son's downcast face, the king asked, "What is it that you wanted to talk to me about? Does it have anything to do with this girl you met with at the ball? Or the reason why you left the house to go to an event of your own accord?"

Adrian looked at the floor and fiddled with the end of his jacket. He ran his fingers through his hair and opened his mouth to speak. He paused when he saw father's expression. "You're laughing at me."

His thunderous laugh indeed filled the room. Adrian felt his face flush with embarrassment. The king had been a bit of a wild child in his younger days. He brawled often with his shipmates, and caused plenty of other kinds of trouble. A bit of that wildness still filled him, even though he did take his responsibilities as king seriously. "It is good that you have found someone you like. A good woman will someday make your days joyous. Just don't go too far. I learned from that disaster. Anyway, who is this mysterious girl? I assume that she is one of the young ladies who just graduated from the academy."

Adrian shifted his feet and started talking. He explained how he noticed the girl at the dance, and how she was so different from the girls he had met before. She made him feel comfortable, something he had never felt before at those kinds of things

His father was leaning on his desk, his eyes focused on him. A proud shiver ran through Adrian as he continued with his story. It had been a long time since he'd been able to keep his father's attention.

"When I first met your mother, it was like that. I met her only a week before our wedding day, but she was a beautiful soul. It was a political marriage, but we did love each other. I hope it will be like that for you." His father sighed.

Adrian loved hearing about his mother. His father tended to avoid that subject around him. It was difficult to tell if it was because he blamed Adrian for her death or if it was just sorrow from the memory of her passing. All of which made it a difficult subject to bring up.

His father continued. "So, what happened at this boating event? You seem to be rather pleased about something."

With a sigh, he told his father what had happened, even the mishap with the lunch basket. He was nervous telling him this, but he was relieved when his father started to laugh again. "This lady seems interesting. I would like to meet her. Go on with the story."

He continued, "And since I did dump her in the water, I said I would invite her to the duchess's horse riding event."

"You. Did. *What?*" His father slammed his hand on the desk, startling Adrian. The king shook his head. "Of all the things to ask for. Do you have any idea what you promised her?"

Adrian shifted as he shook his head. "Isn't she my aunt? Why would it be a problem?"

The king sighed, covering his face. "Do you know who is next in line after you?"

"My cousin?"

"Yes, that . . . woman has been parading her daughter around trying to convince people that her daughter would be best to rule. That wretched woman has trained that girl to be completely dependent on her, so even if her daughter were to be on the throne, it wouldn't matter. The power she has over that girl would mean that it would be like she was on the throne herself. She would be overjoyed if something happened to you. Especially now, since it would establish her daughter more firmly in the minds of the people. Do you see the problem?"

"Then why won't you allow me to be more involved in politics? I would have known —"

His father cut him off. "You are very weak child. Any stress could make things bad for you. These sorts of things are what I was afraid would cause you pain. You have nearly died several times since you were a child. I am trying to protect you. Can you see why I keep this from you?"

As his father continued his rant, anger built inside Adrian. Anger at both his father's accusations and at his own weakness began to bubble up. Already, he could feel his lungs seize from stress as he struggled to breathe properly. Clenching his fists as his father's tirade washed over him, he was able to keep his anger in check until his father's final question. That was the final straw.

"I am only angry because you never tell me anything! You keep everything from me. I know so little about how politics work and who is involved because you keep it from me. It is almost like you want her to become the next in line."

"Enough!" his father roared. Adrian glared at him, breathing heavily. They gazed at each other with an intensity that showed that neither of them was willing to back down. His whistling breath was the only noise after his father's outburst. His legs trembled from the expenditure of energy, but he refused to show it.

They continued to glare at one another until a crash of thunder and patter of rain caused them to jump. His father rubbed his face with his hands and ended the conversation. "If you want to know what your aunt is like, then you should go see for yourself. Go to the event. But this is a warning to you. You will not like what you see."

His father waved him out the door, dismissing him as he would a servant. Adrian stomped across the room and out the door, anger still coloring his thoughts. He ignored Phillip, who watched him stride down the hallway. Despite his huffing and puffing, he didn't stop. His wheezes billowed loudly by the time he arrived at his room. Mathew was waiting for him, and with one look, opened the door and then sent for Abigail.

Adrian stormed over to his chair and collapsed into it. He tried closing his eyes to calm his breathing. He had obtained permission to bring Ari to the event, but the circumstances of how he got permission were infuriating. His father still saw him as too weak to include him. His anger at the conversation caused his lungs to seize, and as he tried to calm it, his wheezing only reminded him how weak he truly was. His wheezing could be heard through the night as Mathew stood watch.

My son does not understand. I fear for him. He has been on the brink of death far too often. He is the only thing I have left of my wife, but even though he looks all right in the moment, I know that his health can fail at any time. I must protect him. If only that woman wasn't around, I would breathe much easier. I fear that his aunt has been corrupted by the one beside her. She yearns for power and is willing to control her child to do it. She is using the problems that surround us to do it. That vile woman is willing to put her child in harm's way to get the power that does not belong to her. Neither my son nor my brother's wife understands the danger. Talk of rebellion between the nobles and the commoners is causing a stir, and danger is forming at our gates. I will not surrender that to anyone. It is my duty as king to rule these people and to protect my son.

King William Henry IV
Missing journal, Unknown date

Chapter Twenty-Three

Private Garden

The duchess's event took place at one of the private parks in London. After the storm a few days ago, the plants had turned to vibrant hues. The muggy air cleared, making it the perfect temperature for riding. During her academy years, Ella had been trained on how to ride, though riding was not her favorite activity. She would much prefer doing physical activities herself rather than nearly dying on an animal that could take off running at any moment. Eleanor and her family had provided a mare for her to ride. The dapple-gray horse seemed to be calm, but you never knew with these creatures.

Adrian had come to escort her, and they began riding from the countess's home. As they rode, Ella was thankful that the Society had custom-made her a saddle in case it was needed. She kept her legs tightly wrapped around the double horn and felt relieved that she was strapped in. Though having a double horn was much more secure, it still made her feel off-kilter. The center of gravity was so small that she felt like she was balancing on a precipice and one wrong move would send her tumbling. Ella was glad the horses were only at a slow walk, and she slowly calmed herself enough to talk to the prince.

Adrian had been rather mellow. He hadn't tried to talk to her at all during the ride. His expression was downcast and troubled. This was helpful to re-familiarize herself with riding again, but was not helpful for the overall mission. She looked around at the streets. They were not crowded at this time of day. Most of the buildings in this area belonged to the nobility and had a decent-sized front yard and space between each house. Ella could hear the two guards that were set to protect the prince walking behind them out of listening range. One was up front to scout ahead and the other behind them. Ella took a deep breath and gently pulled on the reins until she was riding side by side with the prince.

For Ella to speak first would be improper, but she hoped it would be her best option. She asked, "Are you alright, Your Highness?"

His head snapped up at her words. He blinked and shook his head and looked at her, a blush rising on his cheeks. "I am so sorry, Lady Arabella. I have not been the proper chaperone, have I?"

Trying to lighten his mood, she laughed. "I think we are well past the stage of you being able to call me Lady Ari. Though, next time I would prefer to eat my lunch on dry ground instead of in the river."

A smile crept across his face, and his blush deepened. He tried to hide his embarrassment by tipping his top hat to her. "As you wish, Lady Ari. Though I also recall asking you to call me Adrian."

It was cute, and with ease, she gave a short laugh. It was easy to talk to him, and he was more relaxed about the rules of society than most people were. She found it refreshing at being able to tease him, and she raised her eyebrow. "I'm surprised you remember that. You seemed to have been stammering quite a bit at the time. I was worried that you were too embarrassed to remember the conversation."

The redness in his cheeks deepened at her comment. He coughed to clear away his embarrassment, causing her to burst out with giggles. She tried to hold it in, but when he gave her a dismayed look, she couldn't help but laugh again.

"You seem to enjoy putting me in embarrassing positions, my lady," he said, his cheeks still flaming red. This time, she managed to not start laughing again.

As they rode, she kept a keen eye on the guard in front of them to see his reaction. He resolutely ignored what she and Adrian were saying and kept their focus on any possible dangers. She was glad to know there were competent guards around to help. She focused her attention back on Adrian, whose cheeks were still beet red.

She turned to him, and finally stopped her torment of him. "I'm sorry. I just wanted you to relax. You seemed so disheartened, and I only wished to cheer you up."

Ella smiled at his light-hearted laugh. "At my expense, of course."

He was so easy to tease. It was easy to forget that getting close to him was her mission. That thought brought her back to what she needed to do, dousing her momentary enjoyment. Her training helped her keep a polite smile on her face, but she could feel a certain pain at having to deceive him.

"Of course, it would do no good for a lady of my stature to be an object of embarrassment. You, on the other hand, would still be fawned over if you did something embarrassing." Ella paused as she watched his smile falter, then went on. "What were you thinking about so deeply that you couldn't speak to me, Prince Adrian?"

Taken aback at the sudden turn of conversation, Adrian hesitated, pondering what he should say. "I was wondering why there is such a fight for the throne. My father worries about me. He sent these guards because of my aunt, but is there really a need for such measures? Why fight for the throne?"

"Because everyone will fight for more power."

He turned, surprised at what she was saying.

Adrian furrowed his brows, looking down at his hands. "Power, but royalty was born to rule the people. We are here for the good of the people. We were born to that privilege of ruling. If you were not born to that privilege, then you should not try to take it."

Ella could only laugh at the absurdities he was speaking. He truly was naive. "Why shouldn't they? Everyone wants power."

The shock on Adrian's face made her laugh again. "But why? I don't want power. I just want to be a good prince to help my people."

She caught his eye and, with a raised brow, said, "And for that, you need power."

"You don't want power," he muttered.

She laughed at his pout. He was so sincere. So, she replied in kind. "How do you know I don't want power? Most women get married as a business arrangement. Marrying someone of a higher station raises hers as well. This is a form of power."

"You aren't like that," Adrian instantly replied, not even thinking about his answer. This worried Ella. He said this without a thought of who he was talking to and was far too trusting. Considering his position, that was dangerous. She could feel the earnestness in what he was saying. He had honest eyes which always looked at her with clarity and without belittlement. Ella wondered how he had gotten that way.

She pulled on her reins and came to a stop. Facing him, she asked, "How do you know that I'm not like that?"

He pulled his horse to a stop as well and turned to look at her. Then, unable to hold her gaze, he diverted his eyes. "Why would I need power? If I truly help the people, they would want to follow me. Also, I am part of the royal bloodline; it is their duty to follow me."

With a sigh, Ella wondered how far she could go with this conversation. She saw his earnestness and intensity and decided to tell him everything. "What about the French Revolution? If you do not have the people on your side, it has been proven that no matter how noble your line is, they will destroy it." She went on. "Or what about foreign invaders? What about other nobles? Not everyone has the same opinion on how things should be run. That is why we have different political parties. The Whig Party and the Tory Party are on opposing sides. This has always caused friction. And as prince, with a higher authority, there are those who are greedy and wish to take it for themselves. That is why there are criminals in this world."

Adrian recoiled as if he had been struck in the face. Feeling that he needed space, she clicked her tongue and tapped her horse with her riding crop, urging her mount into a walk, leaving Adrian behind in his thoughts.

It didn't take much longer to arrive at the park. Though Adrian was still being moody and irritated, it didn't seem to be aimed at her. When they reached the gate, she waited. One guard was already through the gate when the prince arrived. The others waited for the prince to allow him to open the gate for Ella, as was societal protocol.

While she waited, she could tell that Adrian was distracted because he got too close to the gate and the horse shied away. It reared a little as he pulled back on the reins and tried to calm it.

"Easy, boy, easy," he soothed. The horse calmed down at his touch. He used the hook that was attached to the fence to open the gate and allowed her through. The servant at the gate checked their identities, bowed to the prince, and motioning them onward. Ella tapped her horse's side again and moved towards the other ladies. There was one in particular she noticed who was at the center of attention. The young Lady Alexandria Victoria, daughter of Duchess Victoria.

With a deep breath, she moved towards the group, wondering how she could get information from Lady Alexandria with Adrian trailing behind.

Chapter Twenty-Four

Adrian felt like kicking himself. What had happened during that conversation? Luckily, she didn't seem mad. But considering how good she was at concealing her expressions, that didn't tell him much.

He sighed, watching her gather with the other ladies who were going on the ride. A few were seated on their horses behind men, and others had escorts like he was. There were also ladies who did not intend to ride who were seated under a gazebo drinking tea.

One of those in the gazebo was his aunt. He could instantly pick her out amongst the many ladies who were seated there sipping tea. She had full control of the gathering, and everyone seemed to gravitate toward her. Her regal bearing and commanding presence showed through from her fingertips to her toes, even to the way she was seated. Seeing that she had been born a princess, that was unsurprising. Adrian was curious about her since his father so thoroughly despised her. Though, he couldn't see why he'd thought to warn Adrian about her.

As he turned back towards Ella, he felt as though something was crawling down his spine. With a quick jerk of his head, he looked back at the gazebo, only to see the duchess turn back to speak to the person next to her.

He shivered and rubbed the back of his neck, wondering why he felt that way. His gaze flicked back to the duchess, but he immediately shook his head and looked for Ari. To his surprise, he saw she wasn't the center of attention. Unsure of why he had that reaction, Adrian continued to watch and saw that she was talking to his cousin, Lady Alexandria. He had met her a few times and called her the family nickname, Drina. And from what he recalled, she was a very smart kid. He patted his horse's dark coat and wondered why he never saw her as much. Then he remembered the reaction of his father.

Why did his father dislike the duchess so much?

Adrian was snapped out of his thoughts by a call to start the ride. The few ladies who were riding singly on their horse rode up front with their escorts behind them. Coming up in the rear were those who rode double. He breathed a sigh of relief that Ari had decided to ride on her own. It would have been awkward riding with her. And this gave him a chance to enjoy the ride. Owing to his poor health, he wasn't able to do much, though horseback riding had become his one freedom. His body refused to work properly, and running could send him into a coughing fit, but riding a horse wasn't like that. The horse did much of the work for you. All you needed to do was have balance and know where you wanted to go. This horse was a gift from his father, and he had raised it from a foal. It was the one thing that kept him going and working to get better, the chance to leave his bed and go for a ride.

The cool air, with a promise of fall, brought with it the smell of the manicured trees. This private garden was well tended and Adrian appreciated the work that had gone into it. The greenery was planted in a complex and beautiful pattern that was easily appreciated on horseback. On a horse, none of the ladies had any reason to approach him, which allowed him some breathing room. The two guards hovering nearby felt like a bit much, but his overprotective father might have had something to do with that. He couldn't really complain. At least it was less than four like his father had originally intended to send.

A wonderful thing about being an escort, other than not having to talk as much to the twittering girls, was riding behind the lovely Ari. He thought about how beautiful she was in her velveteen dress. The dark blue fabric brought out her light blue eyes. The fascinating eyes that could see right through him. The short riding jacket, more masculine than her dress at the ball, seemed to suit her far better. Her long weighted skirts hid her feet, as was proper, and the short top hat with a large feather gave her an elegant air. As he watched, he couldn't help but notice the breeze catch some of her curly hair, and she tucked it behind her ear. For some reason he could feel his face flush, watching that motion.

He turned then to look at his cousin. She was still young, only eleven though he could appreciate her horsemanship. She sat easily on the horse, as if she was born to do it. Her light brown hair was tucked into her green riding hat. She was very small for her age and didn't have any of the roundness one could expect for one so young. Adrian felt a sense of unease at this thought until he heard what the girls were talking about.

"You know how many languages, Lady Alexandria?" Ari asked, surprise evident in her voice.

A blush crept across his cousin's face as she said, "Four. French, German, Italian, and Latin. My mother wanted to make sure that I could speak to everyone. How many languages do you speak?"

"Only the one. I doubt I could ever be as talented as you." Adrian could see that she had charmed another person and was glad they were getting along. He did notice, though, that she spoke to his cousin in another tone than the one she used with him.

There were three other ladies who rode in front with Ari and Drina. Drina showed herself to be the perfect hostess and spoke to everyone. It was strange watching them. Somewhat to his surprise, Ari seemed to fit right in with the rest of the ladies that he usually avoided. Yet there she was, jabbering away about some gossip or about some noble man, just like the other ladies. One of the ladies who had been sneaking glances at him, commented, "My, I didn't realize that one such as you could have such company. It is a surprise to have him here. I tend to see Lady Alexandria around more."

Ari smiled back at the girl. "Yes, His Highness had been very generous. He is very kind to all of his subjects, much like his father. He is a great prince."

The girl gave him another glance, then turned to his cousin. "Your mother has been so kind. It has been a pleasure seeing both of you at all the balls. I heard after this, you are off to a ball in Wales?"

With a smile on her face, Drina answered, "Yes. Though on the way there, we will be attending a ball at Earl Gray's house."

Another girl, wearing a brown outfit, was eager to join into the conversation. "How many balls are you going to this year?"

His cousin, with her still smiling face, answered, "My mother wants me to attend as many as possible so I can meet many different people." Though she was smiling, he felt that it wasn't genuine. Her youthful face showed no signs of distress, yet her eyes looked tired.

"Your mother seems to have everything under control," Ari remarked, jumping back into the conversation. The first girl looked at her, then dismissed her with another glance.

Adrian noticed the sad look in Drina's eyes as she said, "Yes, very controlled."

As the conversation went on to speak of how one of the lords had run off with a maid, he dismissed his thought about Drina as a mistake. Then let his mind wander as they rode their horses down the well-maintained path. Though he couldn't quite help it when his gaze kept lingering on Ari.

The group had almost made it around the garden when his ears picked up someone mentioning the Duke of Wellington. That conversation turned out as boring as the rest and only spoke of his rather impressive stature and handsome features despite his age. Adrian had hoped that he could learn something other than facts about his rather impressive military career. He should have known better, as ladies didn't talk about important matters in politics. Yet, as Adrian thought that, his earlier conversation with Ari was brought to mind. She had spoken about how marriages were formed as a way of gaining power, so it would make sense that the women talked about men. That concept changed him. These women weren't just gossiping about marriage because all they could think about was men. It was because this is how they climbed higher than one another in society. He felt as if his mind had been opened. He had been looking at things all wrong. It was just as Abigail had said. He just needed to look without preconceived notions.

After the refreshing ride, his horse came to a stop as the group came to a halt. They had arrived back at the gazebo. It was time to escort Ari back to her home to get ready for the ball later that evening. His cousin came up to him.

"I apologize for not greeting you sooner, Your Highness." She gave a slight bow of her head. Her small frame sat with ease upon her chestnut mare, and she held the reins loosely in her hands. A smile graced Adrian's lips. He was proud that his cousin was such a competent rider. Maybe his father would allow them to ride together sometime if only his father would get rid of his grudge with her mother.

He tipped his head in response. "Drina, it is always a pleasure to see you. Think nothing of it. I hope we can find some time to get together soon."

Again, he felt a sense of unease from her, though she gave him a polite smile and replied, "I will speak with my mother."

Adrian nodded his ascent and turned towards Ari. He noticed she was ready, and he motioned her forward. A servant opened the side gate for them, and Adrian's guards followed them out of the garden. Overall, he was pleased with how the event had gone. Though he was still surprised at why his father had been so insistent on him not meeting with his aunt.

"That went rather well, I think." Adrian said to himself, enjoying the late afternoon air as they rode.

Things are more dangerous than we assume. Many fights have broken out since the reform bill did not pass. The citizens are going to try again, but the nobles will not go for it. We will have another French Revolution on our hands if the reform bill does not pass. As our job is to protect the royal line, would it not be better to give the people more freedom and keep the country under their rule rather than to see the people massacre the royal line? Please advise.

Lady Arabella Cooper;
Codename Cinders
Coded message found in a letter
sent to the Academy

Chapter Twenty-Five

Ella, however, was already upset with how the event had gone. All the information she obtained was just more bad news. The prince was in a more precarious situation than she thought. She was sorting through what she heard, wondering what she could do, when she heard Adrian exclaim that it went well. The polite smile that she wore like a mask nearly slipped at that line.

"What about that event went well?" she inquired.

He opened his mouth to answer her, but then he was halted by another question.

"Was it when it was considered derogatory for me to be escorted by the prince? Or was it when the ladies indicated that they were more interested in your cousin being next in line for the throne rather than yourself? Or it could be when your cousin snubbed you by greeting you at the very end of the event?" She struggled to rein in her emotions at how oblivious he could be.

"When did all that happen?" he asked, confused. She gave him the *'look'*. Her polite smile was plastered on her face, but her eyes glared daggers at him. He tried to backpedal as she refrained from rolling her eyes.

After the intensity of her stare, he could only open and close his mouth like a fish out of water. "But Drina . . . Drina . . ."

Ella's heart clenched as she thought of that child. She sighed. She shouldn't get upset at Adrian. Ella took a deep breath to calm down. He has never had to deal with society. It will be hard to get Adrian all caught up with the inner workings of society, but he does need to understand his cousin's situation. "Lady Alexandria is nothing more than a puppet controlled by her mother. That poor girl. Though that's not all that uncommon, considering her mother's position."

Ella could see concern flood his eyes at her words.

"What are you talking about?" Adrian asked.

Ella sighed, taking a moment to listen to the sound of her horse's hooves on the cobblestone streets as she organized her thoughts. Taking another deep breath, she asked Adrian, "How exhausted are you after attending the ball?"

"What type of question is that, and what does it have to do with Drina?" Adrian blurted. He opened his mouth to continue, but paused as he looked into her eyes. His brows furrowed as he thought about her question. While he organized his thoughts, Ella did as she was trained to, and looked around for any sign of a threat.

When he finally spoke, she looked back at him. "I get tired, but I'm normally tired. I also get swamped by people. I'm not really used to balls."

She nodded, remembering his medical file. "Now, what do you think about an eleven-year-old girl who has to dance with and speak with those swarms of people? Do you think that it would be exhausting for her as well?"

"I guess."

"What about if you have to do it every night for the entire season?" Ella pressed, a touch of pity lacing through her words.

Understanding filled Adrian's eyes, and quickly turned to concern. Ella could tell that he was about to ask something, but he became distracted by movement ahead of them on the road. She turned to look at what the distraction was and saw what was approaching.

"What wrong?" he asked, noticing her concern.

His question was answered by one of his guards moving up to join them, while the other headed to intercept the crowd that was quickly approaching.

"Your Highness, we must leave now. As fast as possible." The guard motioned the prince to head back the way they had come.

They were close enough that Ella could pick out pieces of what the people were saying. "...reform...down with nobility...rotten boroughs..."

She could tell that the situation was getting dangerous, fast. Adrian was arguing with his guard to find out what was going on. Knowing that they needed to leave now, Ella reached over and grabbed Adrian's reins. She then prodded her horse and started to pull him to safety. The guard left behind them was struck by a rock. His horse bolted. At that moment, a few of the people broke past the other guard. Between getting his horse under control and the crowd of people, he was unable to get to them right away. Ella and the prince would have to fend for themselves.

No longer resisting, Prince Adrian urged his horse forward. Now at a gallop, they started to head back the way they had come. Ella was glad she was strapped into her saddle as the horse sped down the road. Every stride it took she felt like she was slipping. Ladies were never supposed to gallop with a horse. Fear of the animal pulled at her until she saw Adrian beside her. Now was not the time to worry about herself.

She looked behind them, wind pulling her hair out of her hat, tickling her neck as she looked down the picturesque street now turned deadly. She could hear the prince wheezing above the clamor of the cobblestone. The stress of the situation was causing his condition to flare. They would need to stop soon.

She breathed a sigh of relief as the group finally stopped their pursuit as they were left behind. But it turned out it was only a momentary respite. Ahead, she saw another group waiting for them. They slowed as the new group approached them. Wearing scarves to cover their faces, these men were very different from the ones behind them.

They needed to escape. Ella looked around for a way off the streets to safety. Glancing around, and found no opening. Fear lanced through her when she realized what needed to be done.

"This way," she called, whipping her horse until it pulled ahead of the prince. To the side was a short gate that a gardener would use, and it was short enough to jump. Praying that she could keep her seat in the saddle, she readied herself for the jump. She could feel her horse bunch its muscles beneath her legs as the powerful animal leaped over the short fence. Relief spread through her as she heard the thump of another horse land beside her.

Pulling on her reins, she turned the horse to see if there were any pursuers. Four of the figures continued to follow them. Their masked faces and dark clothes were easily noticeable. Ella glanced back at the mansion ahead of them. She made a quick decision, yelling to the prince, "Go to the mansion and ask for help. I will ride in a different direction to distract them."

"I can distract them," he wheezed, his fingers turning white as he gripped the reins too tightly.

This was not the time for him to be noble. "You are in no condition to be doing anything right now. I will be right behind you."

He still hesitated. His horse sensed his agitation and shifted under him. She slapped his horse on the rump, making the decision for him. The dark horse shot off towards the mansion, leaving her behind. She breathed a sigh of relief now that he was in relative safety. Ella positioned herself so that there was an ornamental tree between her and the enemies as she pulled out her dagger. Instead of wasting time unwrapping herself, she cut herself loose and fell to the ground in a heap.

Glad to be off the horse and back on solid ground, she shooed the horse away from her. She slipped the dagger back into its hiding place. It would do no good to kill people without getting information first.

Whoever owned this house had a rather impressive garden, which made it easy for a lone girl to hide in it. The maze of hedges was about waist high, filling the garden. In the center was a white gazebo. Plenty of places for sneaking up on the enemy.

She ducked behind a nearby hedge as one of the men approached. As she crouched, she deftly slipped her skirt loop onto her wrist so as not to trip on her overlong riding skirt. Then, flipping up the hem of her skirt, she felt along the edges until she found a small loop on the hem. She pulled, dragging the weights out of her skirt. She was disappointed that she didn't have her fan since it was the weapon that she was most proficient with, but she was glad that there was always a backup.

Instead of the normal lead weights in her riding skirt, hers contained a chain with a weighted end. Wrapping the chain around her hand and holding the weight in the other, she peeked over the hedge.

Two of the men were chasing after her mare, and the other two had started towards the prince. She ducked further when one came close to her hiding spot. Taking deep, quiet breaths, Ella listened as footsteps crunched through the beautifully graveled path. Breathing in time with his steps, she waited as each step brought him closer to her. While she counted, she finished wrapping the chain around her hand, closing her fist around the weight in her opposite hand.

As he took a step past her spot, she jumped up and flipped the chain around his neck. She spun in-between them, causing the chain to twist. Now facing the opposite direction, she had enough leverage to pull the chain tighter as he was pressed against her shoulder. The man tried to choke out a warning and scrambled to pull the chain from his neck. But she held tight. Within a few seconds, he stopped jerking, and she dropped him behind the hedge. She unwrapped her chain and felt for a pulse. A slight flutter brushed her fingertips, signaling that he was still alive. Ella pulled the mask from off his face. Not recognizing him, she quickly memorized his features, just in case. Then she riffled through his pockets, searching for anything that would indicate who had hired him.

Inside his vest pocket was a small scrap of paper. She slipped it into a seam of her petticoats and began to hunt the other three men. As she snuck around, hidden by the hedges, a smile spread across her face. This was what she was trained for.

Chapter Twenty-Six

Adrian slowed his horse after regaining control. The fear that had shot through his veins calmed and his violent wheezes mellowed to a slight rattle. He was almost at the mansion door when he realized Ari had not caught up to him. Jerking the reins, he whirled the horse around, searching. Adrian spotted her horse at the far end of the yard. And she was not on it.

Kicking his horse's sides, Adrian galloped to where he saw Ari's horse. He reined his horse to a halt when he saw two men heading his way.

Where was she? Fear gripped him. He knew it was dangerous for a lady if she fell from the horse. When the saddle slipped, their skirts were known for getting tangled in the horse's hooves. Disregarding the men who were hunting him, he stood in his saddle, hoping to see her fallen among the hedges. It was then that he saw a figure in navy stalking the men.

A very familiar figure.

The figure was dressed in a navy-blue riding habit. The same navy blue habit that Lady Ari had been wearing. He could only watch in awe as the figure flicked a chain around one man's neck, and he dropped within seconds. Then, in defiance of her small frame, the figure tucked the man behind the hedge.

This could not be the same girl who rode with the ladies, speaking with other nobility with such a silver tongue. Yet hints of this had peeked through as he remembered thinking of her as a fey. Her, peeking and dancing among the hedges, dispatching the enemies one by one. The flash of silver in her hand and the whirl of skirts fanned behind her like wings. A smile was on her face as she looked entertained by the mere mortals who tried to trespass her domain. Adrian felt like those in a story who came upon a fairy circle, and becoming entranced, never to leave.

So enthralled by this scene, he didn't notice when one of the men came up by his horse and grabbed Adrian to pull him off. Adrian dropped his reins in surprise as he was pulled backwards by his jacket and fought to keep his seat. He was unable to grab the reins, as his feet were trapped in his stirrups. He started choking as his clothes pressed against his neck. Pain shot through his ankle as the man tried to drag him off the side of the horse. His foot on the opposite side managed to slip out of his stirrup and fall. The horse reared at the commotion behind him and shot off towards the mansion, leaving his master on the ground.

When Adrian tried to stand, he was grabbed from behind, cloth strangling him as he was dragged backward. Feet scrabbling at the ground, Adrian grasped the arm dragging him back, and struggled to pull it off. His frantic breathing sounded like a dying cat as he thrashed about, desperate to breathe. Weakly, Adrian tried one last time to escape. When the world started to fade and he fought for his final breaths, the pressure suddenly vanished.

Gasping for air like a man drowning, he collapsed to the ground as he glimpsed the man who had been choking him being dragged away. Glinting in the light was a silver chain wrapped around his ankle, Ari holding the other end. Using the gazebo pole for support, she leveraged the man closer to her. When he was close enough, she gave him a quick and satisfying kick to the head. Adrian stood and wobbled closer to her, watching as she pulled a pin from her hat and jabbed the man in the arm.

"What . . . was. . . that?" he croaked, still straining to catch his breath.

"That is a drug that will make him forget the next few minutes," Ari replied simply, unwrapping her chain. Then she proceeded to pull off his mask and asked. "Do you recognize him?"

"What was . . .that?" Adrian asked again, his breathing starting to calm down. The look she gave him was the same one she offered when he had said that the day had gone well. He sighed and looked at the man. His grungy face and coal-stained face made it difficult to tell who it was. "I don't think so."

She nodded and started riffling through the man's pockets.

"Who are you?" he demanded. She looked up, then continued to rifle through the clothes until she found something. "Are you ignoring me? I demand to know who you are!"

She glanced back at him, looking him in the eyes. He stood there huffing as she stared back. She held out what she had found. "I was protecting you."

Taking the crumpled scrap from her hand, he read the words written there.

The rider on the black horse must be taken out by any means necessary.

Adrian turned behind him and looked at his black horse. Did his guards ride a black horse? He didn't think so. Of those that rode today, he was the only one riding a black horse. His thoughts flitted between disbelief and questioning. Why would someone do this? And why was this happening? There was no one he knew that would betray him like this.

He turned to Ari, his eyes red-rimmed, on the brink of crying. "Who would try to do this to me?"

It was suffocating. He placed his head in his hands as he tried to breathe. Ari reached over to comfort him. It was too much. He flinched, and pulled away from her. Looking at the girl he liked, he now realized the danger he was in just being next to her. It was just too much.

Adrian shook his head, backing away from her, and heading towards the mansion. He walked slowly across the lawn, his thoughts warring with one another as he tried to understand what had happened and also tried to forget. As he neared the heavy wooden door, a servant was already opening the door from the commotion. The head servant instantly recognized the insignia on Adrian's jacket and quickly bowed.

"Your Highness, to what do we owe the pleasure of this visit?" the manservant asked.

At that question, Adrian paused. What was he supposed to say? He turned behind him to see what Ari would say, but she wasn't there. He remembered he had left her behind. He looked across the garden, the evidence of what had happened had vanished. The men who had tried to attack them could not be seen and Ari was no longer there. His horse, now no longer afraid, had returned quietly to his master.

Adrian smiled at the servant. "There was a disturbance on the road and my horse was spooked, causing me to take a fall. I seemed to have ended up in your garden. Your assistance in this matter would be much appreciated."

The servant nodded and lead Adrian to the sitting room, and called for a stable boy to take Adrian's horse. The quiet stroll through the house forced him to acknowledge the one question he had been avoiding. Had Ari lied to him about everything?

He thought of everything that had occurred just moments before. That was the one thing he feared the answer to the most. What if it was all a lie?

His thoughts finally turned to Ari in the garden, skillfully neutralizing the enemies, and of the final thing she told him — I was protecting you. Yet her actions changed his thoughts from betrayal to, why would she do this if she actually wished him harm? He decided he would get his answers, and no one would stop him. Ari would not get away from him that easily. He would find out everything, and maybe after all was revealed, he would know the reason she had done this.

The fear that my mission was over flashed through my mind. What would happen now? Never had I learned what would happen if our mission was discovered. Sometimes a member told the person later in life, but never during the mission. Adrian and I had only seen each other a few times. And if they did pull me, I would never find anything on my mother. And so, I waited to see what Adrian would do, and focused on finding my mother before I was pulled from my assignment, as I was sure would happen.

    Lady Arabella Cooper;
    Code name: Cinders
    Excerpt from report 98

Chapter Twenty-Seven

1830 December

Ella stood in her room at Eleanor's place, as Clementine prepped her for the ball. She had already sent Harriett, who had been becoming a fantastic ghost, to arrange for a carriage. Clementine was finishing the last touches.

"Viscount Edmund should be at this event," Clementine told Ella as she finished tying her dress. "From the information that was found, he generally does business with this household during the dance."

Clementine circled around the front and made sure that the skirts were laying properly.

"Did you hear if my family is going to be there?" Ella asked.

Satisfied everything was in its proper place, Clementine turned to the dresser and started adding Ella's jewelry as she answered. "Yes, so be careful."

Ella noticed the necklace that Clementine was reaching for and stopped her. "Put on the other one. I fear I many need it this time."

With a nod, she reached for a diamond necklace. She made sure to clasp it very carefully. She handed Ella a pair of gloves and searched through the jewelry box for a bracelet to match. Ella put the gloves on, deep in thought.

Clementine reached over and patted her arm. "The prince will try to speak to you. I think he will understand."

Pulling her arm away, Ella held her hand out so Clementine could put the bracelet on. "I was worried about finding out about my mother, not him." At this, Clementine raised an eyebrow. "It's true."

And she was sticking to that. The prince, who she had come to care about, now felt betrayed by her and there was nothing she could do about it. Instead, she took a deep breath and grabbed her shawl. Adrenaline pumped through her veins as she focused herself on finding information about her mother.

Clementine passed Ella her mother's fan. Flicking it open, Ella felt the Fan Society's symbol and calmed herself. She was ready.

Ella had been lucky to get an invitation to this ball, and if it wasn't for the efforts of Eleanor, she would have never been invited. The bottom floor of the Lyceum Theatre, now devoid of most of its usual chairs, was open for the dancers. Music floated from the musicians on the stage about the room. Along the edges were some chairs and several sets of stairs that led up to the balconies. Here, one would normally watch the actors on the stage, but now they could watch the dancers below. Eyes gliding over to the few ladies that had already grouped around the edges, Ella could pick out a few recognizable faces, one in particular who might be willing to help her.

Sitting on the far side of the room was Lady Luella Jones, Ella's rival from her academy days. Luella's dark hair was pulled back and her emerald-green dress made her blue eyes pop. Her strong jawline was framed by the ringlets, softening the rigidity that Ella knew was more than just physical.

Ella flicked her fan to get her attention. Luella glanced in her direction, then signaled with her fan a "go away" message. Refraining from rolling her eyes, she flicked her fan again. It looked like Luella would shoo her away again, but Ella pointed her fan across the room. Her fan was pointing towards the viscount, who was now headed up the stairs to the balcony. She then pointed toward her stepsisters, who were sitting at the base of the same stairs.

In an instant, Luella flicked her fan in front of her face to hide her expression. Ella watched as Luella stood, letting the men know she was available to dance, and slowly shifted towards Ella. As Ella moved toward the stairs, she could feel some of the ladies' eyes glance in her direction. Effie studied Ella as she came closer to them.

"Oh my, it is Lady Arabella. I am surprised that you managed to get an invitation to such a prestigious ball," Luella said as the ladies who surrounded her, giggling in agreement.

Giving a curtsy proper to a woman of higher rank, Ella replied, "I have friends in high places, Lady Jones. They see my achievements over some ladies with just a title."

Luella's brows furrowed before she managed to hide it. Ella smiled at Luella's annoyance, but was irritated herself as she knew she would have to lose this conversation. It was just difficult to allow Luella to beat her. Having been rivals for the last four years didn't help matters. Flicking her fan in front of her face, she sighed, feeling the emblem on the fan. It was time to lose this round.

A familiar voice spoke up, her stepsister Audrey. "How dare you speak to her that way? Having a few friends in high places does not make you better than a daughter of the marquess."

Having her childhood tormenter in front of her made her snap out a retort. "Of course, Lady Audrey, *stepdaughter* of *Baron* Cooper."

Never one to hold her emotions, her stepsister's face turned a violent shade of red. The grip on her fan rivaled that of her mother's when Ella had accidentally dumped tea on Audrey. Ella hid a laugh behind her fan. It was too easy to pull one over on her stepsister. Audrey was just like her mother, insecure because of how low they were on the nobility hierarchy.

Ella caught the look on Luella's face. The same look she gave Ella when she told her she was ashamed that Ella was a legacy. Happiness doused, the conversation halted. If it ended like, this then she would not have the excuse she needed to follow after the Viscount.

To her horror, or luck in this particular case, her other stepsister stepped in. Effie, always one to aid her sister, spoke. "Now, now. We should all calm down. It is not lady-like to act this way. Didn't your mother ever teach you that?"

Rage ran through Ella as her stepsister spoke of her mother. Her fingers gripped her fan and brushed the emblem again. This was where she had to end it. She had to calm down. Looking at Effie's knowing smile, Ella knew she was waiting for Ella to give herself away. It looked like Effie still suspected her.

Glancing back at the hallway, Ella could no longer see the viscount. She had spent too much time here, and the person she needed to follow had already left. If she took any longer, all the effort she put in would be wasted. Looking at Luella, Ella knew she would also prove to her rival that she was right in thinking that Ella was not worthy of being a Legacy.

Instead of spouting back that the woman who raised Effie had not shown her the points of grace needed in society, she simply said, "I am so sorry. I haven't lived with my . . . mother for a long time."

As she turned and fled, she heard Luella tell the group, "I heard she was a bastard child. I hope she won't be back after being humiliated like that."

Grateful to be away from her stepsisters, Ella turned her thought to her mission of finding the person who sold her mother.

Ella headed in the direction the viscount had disappeared down. As she did, she saw a small door opening nearby. The person who was opening it was Countess Matilda, the woman on the boat who was talking about poisoning and the prince. Ella watched as she went through a different door than the one she believed Viscount Edmund had taken. Hesitating at the base of the steps, she glanced back to where he had gone.

The debate of who she should follow wrestled in her mind. The man who she knew had something to do with the disappearance of her mother or a woman whose conversation might have been about the prince.

The prince. The sweet, naive prince. The prince who was impulsive but open to other people's thoughts. She was going to head towards Matilda's door when she stopped. Remembering the look on his face when he asked who she was caused an end to the battle in her mind. Her lifelong mission to marry the prince was surely already a failure. Someone else would have to marry him now. Sorrow and guilt dripped from her as she turned away from the women and followed Viscount Edmund up the stairs, hoping she was not too late to learn what she needed. And hoping she was wrong about her suspicions that someone wanted to poison the prince.

Chapter Twenty-Eight

Adrian looked over the glamorous theater, which was now being used as a ballroom. He watched the vibrant guests as they moved about the floor. He leaned against the dark wood of the balcony, ignoring his two guards, who, since the incident on the streets, he was never allowed to be without. Nervousness wetted his palms and weighed heavily on his lungs as he finally was let out of the house. There was one thing left to do — he had questions that needed to be answered.

Adrian peered over the railing. The massive chandeliers lit the floor below as he looked at the twirling dancers. The music played a jaunty quadrille, a favorite at the dances, and the dancers moved in time to the music. The floor was filled with people, leaving very little room to move, forcing some into the different balconies.

Having so many people at this event made it very hard to find the one particular person he needed to see.

Then, as if in answer, his eyes were drawn to her. Even now, he couldn't help but watch in awe as she moved with grace and strength. The strength which he saw so violently used before as she took down his would-be assassins.

Shuddering at that thought, he focused on her again. She was dressed in a beautiful blue dress. A beautiful blue that would make her intelligent eyes shine even more. She was surrounded by several ladies that looked like they were ready for war. And it ended with her heading up the stairs behind them in distress.

Turning on his heels, he hurried to catch up to her. His escorts couldn't keep up through the crowd as he wove his way towards the side where he last saw the lady in blue.

Adrian saw a flash of her blue dress as the lady ascended the steps to the next floor. Already winded from his chase to the other side of the theater, he followed her up another flight of stairs. As he did, the crowd thinned, making it easier for him to breathe in the narrow corridors. He did his best to keep his wheezing under control, though he was surprised she didn't hear his wheeze as he followed her. He followed Ari up yet another flight of stairs, though this time she was moving at a much slower pace, allowing him to catch up.

The noise from the musicians and the people started to fade as they went deeper into the theater. Hopefully, they would stop soon. He turned the corner and she was no longer there.

"Why are you following me?" a feminine voice asked.

Adrian jumped in surprise, gasping as he was startled. He stepped backward in surprise, stepping into the emptiness of the stairs behind him. He flailed wildly as he desperately tried to stop his fall. As his foot was hanging in mid-air, a small, delicate hand grabbed his, and pulled him back onto the safety of the landing.

With his feet back on the floor, he could see who had pulled him to safety. The one who he had been hoping to meet since he left her behind in the garden. Ari.

"Lady Ari, what are —" she cut him off before he could speak any more. Her eyes flashed with annoyance when he tried to speak again.

"If you don't want to get us into trouble, then be silent," she whispered. After watching to make sure that he wouldn't speak, she pulled him into a small room. Though it wasn't lit, he could tell there wasn't much room for them to move around. This made him aware of Ari's presence all the more. She stepped closer to him.

He stepped back with a jerk and hissed, "What are you doing?"

"Hush," she snapped, placing her hand over his mouth. "Are you going to tell anyone?"

Adrian pushed her hand aside, glad that the room was dark so she couldn't see him blush. "Tell who what?"

He could feel her hesitation, and he had to strain his ears to hear her answer.

"Did you tell anyone about me?"

His intention was to give her a piece of his mind for lying to him, but the forlorn tone of her question made his heart break. He paused, wondering how long she had been wanting an answer to that question. His thoughts turned as his anger died down. From what he knew of the ladies of society, those who did what she did was considered completely unfathomable. She would be ostracized on the spot.

"No. You saved my life. How could I do that to you?" He couldn't see her reaction; all he could hear was the muted sound of music playing through the walls, this time a waltz.

He leaned closer to her to ask her the question that was burning in his mind when he heard a door close next to them. He jumped. Mood ruined, he tried to question her again when she shushed him. Then she pulled him towards one of the walls. Silence permeated the space, and the darkness made it difficult to see what was happening.

"What are you doing?" he whispered to her. In an instant, she clapped her hand over his mouth. He sighed, pulling her hand away, and strained to hear what she was listening for. And what he heard made his blood run cold.

"The nobles are fighting each other like rats in a sinking ship," a woman's voice said. "All over that insufferable prince."

A man's voice that set Adrian's teeth on edge laughed in reply. "And that is why it is so profitable. They all want to be higher than they already are."

"And you are willing to give it to them. . . for a price." The cool tone of the woman reminded him of some of the mercenaries that came through the palace. They all seemed self-assured of their place in the world. They were willing to do whatever it took to earn money, even if it was morally ambiguous.

Adrian could almost hear the sneer as the man replied to her, "They get what they paid for. Even if it brings them to ruin."

"What are we going to do then? Are we going to sell them as a slave like we did with that one woman? What was her name? That request 10 years ago?" He could feel Ari stiffen beside him at what the woman said. The air around her also seemed to fill with a wave of anger so hot it was a wonder he didn't get burned. He continued listening as horror froze his veins.

"That made us a good profit, but things have changed. Considering the new target's station, it would be better to simply give him poison and be done with it. Or better yet, make the people do it. That would keep our hands clean of the whole affair."

"We still have some poison left over from a few years ago. They wouldn't notice a thing." She sounded so smug. The nonchalance over killing someone, made their conversation seem so much colder. If you merely listened to their tone, it would have sounded like a business meeting. Not a meeting discussing the murder of another person.

He clenched his fists and started to move towards the door. Anger filled his soul, and he wanted to yell at these people.

How could they discuss the fate of someone so casually? As he prepared to barrel towards the door, Adrian was stopped by a hand on his arm. Her hand only lightly touched him, but it felt like a weight. He couldn't wrench his arm away from her. His rage drained away at that single touch.

This woman, how could she do that? She was still crouched by the wall, listening, unaware of what she was doing to him. Not wanting to acknowledge her power over him, Adrian crouched by the wall, intent on listening like Ari was.

"...I'm not surprised it's the duchess. Though that other woman was much more of a surprise," the faceless woman said, continuing the conversation.

The man replied, amused, "And that is why I like her so much. When she first came to me several years ago, I knew that she would be a force to be reckoned with."

"As you say." Adrian could almost see a peeved expression as she said those words. Adrian leaned closer as the voices quieted again. As his weight shifted forward, the boards beneath his feet shrieked in the quiet room. He froze instantly. The voices in the next room stopped.

His thoughts pinwheeled. How were they going to get out of this mess? His breathing became raspier as his lungs struggled to find air. These people were planning someone's death, and they had probably killed before. Many times. Cold fear ran through his veins as the idea of being caught terrorized him.

A small hand grabbed him by the arm and pulled him close to her. His chill of anxiety warmed to her touch. Now facing away from the door, he couldn't see who had opened it. Ari's hand on his arm stopped him from turning around to see. Light beamed through the room, illuminating Ari's face. Her face was now covered by her fan as she gasped at those who had entered.

"Oh my!" the person at the door said

...e found out the pas. . . ord for getting into the upper
fl. . .s. Make sur. . . is done betw. . .n the first . . . third
step. Watch . . . for guard. H. . nder you. Attached is
the passcode Follow ins. . .tions exactly.

U   n   k   n   o   w   n
author
Scrap of paper found in fire pit

Chapter Twenty-Nine

Ella gasped, as she could see Countess Matilda opening the door. Her puffed sleeves nearly filled the doorway as the rest of the doorway was taken up by the massive mound of bejeweled feathers balanced on top of her head. Her chocolate-brown hair framed her face, and by the tilt of her head, you could tell her rank. Grey-blue eyes glinted as she looked down at Ella. The countess flicked her fan in front of her face to hide the shock.

"What do we have here?" the countess asked, amused, her eyes sparkling with interest.

Ella suppressed the anger at the information she had just found out. She knew it was most certainly about her mother. The fear of Adrian being caught repressed the presence of Countess Matilda. She could think about the information later when she had the time. Ella knew this would have to be the performance of a lifetime. She avoided looking at the prince, whose eyes burned into her, and said in a rush. "I'm so sorry, Madame. We were just leaving."

Ella fluttered her fan in front of her face, as if trying to push aside her embarrassment. Shifting her weight from side to side, she made it seem as if she was debating on whether to run away or stay and hide.

The woman laughed. "I've had a tryst or two of my own darlings. Just make sure not to get caught so easily next time. It would be bad for your image. You are lucky it was me and not anyone else."

Ella bobbed, keeping her face hidden, as she thanked the woman who turned from the door. As Countess Matilda turned, Ella could see a man behind her, and she did her best to memorize what little she could see of his appearance. The only thing she could tell was that he was a large man. As the man glanced in, Ella made sure that she kept her face covered by her fan while also kept track of Adrian, keeping him from turning around, as she waited until he left with the Countess.

Just when she thought she could breathe a sigh of relief, the man turned back and asked, "Why isn't the man turning around? Is he not a gentleman as well? Or is he allowing himself to be protected by a woman?"

Adrian started to turn, and Ella put a hand on his arm to stop him. She could feel his tension rising as he clenched his hands. She needed to make the Viscount leave, and soon. Keeping her face covered with her fan, she replied, "It is my duty to protect a noble of higher rank. As well as my honor."

Edmund raised an eyebrow, still suspicious, but finally turned away. Ella strained her ears until she could hear their footsteps echo into oblivion. She sighed and relaxed. Looking up, she was startled by the intense look Adrian was still giving her. He looked down at her hand, which had lingered on his arm. In a flash, she removed her hand and put it behind her back, regretting having let him go.

Bowing her head, she said, "I am sorry for touching you, Your Highness. It would be best if we weren't seen together like this again. Now, if you would please excuse me."

With resolution, she avoided looking at the prince as she moved to pass him. As she did, Adrian grabbed her by the arm and turned her to face him. "You are not leaving just yet." he said sternly.

Ella looked into his eyes. She couldn't understand the conflicting expressions that crossed his face. She struggled for words as she removed his hand from her arm. Then, making up her mind, she decided she would continue to protect this sweet prince even though soon it would no longer be her mission. "You said before that you would not say anything. I would appreciate that, and if you refrain from speaking of this as well."

"I don't fully understand what went on here, but I do know that you saved me once again. Everywhere I turn, I'm constantly kept in the dark. In my position, it is my duty to protect my people. How can I do that when I am being treated like a porcelain doll?"

She watched as his anger radiated out from him. Ella stared into his pale blue eyes, crying out to her in desperation. After his outburst, his breathing had turned into wheezing again — which he continued to ignore as he held her in place with a steady gaze.

Was it really best for him to keep him in the dark? Never had Ella questioned that. It had always bothered her that the secret Society was there to protect the royal line but was never allowed to tell them. How much more good could they do if they knowingly worked together?

And before she fully knew what she was going to say, she spouted, "I believe the Viscount Edmund sold my mother as a slave."

"What?"

"One day ten years agon, my mother had gone out to visit friends. She returned home late and disappeared. I believe. . . no . . . I know that he had something to do with her disappearance."

Any anger he had left defused, and his eyes filled with concern over her words. "I'm so sorry, Lady Ari. Why has nothing been done in the matter?"

Grief that Ella had long held inside shook her to her core. Having someone show concern for her and her outrage that nothing had been done for her mother burst the dam she had long built around herself. Never wanting to burden Clementine, who also cared for her mother, she had always refrained from talking about it. But now it was someone who hadn't known her mother, who still felt like it was horrible. Her unshed tears spilled down her face, washing away some of the pain. The pain of losing both of her parents. The pain of watching as a new stepmother destroyed everything that was her family's. And the pain of being unable to do anything about it.

Looking back into his kind face, she could see he was flustered by her tears. He searched his jacket until he pulled out a handkerchief, handing it to her. She smiled and dabbed away the tears, then handed it back to him. "Thank you."

He had calmed down and her crying had slowed. Adrian looked at her and said, "I know what it's like. Someone who was like a mother to me died. Nothing could be done then, just as it seems like nothing could be done for your mother. Why does that happen?"

Ella cleared her throat and murmured, "The night watch and constables can only do so much. Most are only volunteers willing to try to keep down the crime."

"Then why are there no soldiers or guards in the city?" Adrian ran his fingers through his hair, loosening their pristine curls, and knocking his hat askew.

Brushing his hand away from his hair, Ella smoothed it back and straightened his hat. "Because the people do not want the army in their city. They fear having the militia in the cities will infringe on their civil liberties. Thankfully, now there is a police force."

"We have a police force? I thought it was just dock workers who policed the harbor."

"Yes, Robert Peel just started an official police force in London. They will also police all of London and not just the ports. Though, since it is new, there have been some ups and downs." Ella finished fixing his hair. "Let's head back. We can talk more later, but for now, it would be better if we make an appearance. You head out first, and I will follow later."

"And yet more information that I didn't know," Adrian said with a sigh. He turned toward the door, then paused. "When are you going to find time to explain everything? Like how you knew this conversation was happening and how you learned those skills?"

"I will explain everything at a more appropriate time. You must leave first, and I will leave later so more people do not get a chance to see us together like this." Ella pushed him toward the door. He hesitated, giving her one last look before disappearing into the hallway. As Ella waited, she adjusted her skirts. She was about to head out the door when she heard a voice.

"Yes, *Lady Ari*, is this a more appropriate time to explain everything?"

Standing in front of the door was Effie, her stepsister.

I will gain my mother's attention. If that means arranging my idiotic sister's marriage, so be it. That look in my mother's eyes when she looks at me is just a lie. She looks at me with the same look of disgust that she does when she speaks my father's name. And now that girl Ella is away, she has finally been proud of my efforts to help Audrey. I'm sure that things will change now. I'm sure of it.

Lady Euphemia's Journal
October 1829

Chapter Thirty

Adrian sat in silence the entire carriage ride home. After he returned to the balcony, his worried escorts shuffled him out of the theater. Not resisting, he allowed himself to be guided into the carriage to return home. He sat quietly, thinking to himself about everything that had happened during the ball.

There were some very powerful people who were willing to kill the nobility for a price. There was a plot to kill someone. A high-ranking someone. And the people who were involved were most likely involved in Ari's mother having been sold as a slave.

Ari. The most confusing and amazing woman he had ever met. Adrian could tell she truly did want to help protect him. Also, she wanted to find out more about her mother. Remembering that moment when she told him about her mother caused his heart to clench. And when she asked if he told anyone, that made all of his doubts about not telling someone fade away. The relief from that moment, as well as the sadness when she mentioned her mother, were absolutely true. There was no way those could be faked.

Then what about all of her fighting skills? She took out all the attackers without anyone being aware of it. And successfully listening through doors. And the quick thinking when they were caught, was that real or fake?

Doubt began to creep back in when he recalled her acting skills. What if this was all a lie? He was startled out of his thoughts by the carriage arriving at his home. Struggling to get out of the dark clouds that covered his thoughts, he trudged slowly back to his room with only a vague awareness of what was going on.

His thoughts jangled with each step towards his room. Right foot. *She is nothing but a liar.* Left foot. *She is trying to help me.* Right foot. *If she can act like that, was everything a lie?* Left. *Those tears felt real.* Right. *When was she ever going to tell the full story?*

This struggle went on until he reached his room and sat in his chair with a thud.

"Your Highness, is there anything that I can help you with?" Adrian looked up into Mathew's concerned face and saw Abigail behind him.

Pulling off his hat, he set it on the small table next to the chair. He ran his fingers through his hair as he took his calming breaths. Mathew was going to have Abigail wait while he helped Adrian get dressed. But Adrian stopped him. "No, Mathew. Allow Abigail in."

Mathew bowed and motioned her in, his concern for Adrian still evident, as for once, Mathew's gaze was not locked on Abigail but on Adrian. Adrian sighed and did his best to ignore Mathew as he let Abigail do her job. He focused on her calming presence, still trying to brush away the dark cloud of emotions still weighing heavily on him.

"Your Highness is doing well, though your lungs seem to be aggravated. It would be best if you did not go anywhere for the next few days," Abigail said, noting his expression, leaning over and patting him on his leg. "It would be best to give you some time to think."

As Abigail stood to leave, Adrian asked, "Abigail, do you think me as breakable?"

She sighed, her soft features giving him a small smile. Sitting back down, she searched his face as if it would tell her what answer to give him. Watching Abigail, Adrian waited. Her auburn hair seemed to turn a deeper red in the flickering candlelight. Time seemed to eek on by, and the pressure of the moment built within him. Finally, she spoke.

"I believe that you have not been allowed to see. The people around you wish you to see the beauty and joy around you. When you were a child, it seemed as if you would not make it to the age you are now. And you have already suffered from your sickness. They wanted you to keep your innocence. Now that you are older, it is still hard to see anything beyond the pale, sickly child who could not even raise his head."

Adrian nodded. "Thank you, Abigail. You may go."

With a small bow of her head and murmured thanks, she made her way out the door. As she was about to leave, she turned one last time towards Adrian. "Your Highness, you are no longer who you were as a child. And your actions can change the impressions of those around you. You just need to think that you *are* able to do it."

Mathew watched her go, then shut the door behind her. Adrian sat in silence, ignoring Mathew's worried look. His friend's gaze weighed heavily on him in the quiet of the room. Only the crackle of flames broke the room's silence. Then Adrian shattered that oppressive atmosphere.

"Is there something you wish to say?" Adrian asked.

Mathew paused, then, as if trying to pull himself out of his thoughts, asked, "What happened at the ball, Your Highness?"

"Is there a need to ask such questions?"

Mathew hesitated before answering. "You have been out of sorts since you came back from the horse-riding incident. I know it is not my place to pry, but I'm worried."

Adrian watched Mathew for a moment as he debated what to say. If Ari was just lying to him, then he needed to tell someone about what was going on, but if she wasn't, and he did say everything, then she could be in very grave danger. The fear of putting her in danger froze any words he wanted to say on his lips.

"How did you know it was better to listen from the other room than in front of his doors?"

Mathew looked up, a quizzical look on his face. "Pardon?"

"Have you listened in on conversations?" Adrian asked, blunt in his questioning. Keeping his face as blank as possible, he watched Mathew. Worry crossed Mathew's face until he looked into Adrian's eyes.

Mathew took a deep breath and responded, "Yes. As your servant, it is my job to help assist you in any way possible. And to be good at my position, there are times I need to hear things that I am not supposed to. But I also know not to speak of anything I hear."

Adrian looked back at the events that took place at the ball. Especially the words that Ari spoke regarding her mother. He didn't know if she was lying or telling the truth, but the closer he could get to her, the easier it would be to find out.

"Mathew, teach me how to eavesdrop."

Never had Adrian seen Mathew's face show so much shock as he did after that remark. He opened his mouth as if to say something, then froze in Adrian's gaze. Adrian was determined he needed this if he was going to find out anything more about Ari. He needed to be beside her. This was the only way he knew how to do it.

Mathew sighed; he knew enough about Adrian's stubbornness that when he was in this sort of mood, it was better to go along with it. "Yes, Your Highness, if that is what you want me to do. May I ask why?"

"Lady Ari."

"Lady Ari? Why do you need to learn to eavesdrop because of Lady Ari?"

Knowing that he should keep what he knew quiet, yet still desiring his Mathew to know something, he debated what to tell him. If everything she said was true, then anyone else who learned about her could be in danger as well. When he and Ari were caught, he may have not seen the villain's faces, but he could feel their contempt. They matched the voices he had heard, and he decided not to share that with Mathew.

Instead, Adrian said, "I have a feeling that things are not what they seem."

Furrowing his brow, Mathew replied, "That is the case with most nobility."

"What?"

"To be noble means never showing your true feelings. Every conversation is a business deal. As is every ball, every tea party, and every other event, including courting and marriage."

"Are you serious?" Adrian blurted. He thought back to all of the conversations he had had with nobles. They all had a mask-like face whenever they spoke to him. Or they covered their faces with fans as their eyes peered greedily at him. He shivered at the thought. Was that what made him like Ari so much? She had shown her emotions? Or was it that she seemed so expressive and free? Everyone else seemed as though they were constrained by society, but she ignored these conventions. She spoke first and even teased him.

Freedom. That was the word he associated with Ari. Adrian turned to look out his window. Considering how large the estate was, there were very few lights. This allowed him to see the stars that glimmered through his window. During his childhood, all he ever thought about was being able to go outside and run. That was why he loved riding horses so much. He loved it so much that he named his horse Free Spirit. The outside looked so amazing, but now that he had been outside, he knew beautiful things could hurt you, too. All this time, being on the inside of the window let him see the beauty, but kept him safe.

Adrian looked up at Mathew's concerned face. Now that Adrian understood more about what was going on, he wondered, did he truly want to step foot out of his protected space? He had almost been killed, and who knew what would have happened if those people had known they were eavesdropping on them? What was his choice going to be? Would he go back to being protected, or would he be willing to walk into a dangerous game where he didn't know who was playing by what rules, and the stakes might be his life?

Then he remembered Ari's tears again. Her face that he could not forget. He pulled out the handkerchief that she had dried her eyes on, and he held it in his hand, thinking.

Finally, with resolve, he told Mathew, "Teach me. I will not be coddled anymore."

Chapter Thirty-One

Ella watched as Effie sauntered into the room.

"What are you going to explain, *Lady Arabella,* or should I just call you Ella?"

Ella froze, doing her best to keep her expression as calm as possible. Effie could be fishing for information. She was smart like that. Feeling the weight of her fan, and fingering the emblem embroidered in the lace, Ella breathed deeply and calmed herself. Her weapon of choice was in her hand, a gift from her mother. Now was not the time to let her emotions get the better of her.

Ella remembered her training, and she denied everything. "What are you talking about, Lady Euphemia? You must be mistaking me for someone else. Who is this Ella you speak of? I have never heard of her."

Laughing again, Effie stepped closer. "If that is how you want to play it, I will play along. Ella is my dear stepsister."

Ella tapped her fan in front of her face, trying not to clench her teeth. "Why would you think I am your stepsister? We have only met a few times. Unless you know something I don't."

With a laugh, Effie stepped closer and began to circle Ella as she spoke. "My dear stepsister was taken to the academy with both me and my sister. Though, during her training, she caused so much trouble that she was *supposedly* sold to the Americas to pay her debt back to society."

Ella followed Effie with her eyes, yet refused to turn her body. Effie was explaining the official report. From how the incident in question had occurred, her stepsister knew Ella hadn't been sold. Effie had planned for Ella to become a servant elsewhere. What Effie didn't expect was that Ella would be pretending to be a noble instead of being sent off to the outskirts of England as a servant. If Effie kept pushing, she would lose her cover. She could not allow Effie to win.

"Oh, dear! That is horrible. I'm surprised that you were unable to do anything for your *dear* stepsister to prevent that. Though, I still don't know why you think she has anything to do with me. I am obviously not a slave from the Americas."

Effie's navy blue dress blended into the shadows of the room, disappearing and reappearing as she crossed into the light of the open door. The whole time Effie held her open fan in front of her face, hiding her expression. Only her malice glittering in her eyes hinted at her true purpose.

"She did not need any help. My stepsister would have never allowed herself to be shipped off as a slave or even a servant. And you look very much like her." As Effie said the last sentence, she leaned over Ella's shoulder and whispered in her ear, "I am sad she left our household. However, there were some good things that came of it. I am glad to hear that you are *not* Ella."

"Oh? And why would that be? I thought you missed your *dear* stepsister." Ella didn't turn to look as Effie hovered over Ella's shoulder, but she was relieved when Effie circled around to stand in front of her.

Effie made a beautiful show of a sad sigh. "It is so sad that Ella is still missing. It took a while, but my mother and sister have finally gotten over it. I would hate for them to go through the loss of my stepsister all over again. But I certainly would be forced to let them know if I suspected she showed up. Unless, of course, she could persuade me not to tell them. Call it a blessing from my missing stepsister."

Blackmail. Ella should have known. Even better than having someone to torment would be someone she could extort. Ella would not be able to tell anyone she was being blackmailed otherwise her identity would come to light. And now that she had seen a glimmer of hope in the prince's reaction, it was not the time to be messing with her stepmother. And it seemed as if Effie agreed.

"What sort of blessing are you hoping for?"

Cheeks pulling into a smile that even her fan couldn't hide, Effie said, "That noble you were in here with, he seemed rather familiar. His features are rather *royal*, wouldn't you say?"

Yet again, a chilling grip of fear tingled down Ella's spine at Effie's words. Thankful for her training, her mouth spoke these words in an instant. "He does indeed have *royal* features. But it would be heartbreaking for you if word of them being found here ever got out. For if it *did*, I doubt the blessing of your stepsister will ever come about."

"Oh, I wouldn't dream of it. I was just thinking about how my sister Audrey so desire's to marry the prince. With your help, I think that we would be able to help my sister with her dream. The joy I would receive from that would surely make me forget certain things that I have seen here."

So that was what Effie wanted, Ella thought. If Audrey became queen, then Effie, who had helped her get there, would gain her mother's approval. Poor Effie. Even if she managed to make it happen, Effie's desires would not come to pass. Ella thought about the demands. If she helped Audrey to become the next queen, it would put her mission in jeopardy.

"The time is passing, Lady Ari. I'm sure someone will be coming by. I wonder what they would think if they saw us here?"

This was very reminiscent of the last time she had struck a bargain with Effie at the academy. Ella would have to make a plan later, but for now, it would be best to keep Effie from poking her nose where it didn't belong. "It would be wonderful if this so-called stepsister's blessing helps Lady Audrey with her dream."

Closing her fan with a snap, Effie allowed her smile to show. She nodded her head slightly, and with her dark blue eyes glittering in the dim light, said, "It was a pleasure to meet you again, Lady Ari."

Ella nodded back and watched as Effie disappeared down the hall. Once she had disappeared, Ella let her eyes look down each hallway. There were not any people this high in the theater. Though she could hear some canoodling taking place down the hallway, the few who were still there were doing their best to avoid others. Thank goodness she had received intel on this place before she had arrived. It would have been difficult to reach this section of the theater without the password, let alone with the prince in tow. The final question was how Effie had managed to get this far?

Now was not the time for that thought. Instead, Ella had something she needed to do. She stood tall and confidently walked to the next door. She grabbed the handle and turned, but the door was locked.

This wasn't surprising, but she had hoped it wasn't the case. She bent down as if she had dropped something. As she bent, she twisted her foot so that the heel of her shoe pressed against the floor. This caused the heel of her shoe to rotate and open a compartment in the heel. Reaching in the compartment, she pulled out her small hooks she needed to pick the lock. With a final glance around her, slipped them into the lock.

Within a few moments, the door was open. Taking one last glance around the hallway, she slipped into the well-lit room. The room was different than she expected. It looked like a normal office. If you could call having an office on a hidden top floor of a theater where people shouldn't be normal. In the room was a desk, not ornate, but made with fine materials, a bookshelf, and a few chairs.

She rushed over to the desk. It was an obvious place, but she had to start somewhere. Opening the drawers, she found they were empty. Ella reached inside and felt along the edges. When she reached the back edge of the drawer, she felt a click. It had a false bottom. Lifting the bottom, she revealed the hidden compartment. Inside were some papers. She pulled them out and ran her eyes over them. With a sigh, she put them back. Those papers were just there to lay a false trail.

Standing, she looked around for anything out of place. She noticed something was out of place. The bookshelf. Having bookshelves was not unusual, but usually one would have a matching pair to give the room balance. It made things more aesthetically pleasing.

Examining the floor in front of the bookshelf, she saw scuff marks. There must be some type of mechanism that would slide the shelf forward. Ella looked over the books and studied the edges. Not finding anything, she instead pulled off her diamond necklace. It was a gaudy thing, hideous, but it did serve a purpose. It was large enough to hide a secret compartment. Inside the compartment was powder, not unlike the talcum powder used on her face.

With a soft breath, Ella blew the powder on the shelf. It settled on the parts of the shelf that people touched the most.

Ignoring the powder marks on the side of the shelf for the moment, she focused on the books. One of the plain leather-bound novels had many powdered prints from where it was touched. Considering the lack of marks on any of the other books, this was what Ella was looking for. Ella smiled and pulled the book down. A latch clicked, and she easily opened the bookshelf to reveal a small room behind it. Her smile grew wider as she saw what was inside.

The letter from Arabella was hidden in a stack of
books that I was reading. It was stuffed inside like a
bookmark. After I read it, a thrill ran down my spine.
I could not help but be excited, because now I would
get answers.

Prince Adrian's Diary
March 1, 1831

Chapter Thirty-Two

March 22, 1831

Adrian paced as he waited for Ari. He fiddled with his black mask that matched his thief costume. His eyes wandered over the mass of guests dressed in other fanciful dresses, then looked back at his own with a sigh. Although it was a far more flamboyant costume than what he usually wore, it was by no means the most flamboyant at the ball. If anything, he was underdressed.

Smoothing the black feathers that were attached to his half cape, he danced in place underneath the light specified in Ari's note. Nerves shot through him, and moments felt like an eternity, so much so that he was almost ready to leave the spot to go look for her when a hand grabbed him. The person, dressed as a sailor, began to pull him away to a side room.

Fear flashed through him, and he worried who this person might be. "I'm sorry, but I must return. There is someone waiting for me."

He was startled by the intruder speaking to him in a very feminine voice, "Yes, Lord Adrian. That would be me. Unless you changed your mind?"

Adrian stopped resisting and looked at his captor. Standing in front of him was Ari, dressed as a sailor in pink pants and white stockings, fitting in the masquerade perfectly. Her top made it evident that even though she was dressed in pants, she was most definitely a she. He blushed and looked back at her face, which was hidden under a half mask decorated by pearls and gold flecks. Her hair, normally a beautiful brown, was hidden by a powdered wig. The wig had a large roll of hair on either side of her face and was pulled to the back of her neck by a short ponytail.

"Do you know who I am now?" she asked with an amused smile.

He took a small step back, then cleared his throat. "You were willing to speak to me?"

"Yes, but not here. Follow me."

Adrian followed behind like a lost puppy down a side hallway. Adrian sighed. It always seemed like he would do whatever she asked. He focused on following her and avoided listening to the strange noises that were coming from some of the rooms they passed. Wanting to peek and know what was happening, but too shy to look, he instead focusing intently on the pink bow that held the wig in a ponytail. Even though he tried not to overhear, he could feel his ears turn red, and he kept his eyes glued to the silk bow. He had heard rumors about masquerades, but had never expected them to be like this. She stopped abruptly, causing him to nearly run into her.

"Here," she said, motioning to the door beside her. He looked into the gaping maw of the dark room before him. He hesitated before he took his first step. Why had he allowed himself to be brought here? Earlier, he had followed the instructions in the message. Adrian had escaped the house without anyone knowing and got into a carriage that was waiting for him. This outfit was waiting for him to change into. No one knew where he was.

Now, he was beginning to understand the danger he was in. He shuffled back, away from Ari. His breathing began to grow wheezy.

Ari watched as Adrian moved away from her, her expression never changing. "Glad to see you now have some semblance of self-preservation. Enter if you wish."

She stepped inside the room, not waiting for him to decide before shutting the door behind herself. The rattle of the door shutting startled him out of his fearful panic, and let him think. His breathing calmed as he sorted through his thoughts.

Should he enter or not? For some reason, he didn't think she would stop him if he left. His identity was hidden, and it would not be hard to disappear into a crowd before anyone knew where he was. But he had no idea what was behind the door. One thing was for certain, though: she was giving him a chance to learn more information, and this would be the only chance. If he walked away, that would be the end.

His body seemed to know what he wanted faster than his mind did, and his hand reached for the latch and opened the door.

The room was no longer dark. While he had been thinking, Ari had lit several candles around the room. Now illuminated, he could see it was nothing but an empty space. The smooth white stone of the walls and golden arches were reminiscent of the building's architecture, and the only things in the room were the decorative wall sconces and some paintings adorning the walls. The only furniture was a few ornate chairs.

"Oh."

"Were you expecting something else?" Ari asked from one of the chairs. "We are nobles, are we not? Come sit, please."

Adrian sat in the chair next to her, ever aware of her presence. This time, instead of feeling comfortable with her, it felt like a wall had been built between them. The smile she usually wore was now just as stoic as any of the other nobles. A polite smile they always wore, but never seemed to reach their eyes.

"Are you going to tell me where you learned how to fight? Or how you're so good at acting? Or why you were listening in on that particular conversation?"

He noticed a slight movement and saw that in her hand was a fan. A beautiful, lacy thing she was rubbing with her thumb. It was the only thing he could consider an emotion that showed.

Ari must have noticed his gaze and stopped. "I can't tell you where I learned it. Can you trust me enough to know that I am here to help?"

She showed no sign of emotion. There might have been desperation in her eyes, but that disappeared so quickly he might have imagined it. Adrian wanted to open his mouth and yell about how unreasonable that was until he saw that her expression hadn't changed. She remained stoic, not even as he got angry or was about to yell. Only some sorrow touched the edges of her eyes. She was expecting him to yell at her, then storm out. Not that it would have been surprising since a few months ago he would have.

"You promised me that you would tell me what is going on. Now you say the only thing you can say is that you can't tell me? Answer me. Why did you learn how to fight? Was it because of your mother? Or was that false as well? You have been acting around me. Why should I believe you? Give me one reason to trust you!"

Her expression still guarded, she answered simply, "I saved your life."

That was the one sentence that kept him from fully giving into his doubts. The one piece of hope that he held on to. Hope that everything wasn't a lie. Staring into the face of the women before him, Adrian's hope still held. Those emotions she showed to him couldn't have been faked. He wouldn't believe it. He had to believe that Ari was a mystifying, yet strong and beautiful woman. One that had secrets. But could he stay by her knowing that she would continue to keep those secrets? Even the ones that involved him?

"You had me come all the way here just to tell me that?" Arian asked, bewildered.

Ari shrugged.

Adrian watched as she sat in front of him like a prisoner awaiting their sentence. It was then Adrian realized she was guarding her emotions because she felt that she had to stop Adrian from going closer with her. And if what she just said was true, then her motivation for pushing him away from her was to protect him. It was then that Adrian made a choice. "That is very true. If you are not going to tell me, well, anything, then I have my own request."

He saw the briefest flash of surprise in her eyes, but it was quickly banished. With such a quick change, and her ever stoic posture, it was difficult to see if she had even shown any emotion. If it wasn't for the fingers that were, yet again, rubbing the fan still held tightly in her grip, he would have thought he had imagined it.

"And what might that be?" Even though it piqued her interest, Adrian couldn't detect any emotions in her words. Only a spark of happiness, then worry showed for but a moment in her eyes, that was quickly buried again. This made him smile since it only strengthened his thought that how she was before him was nothing more than a farce. And who he had spoken to at the ball showed her true character.

"I believe I have told you once before. I do not want to be treated like a porcelain doll. I will not watch my life behind a window. And so, I'm going to help you."

"*What?*"

Adrian couldn't help but laugh at her surprised face. He had finally broken that mask she had been wearing. He had his laughing almost under control when she gave him a glare, which started him back into another laughing fit. After Ari took a deep breath, she reined in her emotions and put back the blank face. That drop in her emotionless mask was worth the danger he knew he was putting himself into.

Taking a final calming breath, he spoke, "I will help you on your search to find your mother. Since I don't know what your intentions are, I just have to see your actions. If I see how you work, I can tell if you truly are helping me, as you say. If not, it is my duty as prince to make sure you are put away for ill intentions."

"It may be dangerous."

"Then you will protect me as you say you desire to, but this time I will know who is attacking me."

Ari sighed and murmured so low that Adrian almost missed what she said. "Even if you can see who attacks you, you still might not know who is behind it."

She looked at him with a gaze that could see into his soul before sighing once more. "On the condition that you will follow what I say exactly at all times. No questions asked."

He shrugged. "That's fine." And it was. For the first time since the horse riding incident, the doubt that had plagued him had vanished.

"Then the first thing I need from you is for you to return home without anyone noticing. Can you do that?"

Adrian blinked. "But then, how will I help you?"

"Don't ask questions," she snapped, flicking out the words like a snap of a fan. "Now, you need to return home. It would not be good if you were discovered to be missing."

It was as if they had gone back to the way they were in an instant. A smile graced her lips as she opened the door and pointed him in the direction he needed to go. With the cloud of doubt that had been hanging over him finally cleared, he gave her a polite tip of the head as a goodbye and exited. Grinning, his steps were light as he made his way back home.

Because of the rising political turmoil, as well as what happened to the French nobility, we will endeavor to push the reform bill to go forward. We hope this will further our goal of protecting the royal family. We must help the Whig Party to gain traction, and pull power from the Tori Party. We will do this by . . .

Note written by Madame Briar
Receiver of message unknown

Chapter Thirty-Three

Ella could feel her smile broadening, a faint light of hope now burning brightly. She held on to that happiness as her mind went back to the conversation she just had with Adrian. She remembered first closing the door and hoping that he would open it and yet wishing he wouldn't. And then wondering if she should tell him more.

His behavior had surprised her.

Adrian was changing. Before, he would have had little thought of his safety and walked trustingly into a dark room. Even though his reaction was a bit late, he now realized it was dangerous. It would be much easier to protect him now that he was more aware that he was in danger. Though, his wanting to join her bothered her. And after being unable to tell him anything, she owed him something. But she had hoped by putting on this act with him he would give up on her and stay safe, not chase after her. Ella sighed; it was sweet that he wanted to help her.

Putting her hands to her face, Ella tried to calm down. It would not do to go to her next meeting with her heart in a twitter. She took one last longing look at the door, satisfied that for tonight, the prince would be safe with the people she had sent to protect him. She turned back to the room.

To the untrained eye, this room looked ordinary, but to one such as her, it was more. Ella's eyes roamed the space until she found what she was looking for. Stalking over to one of the wall sconces, the second from the right-hand side, she examined the filigree that decorated it. There it was, so small that unless you were looking for it, it would go unnoticed. Tucked inside the curls was a circle of eyes with a fan in the center. With a gentle touch, she brushed the insignia that matched the one on her mother's fan, then pulled the sconce. It tilted forward, opening the wall that had hidden the passageway.

Taking care to make sure the candle stayed lit, she clicked the sconce back in place. It would do her no good if people paid special attention to this because the flame had gone out. She hurried through the door, aware of the faint clicking noise as the mechanism reset itself.

Now enclosed in darkness, Ella placed her hand on the cool stone wall and followed it. She was reminded of the first time she had entered a passage like this with Madame Briar. Which put a smile on her face; she had missed her teacher. The smile which turned to a frown as she the realization that Madame Briar would be opposed to what Ella was planning. Ella's steps slowed but didn't stop. Despite knowing that Madame Briar would be against it, she still had promised Adrian.

Ella took another step forward. Everything she had done today would be against everything she was trained to do. Everything that three hundred years of the Fan Society had done. She had promised the prince, the very person she had sworn to protect, that she would allow him to see what she was doing. All of their traditions said that the royal family should never know anything. It should all be kept a secret. And yet she believed it was wrong.

Ella's next step was even slower. Then she remembered the prince's reaction.

Ella could feel Adrian's desperation when he said he wasn't a porcelain doll. Having read about him did not prepare her for the real thing. Paper could not truly evoke the necessary emotions and feelings that a person had when going through life. Adrian needed to know. He deserved to know. But it was not her place to say, though he realized it, he had given her a way so she wouldn't have to. As long as he stayed willing to help her without questioning, things could change for him.

Ella's pace quickened. She knew that what she had done with Adrian had skirted the bounds of what she was allowed to do, but what she was about to do would be a very blatant disregard of regulation. Everything she had done up until now had just involved her. What she was about to do would involve someone who was not a part of the Fan Society, nor someone who was protected by the Society. But this was for her mother.

It was too late to change her mind. She was already in the room. The hidden room, much smaller than the one in the academy, was already lit. Clementine grabbed her and pulled her in.

"Let's get ready," Clementine said, helping her out of the costume and making sure the wig was not displaced. "Who knows how long he will wait?"

Ella acted like a doll, allowing Clementine to do her work without resistance. Once her costume was removed, she then removed the corset she had been wearing, trading it for another specialized corset. This one would help conceal that she was a woman. Clementine helped Ella into an outfit very similar to the one she had sent to the prince. After she finished tying on the half cloak, Clementine fixed her wig. Finally, she changed Ella's makeup to appear more masculine.

Clementine looked Ella up and down, satisfied. "You're ready."

"Did the prince get home safely?" Ella asked worriedly, remembering his dazed look when he left.

Clementine tsked, "Who do you think I am? Yes, but I wonder what you said to him to leave him in that state. And why did it take you so long to get here? I had already dropped off the prince, returned here, and had the room ready before you had arrived. I know that how I entered was a more direct path, but still, it shouldn't have taken you that long."

Ella sighed, looking at Clementine, who had her hands on her hips and a pout on her face. The hope that Clementine wouldn't bring that up, was shattered.

"I got lost in the dark," Ella offered, knowing that Clementine would not believe her, but also she wouldn't press the issue for now.

And she was right. Clementine simply rolled her eyes and shooed Ella down another pathway. "Fine, I won't ask, but you may miss him, so go."

And with that, Ella was on her own. She followed the pathway until it ended. Grateful that this was a more well-used pathway so she wouldn't get covered in dust, Ella felt up and down the wall until she found the lever. She pulled the lever, letting the wall swing open. Ella then stepped down and waited until the wall clicked shut and took on the appearance of any other wall.

She strode across the sparsely decorated room and lifted a small hook from the top of the door. Stepping out, she shut the door behind her, resting her back against the strong wooden panel. Her eyes closed as she thought of what needed to happen next.

Her hand brushed the doorframe and felt a small pattern engraved into the wood. The symbol of the Fan Society. It was time. She opened her eyes, stood tall, and walked to the next door. With a final deep breath, Ella stepped inside.

Waiting inside was an older gentleman dressed in a masquerade costume of a soldier. If Ella hadn't been looking closely, he would have looked like any other noble gentlemen. Though Ella knew that what he wore wasn't just a costume. This man was a soldier to his bones. Even though he was sitting on the chair hunched over a cane, Ella could still see the glimmer of intelligence in his eyes. The intelligence of a war hero. His glory days long since passed and reputation stained from a duel gone wrong, Ella could feel his strength of will from the door. Doing what she needed to do was going to be difficult.

Ella plastered a smile on her face. Enclosed in this smaller study room, a tense energy filled the room as she sat across from him. The soldier turned toward Ella, and she could finally see his face. With his high cheekbones and strong nose, he would have been even more imposing in his prime. His dark hair was gray at the temples, and his hunched back might make it seem as if he had lost a step. Though to Ella, it seemed as if a hawk was watching her.

Ella spoke her greeting. She made sure to speak in a lower tone. "Hello, good sir, it is a pleasure to meet you, Duke of Wellington." She held out her hand towards him.

Before her sat the man who had been forced to resign as Prime Minister, though he was still a very powerful force in the Tori Party. He smiled in an affable way that made him seem like a favored grandfather or uncle. He was good at pretending. "It seems you have the better of me. You know my name, but you have yet to give me yours."

Ella kept her polite smile like a mask on her face. "That is very true. I have come to ask you for information."

The duke leaned forward on the cane in front of him, as if intrigued. "You still have yet to tell me your name, and already you are asking for something? Kids these days don't know how to respect the older generation."

Ignoring his question, Ella instead said, "It would be far better for both of us that this conversation never happened. I am here to ask you about your connection to Viscount Edmund."

Chapter Thirty-Four

Clarence House

Adrian had done it. He could now get closer to Ella and maybe even learn more about her. Everything he currently knew about her was mostly through hearsay and rumors. Very little of it was from her own mouth. Now, he would be helping her, and hopefully through that, learn more about her. His thoughts were disrupted by the carriage coming to a stop.

Adrian hopped out. He had already changed back into his own clothes and now hurried down the cobblestone street where he lived. Looking up, he could see his home, a large square building that nearly glowed in the darkness because of its new white stone. The building had just been built a little less than a year ago, and he still struggled to call home. Though, he did find it more comfortable than living in the palace, a building whose size easily dwarfed this one.

Adrian quietly entered the building and found that it was still suspiciously empty of any guards. In one way, it was a relief that they weren't there because it meant he could sneak in, but it was disconcerting since they were supposed to be there protecting him. The only reason he could think that they were missing conveniently was because of Ella. If she was able to get in and out of his home so easily, he thought that if she had wanted to harm him, she would have already done so.

Adrian had managed to avoid detection until he arrived at his room. When he opened the door, Mathew was sitting in his chair, arms folded, waiting.

"Mathew, you scared me," Adrian hissed as he entered and closed the door. "What are you doing in my room? Shouldn't you be asleep?"

Mathew stood and stalked towards Adrian. "You should be asleep, Your Highness. Do you know how worried I was when I came to check on you? When I peered in and you weren't here? You have been out of sorts for days, and then you ask about eavesdropping on people? And now you have been gone for who knows how long. What has been going on?"

Mathew's emotions were written all over his face. Adrian could tell that he was terrified. It had been a long time since he had seen this expression on his face. This expression he wore when Adrian's sickness had gotten so bad that they were unsure if Adrian would live to see the next morning. The expression that this servant, who was more of a friend, wore whenever he tried to hide his fear from Adrian. Adrian knew that Mathew tried to hide the fear so that not only would Adrian keep his hopes up, but so that Mathew himself could keep his up as well.

Now came the dilemma. Could he lie to his best friend? Or would he put Mathew in more danger? Adrian's heart clenched at that thought, and his breathing started to grow raspy. Mathew grabbed Adrian by the arms and gave him such a pleading expression, which only made his breathing more aggravated. The words Adrian wanted to say were there, sitting on the tip of his tongue, waiting for him to spill out his secrets.

"Prince Adrian? Please?" Mathew pleaded one last time.

And the dam broke. A torrent of words tumbled from his mouth that he could not stop. "Someone is in trouble, and I need to help her. I cannot tell you any more than that because doing so would put her in danger. Please do not ask me any more than this. It is better for everyone if you do not."

It was as if Mathew was hit over the head. The stunned expression on his face as he blinked at Adrian only held confusion.

His brows furrowed in confusion. "Is this about Lady Arabella?"

Adrian avoided Mathew's gaze. He tried to control his breathing, though it only seemed to get worse. "I cannot tell you anymore."

As Mathew studied him, Adrian tried not to flinch under the pressure of his gaze. Mathew finally spoke. "My job is to serve you and to keep you safe. How can I keep you safe if you refuse to talk to me?"

The coldness of Mathew's words pierced through Adrian. If he had been pressured this much before speaking to Ari, then he would have crumpled, but now he knew the stakes.

Adrian took a deep breath, his wheezing calming down as he returned Mathew's gaze. "I'm sorry, but I will say no more of this. Do not ask again."

Mathew's look of betrayal pricked at Adrian as Mathew released him. His face was now a blank mask, and he pretended as if Adrian was a guest rather than a friend.

"Yes, Your Highness. I will obey your orders. Do you need any help to get changed?"

"No, you may go."

Adrian watched as Mathew left. When the door shut, the tension broke, and Adrian collapsed into his chair. Placing his head in his hands, he groaned. It felt like his lungs were being crushed by a giant fist as he tried to breathe deeply. From the excitement of talking to Ari, all the way to this depressing moment, took everything right out of him.

But he had made his decision. He took a final deep breath, then stood and started to get ready for bed. It would be much more difficult without Mathew's help, but he couldn't request for it now. This was what he asked for, and now he would have to make do. To avoid thinking about Mathew, he thought instead of how he might speak to his cousin.

My son asked to go riding with Drina. I worry about him. If he stays close to her, he will gain the duchess' attention. That snake of a woman only wishes that my son were dead and her daughter on the throne. Though, he has changed. I don't know how or why, but it makes me worry. Is the change for the better or the worse?

King William Henry IV
Missing journal vol. 2.
Unknown date

Chapter Thirty-Five

Ella could feel his gaze weigh on her as the duke contemplated her question.

"Viscount Edmund? Why would you think that I have a connection to a man like that?" His eyes revealed nothing.

With a small smile, Ella decided to test the waters. "Considering your gambling habits, I would be surprised you haven't seen him, Iron Duke."

The Duke flinched at the nickname, which was not surprising. That nickname came about after his flop of a duel a little over a year ago. How easily the people forget that he was still a decorated war hero. But there was a lot of debate over what actually happened, so who's to say it didn't turn out exactly the way the Duke had planned it? Though Ella could tell from his previous attempts in dealing with society that he did not know how to control public opinion. He was too used to being obeyed.

The duke sighed and sat tall. "I see you have been spending your time reading the gossip column. And even if I did gamble, how would I know anything more about the viscount? Almost every person in high society visits his gambling houses. It still would not mean that I would know anything about him."

Even though he was not as good with the battles of the tongue, he still was still intelligent if his war achievements were anything to go by. And though he didn't have a glib tongue, he was intelligent enough to sidestep most of the round-about talking that the society used. Ella couldn't help but feel she would have to give something here, or else she wouldn't get the information she needed. He was an honorable man, even if he had a gambling problem.

"That is true," Ella allowed, acknowledging his previous statement. "Though not many would know where his true place of business is. I happen to know that, being the man you are, he has allowed you to go to this place. I need to know where it is."

He gave a raised eyebrow. If she had been the duke's soldier, she would have run away from that calculated glance. But instead, she leaned back, mirroring the duke, and folded her hands in her lap, her foot on the opposite knee. As casual as she could, Ella tried to keep her breathing steady while he studied her. Then he answered.

"Even if I knew this information, why should I tell you? This man, as crooked as he may be, has done no ill to me. Also, he polices himself and never steps out of bounds. I have no intention of getting on his bad side."

It was her move. She had to give him sufficient reason to give her the information or else all was lost. Wishing she had had her mother's fan to give her strength, she spoke. "What if I have evidence he was stepping out of bounds?"

"Such as?"

"Being involved in a plot to murder His Highness, Prince Adrian."

Even being as well trained as he was, he couldn't hide his shocked expression at her words. But his commander instincts quickly kicked back in, and he hid his emotions. "Why do you think this?"

"A little birdy told me."

"If you're not willing to offer more evidence than that, then I'm afraid I can't help." Before she could say anything in reply, he continued. "Perhaps you should speak to the duchess's financier."

Ella smiled in reply. "The kingdom will thank you for this one day."

The duke laughed at her words. "I think not, young . . . one. I think that our meeting will stay a secret, just as you have kept your identity a secret."

As the duke looked at her, Ella could tell that he knew she was a girl. When did he find out? She thought back through the entire conversation and not once had he referred to her as a man. He had called her young one or youth, but not sir or gentlemen. The duke stood, giving her a knowing smile. "You do not have to worry. It would be better for me if this conversation never existed, as you said."

She was in shock as he walked over to her and whispered in her ear. "I doubt that this has much to do with the prince. But on the off chance it was, I expect that this will be taken care of. I don't want to have to attend another royal funeral."

Ella nodded stiffly and watched as he left the room. When the door shut, she could only give a sigh of relief. After she calmed herself, she made her way back through the hidden passageway and to the room hidden within the walls, where Clementine was waiting.

Clementine was sitting in a chair, her feet propped up, braiding her hair. But when Ella walked in, she looked at her. Clementine pulled her feet off the chair, and slid it over.

"So how did it go?" she asked as she sat taller.

Ella stalked to the chair and sat with a thump. She began to pull the pins from her wig. She didn't say anything until she had slid the wig off her now frizzy hair.

"I can't believe that people believe the duke has lost his step, Clementine."

Clementine just shrugged, getting up and grabbing the clothes Ella needed to wear home. "People see what they want to see. That is why the Fan Society is able to exist in the first place." She looked at Ella, her gaze speaking volumes. They were close enough that she knew something was going on, but wouldn't pry until Ella decided to speak.

Ella sighed. "For someone who is surprisingly bad at dealing with the public, he sure knew how to dance around a topic."

"Did you get anything from him?"

"Not the address I was looking for, but he pointed me to a person who might have a connection to the seedy side of things. And who it is is very concerning."

Clementine laid the dress over the back of the chair and leaned forward, concern on her face. "Who?"

"John Conroy, the duchess's financier."

Clementine's mouth fell open with shock. "But that would mean. . ." She trailed off at the thought.

Ella nodded in agreement. Her gaze slid to the lamp on the wall, and she watched the flickering flame. The chamber was well insulated from the outer walls, and the silence weighed heavily on her.

"What was nothing but conjecture before is likely the truth. The duchess may be trying to kill the prince."

Walking towards Ella, Clementine knelt in front of her and asked, "What are you going to do?"

Ella, still looking into the flickering flames, whispered, "I don't know."

Gaining the loyalty of Harriett was easier than I expected it to be. Her mother had been scammed several times because of her inability to read, and her lack of math skills. After sending Clementine to teach them those skills, as well as paying her handsomely for any tidbits of information, she was loyal. As long as I did not go against Eleanor.

As the months went along, her pro-activeness became apparent, as well as her talent. And I started to trust her with more things. After this is all over, I hope that she can be trained by the academy where her skills will shine.

Lady Arabella Cooper;
Code name: Cinders
Excerpt from report 100

Chapter Thirty-Six

28 October 1831, Bristol

Adrian was feeling rather refreshed as the carriage drove through the countryside. Though his relationship with Mathew was still awkward, his friend at least had stopped trying to get him to say anything. Adrian was still uneasy about not being able to truly talk to him. Mathew had built a wall between them, and though Adrian could understand why, it still poked at his conscience. But he now had something to distract him.

A note from Ari.

He had been waiting for this. It had been many months since he had the conversation with Ella, and he worried that she would never contact him. But now that it had, what was he going to do? He thought about the words on the note.

Attend the ball taking place on
October 28th in Bristol.

Adrian had asked Mathew if there was a ball scheduled, and there was indeed. The only problem was that the duchess and her daughter would be there. Surprisingly, when he had asked to go, his father agreed. And the conversation didn't degrade into a yelling match. The only stipulation was that since it was a great distance from his home that he take extra guards, as well as both Abigail and Mathew.

This would be the furthest that Adrian had been from home and he was excited. And he would be seeing Ari. He tried to breathe in the fresh country air, but started sneezing on the dust kicked up by the horse's hooves. His gaze turned from the moving scenery to Mathew seated across from him. Mathew still refused to look at him and sat emotionless, looking out the other window.

"I'm sorry," Adrian said in a soft tone. So soft that he was surprised that Mathew even heard it over the rattling of the carriage, let alone answer him.

"I know you are." Mathew looked into Adrian's eyes, then sighed and went back to looking out the window. "But it doesn't change that you are going to refuse to tell me anything."

With a sigh as an answer, Adrian looked out his window, the excitement fizzling out of him. This was going to be a long ride.

The ride took a few weeks. They traveled slowly, because of Adrian's low constitution. When they rode through the city gates, things didn't feel right. The townspeople radiated anger and crowded around the carriage. Upon seeing the royal crest on the carriage, they turned away.

"What is going on?" Adrian asked, worry creeping into him at the strange energy surrounding them.

"I don't know," Mathew said, concern lacing his words as he surveyed the crowd. "Maybe it would be best if we don't go to the ball."

Adrian thought about the note and wondered if this was something the note was talking about. The sense that Ari was involved in something dangerous grew. Considering the current atmosphere, things were more precarious than they had thought. Things could easily get out of control and he could get hurt. But he committed to helping her, and so help her he would. He would not leave her alone when she was counting on him.

"The ball is tonight. It would be a shame to come all the way here and then miss it. How about we go to the ball, then leave early in the morning instead of staying here for the week?"

Mathew nodded but shifted in his seat and flitted his eyes to the crowd, then back to Adrian. His worried expression continued to hold all the way to the inn. He had decided to stay there instead of the manor since Ari asked in the note. The note had told him to say farther away, just in case.

At the inn, exhausted from the trip and unnerved by the crowd, Adrian decided he needed to rest. A young maid came up to the room to bring up refreshments for the prince to snack on. She had her dirty blonde hair tucked under a cap, and her brown eyes were downcast as she walked into the room. The girl kept sneaking glances behind her at Mathew.

Adrian couldn't help but feel for her. The strange atmosphere had made Mathew very protective of Adrian, and he wore the same expression as a guard dog would if someone tried to step foot on his land. He could almost see Mathew growling at the poor girl, who trembled as she stepped towards Adrian. The tray shook in her hands, and the dishware on top of it clinked. Adrian winced as it clattered on the table. With a quick wave, he dismissed the girl, and she hurried out the door.

Adrian smiled with amusement when she squeaked as she passed Mathew. He grew serious as he looked at the tray. Tucked under one of the dishes was a piece of paper. He shifted the dish off the paper and revealed what seemed to be instructions. The handwriting was the same as the other notes that he had received. He was about to have Mathew look for the girl, but thought better of it. Adrian waved Mathew out the door, and he rested as much as he could before the ball.

Chapter Thirty-Seven

Ella brushed her wide skirts, as she looked around the ballroom. The ball was in full swing, as if in defiance of the atmosphere just outside. Ella watched as those of nobility refused to acknowledge what was going on outside. Though as she watched, she could see a few with paler faces and nervous glances at the door. Many would jump when anyone came close to them from behind. It seemed that they all wanted everyone to think that they were not afraid.

Fear and guilt pricked her conscience as she contemplated the disaster that could befall the prince here. She had not expected things to be this bad, but it was too late. Ella would just finish this as quickly as possible. The sooner she got this done, the sooner the prince could be sent back to safety. All she needed him to do was to help during the ball, then her stepsisters would be taken care of so she can take care of other business. She hoped that he was able to follow his instructions. As long as he did, then he should be safe. That last thought stemmed from the guilt she had about Adrian.

Ella had been stalling, and she knew it. It was time to face her stepfamily and hope that everything would work out. It must work out. She rubbed the emblem on her fan and took a deep breath, striding forward. As she headed for the group of girls that included her stepsisters, she could see someone unexpected in the group. Drina. Ella knew immediately that she should head back and rethink her plan, but it was too late. Drina locked eyes with her.

Plastering a smile on her face, she continued forward and gave her greetings. "Good evening, Lady Alexandria. It is a pleasure to be seen by an esteemed lady, such as yourself."

Alexandria gave a perfunctory smile and nodded in acknowledgment. Then Ella turned to the others. "Greetings to Lady Audrey and Lady Euphemia."

Ella could see the gleam in Effie's icy blue eyes as Ella greeted the others. She could almost feel the smugness wafting off of Effie like a noble with too much perfume. But like the trained noble she was, Effie had it all concealed behind her fan. After the greetings, Effie spoke up. "Why would one with a background such as yours feel welcome among us?"

"My background? And what background would that be?" Ella couldn't help but bristle at her stepsister's attack.

Her stepsister gave a twitter of laughs. "Oh, pardon me, I do not believe that we should speak of such things in present company. Unless you wish it so?"

The edge in her voice hinted at her meaning. That she would spill Ella's secrets if she kept provoking her. Ella really needed this night to be a success. She had not been under her stepsister's thumb for long, but it was already grating. She could not mess up this night due to pettiness.

Instead, Ella smiled and bowed her head, hating every second of it. "Of course not. I was just so honored at meeting your friends. I was wondering if you would like to meet mine?"

"And why would we want to meet any friend you have?" Audrey sniffed, hiding her face with her fan as if to block the stench wafting off of Ella.

Jumping into the conversation with grace far above what a girl of eleven years should have, Drina spoke up. "It is better to know more people than too few. Who is this person you call a friend?"

The others nodded, eager to get on her good side. But this was not going the way Ella wanted it to. She needed her stepsisters and only her stepsisters to follow her. If Drina came, who knew where this conversation would end up? She turned to Effie, looking for some help. What she was attempting was on behalf of her. But Effie just turned away. Ella should have known she would get no help from her.

Ella plastered a polite smile on her face and answered, "Lady Alexandria, it is someone you already know. He was my escort at the event in the gardens."

Understanding lit Drina's eyes, and then the understanding turned to something Ella couldn't recognize. But it was enough. Ella then turned to Audrey. "Lady Audrey, this man I know can make your dreams come true."

She sneered. "As if anyone you know could help me with my dreams."

"As you wish." Ella prepared to leave, but Effie called to her. Ella smiled as Effie spoke, and hid it behind her fan. "Yes, Lady Euphemia? Is there something that you need?"

Her cold eye's spoke volumes about what she thought of this situation, but when Effie spoke, her voice was cool and calm. "Yes. I would be happy to meet your friend with my sister. It is only right for those with higher station to help those beneath them."

"Why do I have to go?" Audrey demanded, not even bothering to mask her annoyance.

Effie sighed and whispered in Audrey's ear. Ella watched as Audrey's annoyance changed to joy. "We would be happy to go. Friends, I am sorry, but my sister is right. This young thing needs our help. Please excuse us."

Faking a smile, Ella held in her irritation as she led them out of the ballroom. They followed the corridor into one of the side rooms. Waiting inside, just as he had been instructed, was Adrian. Ella let out a breath she didn't realize she had been holding, then motioned with her hand. "I would like to introduce you to my friend, Prince Adrian."

Shoving aside her younger sister, Audrey pushed her way in. With obvious glee, she gave her most elegant bow. "Your Highness, it is a pleasure to meet you."

Ella had to push down another bought of disgust when Audrey fluttered her eyes at Adrian. Audrey held out her hand for him to kiss. A rush of possessiveness ran through Ella as Adrian took her hand and kissed it. Annoyed at that feeling, Ella tried to squash it. It was no time to be annoyed at what she had told Adrian to do.

"May I have the pleasure of knowing your name?" Adrian asked, far more politely than normal. Or it may have just been Ella's prejudice against her stepsisters.

"Lady Audrey. Though you may just call me Audrey." Ella stood behind her and to the side. She could see the greedy smile she was hiding from Adrian. It was sickening seeing her talk to Adrian like that. Adrian was kind and caring. He didn't need someone as greedy as Audrey beside him.

She almost couldn't hold back a smile when Adrian replied, "I'm sorry, but I cannot speak to you in such a familiar way."

Undeterred, Audrey just moved closer to him. "Are you sure, Your Highness? I don't mind. It would be positively enjoyable for you to say my name."

She fluttered her eyes again, and Ella nearly gagged. Audrey must have learned that from Lady Victoria. Ella wanted to smack her stepsister across her snooty face with her iron fan, but she merely smiled and tightly clenched her fan. As she did, she prayed silently that she could keep up this farce.

Effie, standing next to Ella, was looking very confident and smug. As long as Ella could keep her cool, Effie and Audrey would soon lose those looks of superiority.

Adrian smiled a polite smile at Audrey. Not the joyful type he routinely gave to Ella, which made her happy. Adrian said, "We don't even know each other."

The greedy smile was still on her face when she replied, "But you will. Come dance with me."

Pulling him along behind her, Audrey pulled him to the dancefloor, leaving Ella and Effie behind.

"I have introduced them, and that is all I'm going to do. It is the prince's decision where he goes from here. Now that I've kept my word, are you going to keep yours?"

With obvious effort, Effie refrained from rolling her eyes and muttered, "Yes, yes, yes. We have a deal. I won't tell anyone, even if the prince does not marry Audrey."

This was what she was waiting for. For all the terrible things she has done, Effie had never broken a promise. Having watched them for many years, Ella had heard Effie make promises and, even though she danced about them, had kept them, true to her word. Now that Audrey was out of her hair, it was time to see if she could change Effie's mind.

Chapter Thirty-Eight

Adrian was already feeling uncomfortable around Audrey. He tried to loosen her grip on his arms, but she was like a lion, keeping tight to its prey. Then he tried telling her she had a rather strong grip on him. But she ignored his words. The vice-like grip she had on him reminded him of when he first started attending balls. There, he felt like the women around him just wanted to claim him for his title and cared so little about him.

Now he was starting to understand that this was how things worked. This lady wanted to have control and power. Adrian didn't know her reasons, but he couldn't help but wonder.

He stood still, causing Audrey to stop beside him. "What is wrong, Your Highness?"

Adrian looked into her eyes, hoping he could see the reason why she was doing this. Adrian only felt a distance, much as he had the other times he had spoken with nobles. He couldn't help but feel pity for her. He had seen the emotions peek out from behind Ari's mask, the mask she wore around society. He didn't think she had one since she was always so forthright with him, but hiding your feelings was what everyone in society did. And even though he understood that this was how society functions, he didn't want any part in this.

Adrian gave Audrey a calm but determined look. She relaxed her grip, and he slipped her hands off his arms. Then he took her hand. "Lady Audrey, I understand that you wish for my titles in order for you to better your life. But this cannot and will not happen. I hope that the man you will eventually marry will be able to see the woman beyond that mask you wear, but that person is not me. Please refrain from acting so casually with me again. I wish you well."

He turned on his heel and headed back to the corridor. He tried to forget the stunned look on Audrey's face, as if he had just struck her. Instead, he focused on getting back to Ari. He had completed what was asked of him, and now he wanted to continue helping her.

As he approached the room, he could hear murmuring voices. His curiosity burned within him as he wondered what they were saying. He didn't want to burst in and interrupt them. Adrian knew that whatever they were talking about, Ari wouldn't tell him any of it.

He started to lean closer to the door to listen, but stopped. Remembering what Mathew had taught him, he instead went into the next room. According to Mathew, especially in winter months, sound traveled through ducts that went throughout the building to keep it warm. Most ducts were used to heat two rooms. If you were in the room adjacent to the room, you could easily hear what was going on next door. Now that it was October, the ducts were opened.

He strode across the room to the vent and leaned down, listening. Adrian could hear what Audrey's sister was saying. "How dare you speak of her that way! You don't know anything."

Adrian could almost feel the ice in her voice as she spoke. Yet those words also conveyed anger and sorrow. Then Ari spoke. "It is true, and you know it. When are you going to live for yourself instead of living to please her?"

There was a loud snap of a fan closing, causing Adrian to jump. Then the other girl spoke again. "What do you know? Your father is dead, and your mother disappeared. You have had no family for years. What do you know about mine?"

Sorrow filled Adrian's heart. It was true what Ari had said in the theater with her tear-stained face. This girl somehow seemed to know about Ari's past, the past that she had refused to allow Adrian to be a part of. It was like her life had been the opposite of his. He had been surrounded and protected his whole life while she was alone. It forced her to grow strong.

A pause filled the space, and Adrian could almost feel Ari's gaze. This was the same gaze she had given him. The one that seemed to pierce his soul. "Oh Euphemia, does your mother even know that you don't like being called Effie?"

Yet again, there was silence from the other room.

Ari spoke again. "Euphemia, I hope you take what I say into consideration. You could be so much more than this."

The lady, Adrian now knew as Euphemia, spoke. "Why are you telling me this? Is it because you hate me? If so, then why do you pretend it is for my own good? I tormented you for years."

"And aren't you tired of pretending? This farce that you put on, doesn't it hurt, keeping it up for so long?"

Adrian could hear Ari's pain and could feel the sincerity in her words. Was this why Ari allowed him to help, so that he could find out? And after that, she wouldn't have to pretend anymore?

He was brought back to the moment as Euphemia spoke. "I'm done with this."

He heard footsteps headed out the room, and the door slammed shut. Then, almost inaudibly, he heard Ari's heavy sigh. At that, Adrian knew he had listened to too much and it was time to head to their meeting point. Leaving his listening post, he headed out and back to where Ari would be waiting for him.

Conroy, my dear Conroy, he saved me from heartache after the death of my second husband. I am saving the image of him by making sure that my daughter is the one set on the throne. And when she is on the throne, I will make sure that she stays by my side. That weak prince is not good for the throne. My daughter is perfect in every way. I made sure of it. Conroy has helped me so much in preparing her. She will be a shining jewel on the throne, with me by her side. I will make sure nothing can touch her there.

Ink splattered page
Journal of the Duchess of Kent

Chapter Thirty-Nine

The conversation with Effie had left Ella unbalanced. She had just gotten her breathing under control when Adrian walked through the door. Joy flooded through her as he appeared, but it quickly turned to fear. Had he overheard what she had said to her stepsister?

In an instant, she had flicked her fan open in front of her face. It would be bad if her face gave away her emotions right now. The intense fear of what could happen if he found out any more about her still caused a chill in her bones. The fear that after learning the truth, that she was using him just as much as the other girls and the worry that he would find out gnawed at her. She had grown close to him, even though she kept secrets from him. And if he left her, just like her mother or father did, it would hurt. But she could not give up all of her secrets. Those were not hers to give.

She relaxed when she heard him speak. "So, what next?"

Ella gave him a genuine smile. He must not have heard what she and Effie had said. Though, even as relief washed over her, a prick of guilt stabbed at her. Not letting her smile falter, she replied, "Next, you go enjoy the remainder of the ball and then head back to London. Things are rather tense here, and it would be bad if you got caught up in it."

He gave her a large smile, his eyes shining with that happy glow he always seemed to have. "That is too bad, since I promised you that I would have to stick by you. Don't you remember?"

Her hope that he would go without a fuss was shattered. She should have known better. She had remembered the promise. That was the problem. Ella had hoped that he had forgotten, but then again he had been rather stubborn lately. She sighed. "I don't suppose that you would go home if I ordered you to?"

"Nope." He grinned.

Ella looked into his eyes, hoping to find doubt. She could not. Ella sighed again, calculating. "Fine, but you must do exactly as I say. This could be dangerous. But *if* you are willing to listen to me and follow my instructions, I will keep you safe. And you *will* leave tonight. As soon as the ball ends. Do not wait until tomorrow."

He stepped close to her. "I can agree to that. And if you want to keep me safe, then I must stick close to you so that I can listen to your orders."

Glad her fan was still in front of her face, a flush graced her cheeks and she smiled. He was teasing her. After all the odd interactions they had recently, she had worried that they would never go back to what they were. But here he was, teasing her. She couldn't allow him to have the last word, now could she?

"If we stand too close to each other, I fear you would catch my dress on fire, since your cheeks are so hot. And it would look strange to a passerby if you stood this close to me."

She closed her fan, and using the tip, gave him a gentle push so he stood an appropriate distance from her. Then she headed for the door, leaving him behind in a stunned silence. He trotted up to catch up to her. "So, where are we headed?"

"There is a man we need to see."

"Who?"

Ella smiled. "The duchess's financier."

His shock was evident on his face as he came to a halt. Then he gathered himself and hurried to catch back up. He strode next to her, asking, "Why? What does he have to do with your mother?"

"I don't know yet," Ella answered truthfully. The only thing knew was that he was connected to the viscount. Ignoring Adrian's curiosity, she continued until they reached a room on the second floor. Ella stopped short. She needed to instruct Adrian so that he could stay safe.

"I want you to listen and keep calm. If you don't, your breathing could give us away. I am trusting that you can stay calm."

A happy smile burst from Adrian, like a flower opening to catch the rays of the sun. Ella felt her heart skip a beat. Warmth flooded through her when she grabbed his hand and pulled him behind her into a side room. This room had not been used this night, and the lights were not lit. She was relieved. This meant that her blush would not be seen by Adrian. They crept through the darkened room. Adrian stubbed his foot on a chair and gave a small cry.

Quickly, Ella reached over and covered his mouth, shushing him. She could feel her hand move when he nodded, and with reluctance, she removed it. Clasping her hand to her chest, Ella tried to calm her heart. This was not the time to let her emotions get the better of her. Clementine always said that if she got too emotional, it would interfere with what she needed to do. She closed her eyes and took a deep breath, thinking back to her training.

When she opened her eyes, her heart had calmed. With a gentle touch, she pulled Adrian as she went to the back of the room. Using her other hand as a guide, she slid it along the wall. She hoped that the vent would connect to the other room, but she had no such luck. She couldn't find it.

Thankful once again that it was dark, she dropped Arian's hand and reached under her skirts. This time, instead of wearing many thick layers of petticoats, Ella was wearing a crinoline. It was designed by a friend of the society. The crinoline was a cage-like structure that gave the skirt volume instead of having to use as many layers of skirts. And it was a perfect place to hide things.

She pulled out a small horn. Normally, this would be used by those who were hard of hearing, but was is also good for listening through walls.

Placing the small end in her ear and the wider end on the wall, she listened.

"... Pinney should be arriving soon... best to ... avoid ... unrest." It was a male voice. The same voice that had spoken to Countess Matilda in the inn. The one who had made a deal with her.

Another voice was recognizable as the duchess's. "But I must see him. . . important. . . politics . . . my daughter."

"It is dangerous. . . we should." the man replied. They seemed to be arguing over staying or leaving because of politics. If only she could get in there to hear better.

Her thoughts turned to Adrian; perhaps he could help her. But no, she shouldn't use him this way. Although he did say he wanted to help, and this could be something less dangerous. And Ella might be able to leave him behind in the relative safety of the ball. Since she couldn't use another society member, since this was an unauthorized mission. And if she didn't want it getting back to Madame Briar, Ella could use outside help. This was exactly the thing that she thought they should do together anyway.

Having made the decision, she led him through the darkness to the door and, before opening it, spoke quietly. "Do you think you can help me?"

"What do you want me to do?" Adrian asked eagerly.

Ella hesitated. This would push the boundaries further than she ever had done. This would put him directly in the path of someone who was in opposition to him. They would become even more aware of him. But it needed to be done. If not, Ella would never find her mother. And if all went well, she would also find out who was trying to poison Adrian.

"Please," Adrian pleaded, his voice quiet but full of intent. "Please, let me help you. Let me do something."

That made the decision for her. Ella could not deny that she needed him. And she could see that he needed to show that he could do things, too. Besides, this was going to be easy. "Do you think you can get them out of that room somehow?"

"Yes," he answered in an instant.

Ella was wary that he answered so quickly, but she would have to accept it. "When you get them out, make sure that they are facing away from this door. And after they are out of the room for as long as you can keep them out, you head directly back to London. Do you understand?"

"Yes, I understand."

"Straight back to London. Do not stop to see what I'm doing. Do not wait for me. Tell your servant to pack only what is necessary and head straight to the next town. Do you *understand*?" Ella said the last word with emphasis. He had no training, and if this thing blew up in her face, he had to be safe. Adrian was safe enough here for the moment, but there was so much anger in the town. It only needed a little spark and it would ignite into violence. She would not leave him in the flames.

Adrian held her hand, and she could feel his honest gaze. "I promise."

Ella couldn't help but feel a sense of foreboding when he released her and headed out the door.

Chapter Forty

Adrian did not feel as confident as he had pretended he was. And he forgot to ask her who he was even going to talk to. His breathing was turning raspy at the thought. No, he must not panic here. He was not going to be sheltered anymore. And Ari wouldn't have asked if she didn't think that he was at least capable of talking to these people. And it was too late to back out now. Before he could even think about what he was doing, he knocked on the door.

The door opened to reveal an unknown man. He looked to be nobility, or at least a high-ranking individual, so why was he opening the door himself? It was strange since normally a servant would open the door on behalf of one with a high rank.

"Who is it?" the man asked, next looking at his clothes and seeing what he wore. "Your Highness, I apologize. I did not realize that you would be here at this event."

Adrian cleared his throat as tried to come up with something to say when a woman spoke from within, "Conroy? Who is it?"

Adrian looked behind Conroy then saw a familiar face of his aunt, the Duchess of Kent. She was standing behind Conroy.

Watching how she stood, Adrian could feel her regal air. She must have been the reason why Ari had sent him here. He could speak to his aunt. Now to figure out a way to get them out of this room.

"Aunt Victoria, I was wondering if I could speak to you." He could feel an irritation radiate from Conroy, though his face held a pleasant expression. Some of that anger dissipated as the duchess placed a hand on his shoulder. He moved to the side to allow her room to speak to with Adrian.

Her face held the cool mask of pleasantness like all the other nobles Adrian had met, but for some reason, the hair on the back of his neck rose as he stood in front of the two of them. He felt as if he was a sacrificial lamb that had been sent to the wolves, and they seemed ready to pounce. Yet if anyone was watching them, it would seem as if they were having a pleasant conversation. It also felt odd that they hadn't invited him in and were making him wait in the hallway.

Adrian's breathing started to get raspy again, which caused him to get nervous, which made his breathing get worse. He thought that he could see his aunt's lip curl into a smile for a moment, but it was gone so fast. Those feelings that he had had grew with each passing moment as she answered.

"Oh, my poor nephew, you sound so horrible. Please come in and sit." She gestured to the room with a smile on her face. The face that he had thought was so kind as a boy, but with what he knew now, made his heart race with fear at what she might be truly thinking. He looked into the room, which felt like a spider's lair, and saw movement in the corner of his eye. Ari had stuck her hand through the door, and his panicky breathing calmed.

"I'm sorry, Aunt. As you can see, I'm not feeling well. The crowds below are getting to me and there are too many women who want to dance with me. I was hoping to stave them off if I were to dance with you. Would you be willing to come dance with me, Aunt?"

Surprise flickered through her eyes, and she turned to Conroy. The man shifted to look at her. Adrian couldn't see the expression he conveyed, but he knew that they were somehow communicating. He clenched his hands behind his back, trying to refrain from running his fingers through his hair. The wait felt like it stretched into hours instead of just the minute that it took for her to answer him.

"My dear nephew, of course I would be willing to dance with you, but I am currently having a problem. There's a new judge coming into town, Charles Wetherell, and I have been wanting to visit with him. The mayor will be riding in with him tomorrow, and I need to see the judge before I leave for the next city. But because of time constraints, the only time we could visit with him is when he is being introduced by the mayor. The mayor has been trying to stay neutral. He is part of the Whig Party and I have been known to side with the Tory Party. If the two of us were seen together, it would be seen as a *faux pas*. It would be a help if you would be willing to use your influence to help me get an appointment with him."

This was what his father was talking about, one of the reasons he hated Adrian's aunt. Her ambition was voracious. Adrian saw Ari's hand flick again in the corner of his vision. He needed to get them out of this room, and from the look in his aunt's eyes, she would not leave until he said yes.

"Well, it would be rather difficult to do at this moment."

"Tomorrow would be perfect," she insisted with a smile.

"What I meant, aunt, is that I am not feeling my best, and I was planning on heading home as soon as possible." Adrian floundered at his attempt to get out of a promise, but she had sunk her claws in deep. She was not going to let go. Her smile became even more sinister and he knew she would not budge on this matter.

Before Adrian could say anything more, she said, "Then it would be best to stay the night here, allowing for you to rest. Then you could introduce me tomorrow, and head home when you feel up to it. You would be willing to do something this simple for your aunt, wouldn't you? And as thank you, we can do one dance together, and then we can send you home for a nice rest. What do you think?"

His chest felt tight as he listened to what she proposed. Adrian could not escape it. He would have to break the promise he made to Ari. If the duchess made a fuss, it would cause problems for his father. He would just have to make sure he left as soon as possible. Pain pricked at his heart, as he knew what he needed to do. Once he acknowledged her, it would be like a promise. And judging by the intensity in her eyes, she would make sure that he upheld it. Holding out his hand, he gave a small bow. "I would be honored to have a dance with you."

The duchess placed her hand in his and allowed herself to be escorted down the hall. Now all he had to do was to get the gentleman to leave. When the duchess spoke, solving that problem. "Lord Conroy, would you mind returning to where we are staying? We can finish discussing this when I return."

Giving her a bow, he replied, "Yes, Madam." Though his response was polite, Adrian could feel irritation in his voice. The duchess didn't seem to notice or didn't care. If the feeling his aunt gave off was like a beast, then the man was like a serpent. Shivers ran down Adrian's spine.

His aunt turned to him and motioned in front of her, "Shall we?"

Adrian nodded, leading her to the dance floor, and hoped that he had done what Ari needed. And hoped that she would forgive him for not leaving as he had promised.

Chapter Forty-One

Ella watched as Adrian led the duchess away, breathing a sigh of relief. Standing behind the door had been nerve-wracking, not knowing what he was going to do. She wouldn't have been this nervous if it was someone from the academy, or even Clementine. But waiting for Adrian was like watching a glass figurine on the edge of a shelf while people were tromping through the house during a storm. Ella couldn't really hear what they were talking about, but she did hear him start to wheeze and stuck her hand out. It was the only thing she could do without ruining everything.

When Adrian led his aunt away, she relaxed. He had led at least one away and was heading towards the ballroom, where he would be safe. Once he finished with his aunt, he would be heading back to London and everything would turn out fine. All that was left was for the man to leave and for her to search for information.

Ella was rewarded when, within a few minutes, the man walked past her door. Her wide skirts made it so the door had to be fully open for her to leave, so she counted to ten and then slipped out.

It would do her no good for him to catch her in the open, leaving a dark room.

After leaving the room, rather than searching the room he vacated, Ella followe Conroy. He was headed toward the dance floor, but instead of lingering on the floor, he headed towards the exit. It would be difficult to follow him without making a scene.

Looking across the dance floor, Ella spotted Harriett. After training her at Eleanor's house, Harriet had become an excellent ghost. It was good that she had brought both her and Clementine along on this trip. She had practiced her acting enough that she could get close enough to get the needed information to Adrian. Harriett had managed to sneak into the ball during the chaos of preparation and was dressed as a servant, making sure that she was in an open space so she could see Ella when she arrived.

Harriett was hovering near the entrance, keeping watch for Ella. Flicking her fan open, Ella waved it to get her attention. Within a few moments, she locked eyes with Ella and nodded slightly in acknowledgment. Ella tapped her fan to her cheek, made a motion in front of her face, then pointed in Conroy's direction. Blinking her eyes in acknowledgment, Harriet followed him out the door.

Confident that Harriet could handle herself, Ella went back to the room that the duchess and Conroy had met in. As she suspected, there was nothing of importance, and she headed back to the ballroom. By the time she returned, the prince had left. Believing that he was on his way home, Ella relaxed and enjoyed her time dancing until the ball came to a close.

Adrian woke up the morning of the next day filled with dread. After dancing with the duchess, or at least his attempt at dancing, his nerves were taut. He was never really trained to dance, nor was allowed to because of his health. Adrian did his best to copy the others in the dance. All he had managed to do was to humiliate himself. By the end, he was too tired to do anything else, and he had headed home. All with the duchess making sure he kept his promise to meet the next day, and letting him know his father would be in a difficult position should he refuse.

Adrian paced as the meeting time approached, his breath whistling with each turn. Mathew entered tense as he stalked through the door to help Adrian get ready. "I don't know why you are going to this meeting with the duchess. Things are getting bad out there, and it would be best if we immediately returned home."

Looking back at Mathew, Adrian sighed. He thought about how to explain this to him, then thought better of it. "Once this is done, I will head straight home."

Mathew had already laid out Adrian's clothes on the bed and now headed towards Adrian, his face in a stoic mask. Adrian could see Mathew's jaw clenching as he helped him with his shirt. "Why does it feel like you came all the way out here because of Lady Arabella?"

"It's not her fault I got in this mess. She told me to leave right after the ball." Adrian snapped his mouth closed. Mathew looked up at him, his irritation only being held in check by his professionalism.

"So, coming here *was* her fault. I figured as much. That woman has you wrapped around her finger. I don't know what she wants from you, but it's not good. Look at the mess you are in, Your Highness."

Adrian turned away from Mathew and picked up his jacket. He ran his fingers through his hair, then turned back to him. "I have already said this is not her fault, it's mine. I will not speak anymore of this. Let's get this meeting over with so we can leave this town."

Mathew watched as Adrian donned his jacket in silence. Matthew kept that silence as he helped Adrian adjust his jacket and grabbed his top hat. He then led Adrian to the awaiting carriage, still silent.

Once he was seated, Mathew placed his hand on Adrian's arm and said, "I still don't like that you aren't bringing me. Just promise me you will make it back safely. If things get bad, don't worry about anyone else. Get yourself back here. You are the only prince we have."

Mathew glanced at the guard and gave them the "look" that said, *I will kill you if you let anything happen to him*. He turned and headed back inside to where Abigail was watching from the doorway.

With an acknowledgment from Adrian, the driver headed off down the street, which was devoid of people. Sweat trickled down Adrian's neck and his chest tightened as they drew ever closer to the mayor's mansion. It wasn't until they arrived at the mansion that they found people milling about. Some stood watching, while others wandered the streets. They seemed to be waiting for something. He was thankful for Mathew's insistence to go in an unmarked carriage, and though the guards did gather some looks, they were able to pass without much trouble.

With the emptiness of the streets, they quickly arrived at Queen's Square. It was a beautiful area, built like a square as the name suggested, and in the center held a park, while all the buildings faced in towards it. The Mansion House, where Pinney stayed, was on the corner of this square. The carriage followed along the street, looking at the houses that were buttressed up against each other, causing the street to be shadowed in the morning light.

A few onlookers in the square peered into the carriage, but after seeing him, they looked away down the street. Others peered out through windows in the buildings, curtains flicking open at the corners every few seconds. Something big was happening today. The air was thick with it.

As the carriage came to a stop in front of the mansion house, he hesitated in the shadow of that stately building. The edgy feeling he had felt all day gnawed at him. Should he stay or should he go? Would the duchess allow him to leave without repercussions? What would Ari say if she found out he broke his promise? These questions haunted him as he exited the carriage and entered the house.

Chapter Forty-Two

29 October 1831, Bristol

Ella walked through eerie streets. At this time in the morning, many people should be busy, going about their day. Now, the people on the streets hurried into buildings as quickly as they could. They didn't stop to talk or to laugh. They kept their heads down and shied away from others on the street. Ella knew this was due to the anti-reform judge who was visiting today. Security was tight, and they changed where he would arrive, but in this city, a secret of that importance could not be kept for long. Especially with sympathizers about.

Considering how the people were, Ella was grateful she had Clementine and Harriette to help. The Society was worried about riots in the streets and had sent Ella here to keep an eye on things. It just also happened to coincide with when the duchess would be here as well.

And if the duchess was here in town, then her financier Conroy would be too. Conroy was involved with the viscount. But how? Is he involved in a plot to kill the prince? Was there even a plot, or was this feeling just her nerves? Her choice was very clear.

She would have to get close to Conroy and see if he would lead her to the viscount. While she would be doing that, Harriett and Clementine could keep an eye on the crowd by the entrance.

Deep in thought, though still alert for danger, Ella arrived at Queen's Square. The Mansion House, where Pinney stayed, was on the corner of this square. Ella followed along the street, looking at the houses that were buttressed up against each other. As she came up to the corner, she brushed her skirts to make sure they were properly laid and in an attempt to remove most of the dust that she had collected on her walk. She was wearing Harriett's servant uniform that had been altered to fit. Though it was a little short, she tried to hide that with an apron and extra fabric on the bottom. She had donned a white shirt over the top of the housemaid uniform and now held a basket of fresh bread that they had prepped for the disguise. All that was left was to hope no one would notice.

Ella kept a careful eye on the people who were on the streets and made sure to avoid them as she walked slowly to the mansion. She waited for an opportunity to enter. She fiddled with the fan she kept in her sleeve to keep her nerves down. The ominous feeling and the men in the streets pressed on her, and she made sure to keep note of everything that was happening.

It was only a few moments later that she saw an armed escort for an unmarked carriage. Considering how people were in the streets, it must have been a nobleman who was trying to go unnoticed in the streets. Ella quickened her pace and watched a young man exit the carriage and enter the building. The armed escorts left with the carriage, and Ella assumed they would be back later to pick him up. With the commotion of a newly arrived guest and the tension in the streets, it would be difficult to distinguish one maid from another. As the carriage drove away, Ella hurried through the gate.

When she arrived at the door, she ducked her head and kicked the door with her foot, as if she was having a hard time both opening the door and handling the basket. One of the head servants cracked the door open, took a look at Ella, then looked behind her to the street. The woman hurried her in and motioned her to the kitchen.

"What are you doing, child? How did you get stuck outside? You stupid girl. How in the world did you get hired? It is dangerous to be out right now!"

It was obvious to Ella that this woman was terrified of what was going on outside. Those who were just servants could do nothing but try not to drown as they tried to survive the storm. The woman glanced curiously at Ella, who had kept her head down. "I don't recognize you, girl. Who —"

The woman was interrupted by a ringing bell. She stopped her question and looked for the sound. In the moment that she turned, Ella had left the basket of bread and headed right through the door. On her way through the kitchen, Ella grabbed a rag and headed up the servant's stairs. As she climbed, she pulled off the white top. Upon arriving on the second floor, she started wiping windows. When no one was in the hallway to observe, Ella would move around the building, searching for where the meeting would take place.

It didn't take long for her to arrive at the front of the mansion. Her breath caught as she looked out at the street below. Through the window, her gaze turned towards the front gate of the town and in the distance, she could imagine the massive crowd by the front gates, waiting for the judge to arrive. The fear she had shoved to the back of her mind broke through to the front. Its cold grip clutched at her heart as she silently pleaded that her friends were safe.

She could not lose her family again. Especially when she was close to finding her mother again.

Her mother's painting in the hall of legacy floated through her head. She was so close to finding out about her. Ella had gone too far to pull back now. Everything she had risked, including putting her friends in danger would be for not if she failed this task.

Touching her fan, she gathered her fear, tucked it back in its box, and shoved it deep into the recesses of her mind. This was not the time to fall apart.

She got herself under control, none too soon, as she heard murmuring voices approaching from behind. Looking around her, Ella headed through an opposite door. With a quick glance, she could see that the room was an office. The office that they were headed towards. She ran through several plans in her mind, dismissing those that wouldn't work.

It took only a moment to formulate and decide on a plan; and just as quickly, she enacted it. Folding the rag she held, she tucked it into her skirts. She then smoothed her skirts, making certain that they were brushed free of dust. Taking a deep breath to calm her nerves, she strode to the door that the voices were coming from. As the voices made their way closer, one voice sounded familiar. With head bowed, she opened the door, allowing them to enter.

As they passed, Ella lifted her head and her eyes locked on Adrian. Feeling the heat of Ella's gaze on him, his eyes found hers. Shock flooded his features, and he struggled to regain his composure.

"Your Highness? May I ask what your concern is?" the manservant questioned. He turned to follow where Adrian's line of sight was with concern.

"It's nothing. I just didn't realize she would be here is all," Adrian responded.

"Who, Your Highness?" the manservant asked, as he tried to conceal his confusion.

Ella stepped forward, her head down. "That would be me, sir."

The manservant's confusion quickly turned to a stoic face befitting of a footman. His eyes looked her up and down as he tried to place her. "And who are you, young maid? And why are you here?"

Quick on the uptake, Adrian chimed in. "She is one of my maidservants. She must have arrived after I entered, but she must have arrived before us to the meeting room."

The man raised his brow but did not comment. Instead, he motioned them further into the room to wait. Ella went to stand behind Adrian by the wall.

This promised to be an interesting meeting. Fear as well as anger warred within her, kept concealed behind the careful mask of a demure servant. She and Adrian would have words once this was over. Knowing who was involved in this meeting, it would be difficult to make it through without giving herself away. And since she wasn't supposed to her here like this, people could easily realize that she didn't belong. She would have to hope that they would be distracted enough not to think too much of a servant.

She fiddled with the edge of her fan and fell into her training, keeping careful watch over the room.

Chapter Forty-Three

Adrian's neck itched as he felt Ari's presence behind him. Shame for breaking his promise filled him, though it wasn't as though he could have told her he was stuck coming to this meeting. He had no way of contacting her. His guilt, though, was giving over to his relief that she was here. He knew he shouldn't look at her, but her presence pulled at him. He turned his chair slightly so he could see her from the corner of his eye.

Even knowing how dangerous of a position he was in, he couldn't help but think about her. He sighed. How was he ever going to be of help to her if he kept getting stuck in his love-struck thoughts? Taking a deep breath, he followed his breathing exercises as he looked out the window. The room was situated so that the guest could look out the windows, but the person at the desk could not. Adrian would have hated to have his office lay out like this, if he ever got one.

Any other day, he would have been happy to look out the large windows at the park below. Today, instead of noticing how beautiful the day was, he could only see the sparse streets below.

He remembered the few people he has seen in the streets and wondered why they were so angry. What was causing them to act this way? What was that ominous feeling that was hanging in the air?

Before he could think of an answer, the door opened and in walked his aunt, his cousin, and the man he met last night. Conroy was his name. His aunt was ever the duchess, and if she was nervous about the commotion outside, she didn't show it.

Drina, ever composed for someone so young, seemed less nervous about what was happening outside and more concerned about her mother. She stood composed, but Adrian noticed that she would flick her eyes in her mother's direction whenever her mother moved. It was as though she was concerned that she would get reprimanded if she did something wrong. Remembering what Ari had said about her, he examined her eyes and could see some shadows beneath them, cleverly concealed by powder. His poor cousin. He would have to do something about that when he got home. But now, it was time to make it through this conversation.

Conroy told the manservant to make sure the carriage was ready to go at a moment's notice. As Conroy and the servant spoke, Adrian could feel Ari tense behind him. Confused at that reaction, but rather than reacting himself, he instead greeted his aunt.

He plastered on a smile and grasped her hand. "It is a pleasure to see you again, Duchess."

She nodded and took her seat, without waiting for him to greet her daughter. Adrian's eye twitched with annoyance at her dismissal. Now that he was getting better at understanding things, he understood this was a snub at his authority.

He bristled at the insult but refrained from arguing with her. Ari was watching. Her calming presence soothed his rage. Turning to his cousin, he greeted her. Adrian could see a few emotions run through her expression. Joy, anger, fear, sorrow, with a constant flicking of her eyes towards her mother, all taking place within a few seconds before her stoic mask recovered. With grace far above her years, she accepted his greeting. She gave him a pleasant smile before turning to be seated.

The tension in the air was thick enough to touch as they waited in silence. It almost felt in mimicry to the tension outside. One small tug and the thread would break. Just one spark and an eruption of flames. One step to the edge of oblivion.

The clang of bells erupted outside. The startling sound caused Adrian to jump, and he looked out the window. A carriage was traveling dangerously fast through the streets, people were leaping out of its way. The ringing bell was the authorities that were escorting the carriage as it hurried towards the gates of the mansion. When the carriage arrived, the gate was thrown open to the men, allowing them onto the grounds. Two men were escorted by several of the authorities as they entered the house. The other stayed out to guard.

A mass of people followed behind them and started crowding the square outside their gates. The empty streets now flooded with people. The quiet before the storm was gone. Now the storm had arrived, and it was enraged.

Adrian could feel his chest tighten. This was what Mathew and Ari had been worried about. They had both been pushing him to leave before this had happened. And now he was in the middle of it and there was no way to get out of it. He could only hope that Mathew and Abigail would be safe. His fists tightened into a ball as he was unable to turn his eyes away from the window. He could hear his labored breathing beating in time to the racing of his heart.

Then a hand rested on his arm, and Ari's face shone before him. "Are you alright, Your Highness?"

Like a cool compress on a fevered head, the raging fire of fear mellowed to a dull roar. His breathing had calmed to a slight wheeze when he answered, "I will be fine."

His expression seemed to mollify her as she walked back to her position by the wall. Now that he was calmer, he could feel her tension behind him. Ari was worried. Adrian knew he had to do something about this situation. He turned to his aunt, who was now hiding her distaste at what was happening outside behind her fan.

"Such a scene at such an insignificant problem." The duchess stood and looked down at the people crowding below. "Quite the racket. How dare they treat us in such a way . Don't worry, my dear, when you are queen, there would be no way they will they cause such a scene."

"What did you just say?" Adrian asked. With the riot outside, this was what she spoke of? Her daughter becoming queen, in front of the crown prince? Fury was building inside him. He did not know everything about this situation, but people didn't riot in the streets for insignificant things. Did she not see the danger of what was going on?

She turned to him and feigned surprise. "Oh, so sorry, nephew. It was a slip of the tongue."

He heard a smile in her voice and knew that this was no slip of the tongue. She knew exactly what she was saying and to whom she was saying it to. Before he could react, Drina spoke. "Mother, please do not say such things. We are in a terrifying situation. Can we wait for this conversation until the lord of this mansion arrives?"

Adrian turned to look at his cousin. Though her words were calm and clear, her hands were white as she clutched her fan. The duchess rushed to her daughter and cooed over her. Making a fuss over the situation and putting on a show for the others.

As this exchange happened, Adrian couldn't help but notice his aunt showed a flicker of annoyance before she went over to her daughter. He also noticed that when Drina showed a trickle of fear, it was not at the situation outside, rather it was at her mother.

The door to the office opened, putting a halt to the duchess's charade. In strode Mayor Pinney, along with Judge Wetherell and several constables. Pinney came in with a whine. "How dare they throw rocks at my carriage. This is outrageous!"

Wetherell strode in, less frantic and frazzled than Pinney. When he spoke, his words were calm, yet had a tone of superiority to them. "This is why it is better for the nobility to control them. If every time they don't get what they want, they throw a fit, it would be better to keep things as they are."

Was this what most of the nobility thought? Adrian asked himself. The people were not the type to just revolt. The last time there were riots was more than fifty years ago. And it was because of politics and those in charge not listening. But then again, was he any different? There were so many things he didn't know, and yet he still believed that he should be prince.

He walked to the window and looked out at the crowd below. There was so much anger. This night was going to end in sorrow.

According to witnesses, Mayor Pinney attempted to speak to the crowd twice, to no avail. By the end of the day, the Riot Act was enacted, and chaos ensued. Looting and rioting filled the streets, and the soldiers had little control. It was a poorly controlled situation, with a few protesters dying by soldiers before the riot even started. Will Mayor Pinney be able to wriggle out of this mess or will he be court-martialed? Find out in the next edition after the trial.

Newspaper clipping from November 1832
Unable to see byline or newspaper title.

Chapter Forty-Four

30 October 1831, Bristol

"You should have gotten some rest while you had the chance," Ella said, watching Adrian. He had been provided a room to rest, considering they were now trapped inside the Mansion House. The tense day had now turned into the dark of early morning before the sun had risen. The only thing that had been constant was the yells of the rioters.

Adrian, instead of laying down as he should have, was looking out the window. Ella came to stand beside him and looked out. Fires dotted the once pristine park, where people carried torches or lanterns. Others carried tools they had stolen from the blacksmith. People were breaking into the government buildings around the square and looting stores. It was chaos.

Ella turned to Adrian. "It is time to go. It is getting too dangerous here. The rioters aren't stopping. We suspect they may come here next."

She reached for his arm to lead him away, but he continued to stare out the window.

Adrian turned to Ella. The flickering flames outside made him appear as though he was being tortured by flames.

"The whole day I have been unable to do anything for my people. I am a prince, and it was always known that I would one day rule. I was always sickly, and so many didn't believe that I would live this long. But I have, and with my father's advancing age, it seemed as though I would end up becoming king. I believed that everything would be alright. That even though I wasn't fully trained, because of illness, it would still be my right to rule. Now I'm learning about how the world really is. And so, I have followed you, trying to learn all that I could. I thought if I truly understood the people, or at least understood enough, I could become a great king. And then today happened."

"What happened today was not your fault." Ella insisted, gripping his arm. "It is not. You didn't know what was going to happen. You haven't dealt with these situations before."

Adrian shrugged off her hand. "Is that any excuse for not knowing what was happening here? Three times their petitions have been denied. And then a judge who goes against everything they want is sent here? It's like a slap in the face. It's no wonder the people are rioting."

Her heart pounded in her chest. She felt for him. He had been innocent in all of this. She came barging in, thinking that she knew everything, and had shattered his world. And when his world was shattered the first thing it revealed was fire and destruction. That look of sorrow filling his eyes broke her heart. Going against orders to reveal the truth had been wrong. And now she put him in a dangerous position.

A noise from a nearby room startled her. She looked out the window and she could see Judge Wetherell climbing onto the roof to escape to the nearby house.

This was no time for moping or self-pity —she would protect Adrian. That meant getting out of this house. Before, it had been a safe haven, but now it was quickly becoming a target.

"Adrian, we can ponder this when we are safe. It is time to move. Now!" This time, as she grabbed his arm, he allowed her to pull him with away.

Adrian shook himself out of his sorrow as he was dragged along. "How are we going to escape?"

Ella gave him a grin as made their way to the attic. Adrian started to make his way to where the Judge had escaped. Ella pulled him the opposite way. "You will have a hard time climbing across the roof. I have a better idea."

She strode across the attic to a maid's room and went to the chest at the base of the bed. Throwing it open, she riffled through until she pulled out a dress.

The look on his face as understanding flooded his features was priceless. "No, no, no. There is no way. I am not going to wear a dress. Besides, how does it help us to get out? You're not expecting me to walk right out of here. Are you?"

"The rioters are allowing servants and women to escape from the mansion. They aren't looking for you in particular and won't focus on you enough to notice. You are small and skinny enough to fit into a dress. In the dark, no one will ever know. Now, get dressed."

She didn't wait to see his reaction as she exited the room to look out the window. It was a silly idea, but she was sure the plan was going to work. She had to believe in it. Watching to make sure that they were still allowing servants out peaceably, her eyes caught a glimpse of a particularly angry group of rioters. And they were headed straight for them.

They had to leave now. Ella headed back to Adrian and burst through the door... to find him with his arms up stuck in the dress.

Her face burned with embarrassment, and she was grateful for the darkness of the room. Clearing her throat, she pushed down her embarrassment and hurried to help him. After she helped him pull it over his head, she looked at the laces. It would take far too long to do them, so she pulled an apron and a bonnet from the chest and put them on him.

As fast as they were, it was still too late. A crash could be heard from the front of the house. Men were shouting, and a gunshot went off. Ella changed directions. While the prince was supposed to be resting, Ella had wandered the house looking for ways to escape. While she did, she had found another exit on the side of the house. Adrian struggled to keep up as she pulled him down another set of stairs. Upon reaching the bottom, to find there was another group of men gathered around the side door.

"Keep your head down. I will do the talking. When you are out, head back to the inn. Don't stop for anyone," Ella whispered.

He ducked his head dutifully, pulling his bonnet further over his face. With a sigh of relief, she headed for the door, keeping her head low and pulling her fan halfway out of her sleeve for easy draw. As she continued past the bottom of the stairs, she kept moving through the men. She had hoped they would escape without incident, but her hopes were dashed when they grabbed Ella's arm.

"What is a pretty lass like you doing here?" That man had a stout frame from doing heavy work and wore smoke-stained clothes. He also smelled drunk, the foul odor of cheap beer pouring out of his mouth as he spoke. "Want to stay with me, missy? I can give you protection."

Disgust filled Ella and she rapped the man's wrist with her iron fan. It gave a satisfactory crack as she pulled Adrian free. The man howled as he clutched his wrist. That horrible man was using this riot as an excuse to do what he wanted. Ella wanted to whack his head to knock some sense into him, but protecting Adrian came first. Another crash came from deep inside the house, urging her on. She refrained from sighing when Adrian waited outside the door for her, shifting from foot to foot.

"I thought I told you to head to the inn." Ella spouted, grabbing his hand again and hurrying down the street.

Even though she was annoyed that he didn't leave like she had instructed him to, she couldn't help but feel happy that he was beside her. And happy that she had an excuse to hold his hand as they weaved their way through the crowd. Once she got him to the inn, he should be safe and out of the rioters' way. Their attention seemed to be centered on the civic buildings around Queen's Square. The inn was several blocks away from the square.

Glancing back, Ella could see that the looters were already relieving the wine cellar of all its casks. She sighed in relief; looting would keep those men occupied while she and Adrian made their escape. Ella slowed so Adrian could take a breath. They had not gone far from the Mansion House, but already she could hear him wheezing from exertion. If they had to do any sort of running, they would be in serious trouble. She doubted he could run at full speed for longer than a few seconds. And he could collapse after that.

"Once we get farther away, we will take a rest. It shouldn't take long to —" Ella cut herself short when she saw something across the street.

Conroy was helping the duchess and her daughter into a carriage they had stashed nearby. They had escaped the mansion just before Adrian and Ella had made their escape, and seemed no worse for the wear. Conroy finished helping them into the carriage but did not get into the vehicle himself. Conroy, the man Ella now knew for certain to be the man who spoke to Countess

Matilda. The one whom the Duke of Wellington had told her about.

An eagerness to follow him pulled at her feet, before she even knew what she was doing. She quickly came to her senses and stopped, looking behind her. Adrian was in danger. Danger that she had put him into. She forced herself to turn away. Guilt at not going after the man who could lead her to her mother ate at her, just as that same thought brought more guilt at putting Adrian further into danger. The carriage went on its way, and Conroy moved down the street, glancing once behind him and hurrying down an alleyway.

Her heart was split in two. Her mission or her mother? She could not take another step forward to lead Adrian away, neither could she step to the side to chase after Conroy.

With a gentle tug, Ella felt a squeeze on her hand as Adrian led them down the dark alley to follow Conroy.

Chapter Forty-Five

Adrian didn't think as they followed Conroy. All he focused on was his breathing. After a moment's rest, they needed to keep moving, but Ari had stopped. She had become so focused on Conroy that Adrian knew this must have been the man she was looking for. He also left on foot.

Adrian watched Ari's face alternate between guilt and desire as she stood and watching him get further away. The guilt, Adrian was sure, was because of him. He had stayed and now was in this predicament because of him, and now Ari couldn't do what she needed to do. Instead, she was stuck making sure that he didn't get into danger. All his hope that by his coming here, he would be able to help Ari was squashed.

Yet again, he had to be protected. Wasn't this what he had been trying to change?

Taking a deep breath, he pulled her down the alleyway where Conroy had left. Seeing what had happened recently, he was not going to sit sheltered. He made the choice. No more would he be a porcelain doll to be kept safe on a shelf while the building crumbled around him. He would defend his home. If that meant putting himself in danger, so be it.

Adrian did not realize how difficult it would be to tail him. First, it was dark. It was still early enough in the morning that the sun hadn't risen yet. Then, with all the people on the streets shouting, you couldn't hear anything. The torches cast flickering shadows, causing Adrian to flinch or think it was someone coming from the side. And, since they were so close to Queen's Square, the crowd here bumped into him. This tangled his legs in his skirts, much to his embarrassment.

He tripped on his skirt once again and looked at Ari, hoping she wouldn't notice. When he looked at her, Ari's face was beaming. In the midst of a riot, following someone who dealt with people who easily plotted about killing others, she was smiling. Smiling! Adrian was glad he made the decision to follow Conroy. He had made the right choice. That made him smile as well.

That is, until Adrian looked back for Conroy and realized that he could no longer see him. Adrian had spent too long looking at Ari and had lost him. As he slowed down, not knowing where to go, Ari pulled him onwards. He smiled again; even amidst a disaster like this, she was there for him. Squeezing her hand, he followed her. Just as the morning light was peaking up over the horizon, Conroy stopped to speak to someone.

Ari pulled them to a halt and ducked behind some barrels. Peering between the barrels, they could see that he was talking to a soldier from the 14th Dragoons. They were part of the army regiment that had been called to suppress the riots.

What was Conroy saying to him? It didn't take long for their conversation to end, and he moved onward. This continued for much of the day. Conroy would wander around for a while, then stop to speak to someone, usually a soldier from the 14th Dragoons, but there were several others. Always, though, the commotion kept them from hearing what he was saying. A few times, Adrian tried asking Ari if she knew what Conroy was doing, but he was always shushed. He wanted to snap back several times, though better of it considering her look of concentration, thought better of it and continued to follow along.

The sun rose and had started to fall before things got really interesting. During the day, he had managed to change into a shirt and trousers. How they got it, he wished he could wipe from his memory. He also changed his bonnet for a hat that had fallen on the streets during the rioting. Now that he wasn't bothering with the skirts, he could focus on what was going on around him, and it horrified him.

They had passed by a blacksmith's shop —door was torn off its hinges, and the owner knelt in tears at his empty smithy. The looters had stolen his livelihood, so they could loot another building. Passing more people, he could see through windows as people huddled together, hoping the looters wouldn't come in. Others goaded the rioters as they sought for excuses to raid another place. The exhaustion of the day, as well as his growing tension, wore on him as he witnessed scene after scene of people that he was unable to help and those he failed.

Adrian walked as though in a trance. Shock had set in and he felt as if everything around him were moving images he merely saw through a window, even though he was standing in the middle of it.

During the afternoon, some of the people's anger had quieted, but now as darkness fell, the flames of anger blew hot once more. They continued to follow Conroy, but he did something different this time. After leading them all day, he finally went into a building. They had wandered around Bristol for the day, and most of the buildings had started to look the same, and this one was no different. Just another building shoved in with all the others on the street.

Adrian's breathing started quickening. This was it. After all the time they had spent wandering, this was where Ari had wanted to go.

He was about to follow Ari toward the building when she stopped him with her outstretched hand. "This is where you stay."

"After all this? We followed him together all day, and yet you want me to sit it out? *Why?*" He had managed to keep his voice to a breathy whisper as he let out his frustration. Over the course of the day, his emotions had been building up at being unable to do anything, and yet when they were about to do something, she told him no.

They were hiding at the corner of the street. Ari pulled him so he was looking at her rather than the street. As she took his hand, his anger calmed, but he held tightly to some of that anger in pure stubbornness. He was not going to let this go, even if she looked at him like that.

"Please. You don't have the experience that I do. And listen to yourself. You are exhausted. If we get into trouble, you would only slow me down. And I would do anything to keep you safe." As she spoke, he could not keep his anger, and it died to embers.

She was right. Every time he inhaled, he could hear the whistle in his breath. And now that they had stopped, he could feel the soreness in his muscles. It was far more physical exertion than he had ever done, and his legs were already shaking. He had sunburns on his face from being outside for so long. When Ari said he would slow her down, it was like a blow to his heart. Even though it had felt like a lifetime, he had only just started to understand what was going on. He was like a newborn chick, and he wanted to jump into the lion's den? If he did, Ari would get hurt because of him. Of that, he was certain. Just as she had jumped in to save him from the looters, she would try to save him from these men. And unlike the looters who weren't focused on killing, these men were.

He bowed his head, and she turned to go. Before she could release his hand, he gripped hers once more and implored, "Stay safe, and promise me that after this is over, you *will* tell me everything. I deserve that. You have kept too many things from me for too long."

Ari gave a slow nod. "As you command." Then she was gone, leaving him behind in the empty shadows of a forlorn street.

Chapter Forty-Six

Ella wiped a tear from her face as she left Adrian behind. Soon, she would have to pay the dues for what she had done. After everything she they had been through and what she must tell him, he would certainly leave her. But, she did not have to think about that now. She could only hope that he was as safe as possible while she went to find information.

She looked down the streets and took it all in. As was common, the houses that lined the streets were built with common walls. It was difficult to differentiate between them unless you already knew which building you needed to go to. And yet something was different about this street. Confusion blossomed in her mind as she tried to place why this street seemed odd. It looked like every other street, except for the people. There was no one here but for the two men who stood by the door that Conroy had entered. Ella had just spent the day wandering the city, and there were always arms of people this close to where the riots were happening.

Though it was dark, she couldn't see any signs of life. No flickering of candles in windows. No faces peering fearfully through the glass. There were no signs of looting. No trash in the streets as the looters went on rampage. No doors smashed open or slightly askew from being torn open. It felt eerie that no one was on the street. Other than the house in the center. She had a plan.

Pulling off her white bonnet and apron, she tucked them in her skirts. Grateful she was wearing the black dress of a servant, she crept across the road. She kept steady, even breaths. Even though her heart was racing, she had to go slow. Speed would be noticed by the men, and it was only her training that kept her from running.

When she arrived at the house that was on the corner, she crouched in its stone doorway. It didn't provide much cover, but she would take what she could get. She glanced down the street one more time to see if the guards had noticed her and got to work.

Ella reached to her ankle boots and twisted the heel. She retrieved her lock picks and went to work unlocking the door. This one was quite easy and within a few moments, she was in. Replacing her lock picks, she stood and slid through the open door. Now that she was in, things were going to get harder. Every step she took would be one step closer to the enemy and one step further from safety.

The only question: was it worth the risk?

Ella pushed those thoughts away. She needed to concentrate. One wrong move and things could get dangerous fast. As she crept up the stairs, she made sure that all was still quiet in the house. Taking a leaf from Lord Wetherell's book, she took to the roof. Using her apron, she wrapped her skirt and tied it around her waist. It would not do to fall off the roof because she caught her foot in her skirt. Then on to the roof she went. Ella had spent many childhood days climbing trees. And, as Clementine constantly reminded her, also falling out of them. Tonight, she could not afford to fall.

As was common of the houses in town, the roofs were pitched and had wooden shingles. Moisture from rain and humidity would make the shingles soft and slick. Luckily, it hadn't rained recently, and the roofs were in good repair. She made her way across the roofs, testing each footing before placing her weight. It was slow going, but it was worth it.

By the time she had arrived at the desired house, time had passed and the pitch black of midnight had overtaken the sky. Ella inched down the pitched roof. Suddenly, her feet shot out from under her as a rotting shingle broke free. She rolled to the edge of the roof, just managing to catch herself before she slid off. The broken shingle clattered to the ground below.

Ella held her breath, waiting for there to be a cry of alarm. Fear lanced through her but her breathing calmed as no alarm was sounded. Releasing the tension in her muscles one by one, she peered over the edge. Though hard to see, the guards were still standing by the door. She looked below her to the house, finding the window she was looking for. Gripping the edge of the roof, she dangled her legs over the oblivion below, feeling for the window's stone ledge. Once her foot was on solid stone, she relaxed her grip on the roof and put pressure on the side walls of the window. With a small squat, she reached with one hand and lifted the window open, and slid in.

Ella breathed a sigh of relief as she shut the window behind her. Ella turned around and surveyed the room before her. Lighting was poor, so not much could be seen. The darkness outside did little to illuminate the room. Vague lumps seemed to be furniture. On the far end, light trickled in from under the door. The only light that had been on.

Moving carefully, Ella made her way across the room and pressed her ear against the door. It was difficult to hear, but she could make out some words. She could hear two men speaking. One was Conroy, the other must have been Viscount Edmund.

Chills ran down her spine as she listened to his voice. The Viscount was congratulating Conroy on the good job he did today and would be rewarded for his deeds. The viscount's voice had a certain charm, yet Ella knew that what the viscount was doing was never good. It disturbed her that the calm tone would stay the same, whether he was talking about going for a morning stroll or killing someone in the dark.

Ella didn't hear much of the conversation since the Viscount was ordering Conroy to leave. It must have taken her longer to cross the roofs than she had thought. Ducking behind a bookshelf in case Conroy decided to exit in her direction, she held her breath for a count of ten. No one came through the door.

Relief washed over her as she stalked back toward the door. She pressed her ear up against it, but could hear nothing. No one talking, not even the scratch of pen to paper. Dare she take the chance? She had to leave soon. Ella had left the prince alone for far too long. It was dangerous out there, and she had left him in the streets unprotected. As she reached for the door handle, a voice spoke from within.

"Come in, Arabella Cooper, or should I say Ella?"

It was as if she had turned to an ice sculpture at those words. Was the viscount really talking to her? How could he even know she was here? How did he know her real name? And if he did know she was here, what about the prince? In that instant, Ella turned to leave through the window, heedless of the danger she was putting herself in.

But she was stopped short by the voice speaking again. "There is something you need to see."

Fear creeped down her spine at the many implications of that sentence. The one that echoed the loudest was, what if he had already captured the prince? She had to find out. Inch by inch, her hand reached for the door. And then she opened it.

The headquarters have been constantly moved, as ordered. Plans should move forward. Soon, the chaos will be far too great for those here to put a stop to it. The next step is underway, and as long as there are no missteps, it should all go as planned. A bonus has also been added to the mix. Make sure that there are no mistakes. If there are, death will follow.

Unknown note mixed in old
papers with a mark
Unknown recipient

Chapter Forty-Seven

Adrian shuffled in the darkness. He had watched Ari cross the street and vanish into a house. After that, he didn't know what had happened to her. He kept peeking around the corner, trying to see her, then worried that he might be seen, pulled back and paced some more. The sky had turned to black, and it was getting difficult to see much of anything. He almost jumped out of his skin when a light appeared in front of him. He turned to get away when a familiar voice spoke.

"Prince Adrian?"

Adrian looked at the figure holding the lantern, eye's adjusting to the light. Shadowed by its glow was Drina. She was dressed in a modest dress, with no extra ruffles that was the fashion. And instead of massive puffed sleeves, hers were smaller, more to the size he had seen amongst the commoners. Though most of that was beneath a black overcoat that was simple yet practical. Even in these clothes, she still had a regal bearing. Her eyes glinted in the lamplight, revealing concern for her cousin.

"Drina, what are you doing here?" Adrian asked, worried. A young girl was in the streets, at night, with no one around, during a riot. Relief spiked through his fear that at least she seemed unharmed. He glanced back in the direction that Ari had gone, and realizing that they shouldn't be here, pulled Drina away from the street. "You do realize that you are wandering around in a riot? What if you had been injured?"

With a sniff, she pulled her hand from his and wrinkled her nose. "Yes, I do realize that, thank you very much. I could say the same for you, but you could scare everyone away with that smell. Where did you get those clothes? They have a rather alarming scent."

Adrian's face flushed. It was not his fault they smelled this way, but how could he explain that to Drina?

Before he could speak, Drina did. "It must have been during your escape. Mother and I had escaped before you, but I heard that not long after we left, looters invaded. I am sorry, cousin."

She was acting very different from how he had always seen her. Yes, she had always had that regal air about her and was intelligent, but walking with her in the middle of the streets, she seemed more alive. It was like when Ari was gathering information. Her eyes twinkled, even when she wasn't speaking. Just as Drina's were right now. It was as if the chains that had bound her were released, and she was fearless. As Drina spoke, he didn't realize where she had been leading him until they arrived at the house at the end of the street. Tied to the knob of a door were two horses.

Confusion overcame him. "Why do you have two horses?"

Her cheeks flushed. "My guard had decided he had had enough, but I forced him to leave his horse so I could give it to someone who would help me."

Adrian, still confused by the conversation, asked, "Why are you here?"

She sigh, with an attitude that was far too mature for her age, spoke. "After hearing what had happened, I had hoped to send aid to you."

Shifting from side to side, she stood next to her horse. It was then he could tell why she had approached him. "And you needed my help to get onto your horse."

Drina blushed and nodded, seeming more her age. He smiled and he went over to help her. Lacing his fingers, he held out his hands so she could get into the saddle. It was a sidesaddle, and he wondered how she managed to get down in the first place. It usually took two people to help a lady down from her saddle. But at the blush on her face, he decided not to. Instead, he asked, "Where to?"

"I didn't actually think I would find you. I was hoping to go to the headquarters of the volunteers and see what I could do in hopes of finding you there. But everyone I asked for directions kept telling me different places. And I don't know the city very well and I never could find it. So I ended up here."

"Well, that I can help you with," Adrian said as he swung up into the saddle of the other horse. "This way, cousin."

In the course of all the walking he had done that day, he had noticed that the headquarters for the volunteers had moved several times. But he thought he knew where it had been last set up.

Happy to be riding instead of walking, he headed towards the square. Suddenly he realized the danger. He spoke to Drina. "Last time I saw it, it was near the square. It is very dangerous there."

Drina gave him a warm smile and answered. "A lady is always prepared." From inside her skirt, she retrieved a small handgun. Adrian blinked in surprise. Where would she have gotten a gun? Or rather, why would she have that?

"Do you know how to use that thing?"

"Of course, I do. If any of those looters so much as touch me, I will make sure they regret it." After all of his interactions with her, she had seemed rather meek, but now that she was away from her family, she appeared so brave and confident.

"Why are you afraid of your mother?" He couldn't help it. The words just spilled from his mouth before he could rein them back in.

Adrian could see her back stiffen and her mouth tense. Her composer failed for a moment when he had asked the question, but she had too much self-control to let her emotions remain seen by others. Watching her for a few moments, he felt as if she was staring deeply into his soul. And he wondered if all girls could do that. Finally, she answered, "I am not scared of my mother." She quickly added before Adrian could reply, "But I am afraid of what she is becoming because of *him.*"

"Who?"

"Conroy. He is an evil man. He cannot be trusted. He twists people around with words and makes people think that it was their own idea. Avoid him, for your own safety. Please, cousin."

Despite following him all day, Adrian had never thought of him that way. Yes, he didn't think of Conroy as a good man, but he thought of him in the way that Drina did. The fear that he saw on her features was not directed at her mother but at Conroy. His cousin, who was calmly riding through a city that was violently rioting and looting, was terrified of Conroy. A chill ran down his spine as he thought about leaving Ari alone with that man.

"I will. Though, I just realized that you were originally going to look for me. And you found me, so why do you still need to go to the headquarters?"

Her riding turned stiff, and she cleared her throat. "Because I saw the blacksmith. And I had actually lost hope of finding you. I figured that I could talk to the guards at the headquarters, maybe they would have seen you. My main goal, though, was to talk to them. If they were to throw some of the looters in jail, they would recover some of what was taken. I was going to see if they could return the tools back to the blacksmith."

The blacksmith . . . he had seen him as they were following Conroy. Adrian had lost hope that he could help him, yet his eleven-year-old cousin had figured out a way to help. Already, she was far better at helping the people than he was.

His thoughts were impeded as he coughed from something he inhaled. The thick scent of smoke filled his nostrils. With a quick motion, he brought his shirt up to cover his face. The stench of his shirt did little to calm his protesting lungs as he tried to not cough. His eyes watered as he turned to look at his cousin, who had reined to a halt. She was looking at the square in horror.

It was on fire.

Chapter Forty-Eight

As Ella entered, she didn't know what to expect. She certainly did not expect was to see the viscount sitting in his chair, looking away from his desk, gazing out the window. He wasn't looking at her. Could she steal some information while she was here? Or should she escape? Yet again, her decision was made for her by the viscount.

Still facing the window, he spoke. "Hello, my dear. Welcome to my office. Getting here was your goal, was it not? Was it everything you had hoped for?"

He stood and turned to look at her. The viscount looked very different from she expected. For someone who had done the things he did, she had expected him to look ugly, or at least like a villain from a storybook. Instead, he looked like a swashbuckling rogue, with handsome features and a charming demeanor. He had a scar that ran down his face across his eye. It was a shame someone had missed. The scar, however, only seemed to enhance the roguish features and made him even more charming. When he spoke, it was in a smooth confident voice, like he had control of everything and knew far more than he should.

This was a conversation she had never expected to have. And so, she thought that it was better to see what he thought he knew, and play off of that. "What do you think I'm doing here?"

The viscount's smile was amiable, like they were having the conversation on a walk in the garden instead of in the dead of night in a hidden office in the middle of a riot. Ella knew had to keep her calm. She knew that if she let anything slip, she would lose the information she needed.

"You, my dear, are looking for information you believe that I have. Against orders, I might add."

How did he know? Sweat trickled down her spine as she kept up her mask of calmness. This conversation made it seem as if he knew about the Fan Society, but he couldn't possibly know about them, could he? The only information that the Society had about him was that he ran the black market for the nobility and the rich. And that no one dared to cross him. The Society left the viscount alone, because he never tried to go beyond his reach. The nobles were the ones who came looking for him, not the other way around. And knowing that, they were able to catch those who were into nefarious dealings. Dealings like the one with Conroy.

"Against whose orders?" Ella asked. Maybe she could find out who he thought she was working for. She touched her fan that was hidden in her sleeve for comfort. Ella was going to need all the help she could get.

Viscount Edmund wandered around to the front of his desk and sat back on the edge of it. It was a casual move. He did not fear her at all. And what he said made her blood freeze.

"That quaint Fan Society, little Cinder."

How did he know of them? *How?* The Society's knowledge of the Viscount was nothing more than a basic idea of the things he sold. And yet he *knew* of them. The secret society was secret no longer. Realization dawned on her of what he had called her through the door. Arabella Cooper. He knew her true name all along. And how had he known of her codename? Her training was the only thing that kept the fear from her face, as she furiously tried to think of a way out.

"Oh, don't worry, dear girl. I have nothing against the Society. In fact, they are rather useful." He had pushed himself from off the desk and stepped closer to her. With each step, Ella had to try not to flinch. She could not end the conversation here.

"Then why not give me information?" she offered. This was her last chance if she was going to find out information about her mother. It would have to be now, while she was still keeping his interest.

His mouth curved into a grin as he leaned backwards to his desk and plucked some papers from it. Still leaning on his desk, he flipped through the papers, then, finding what he was looking for, tapped them. "Ah, here we are. The plot to kill the prince."

So, it was true. The information she had shared with the Duke of Wellington was true. There was a plot to kill the prince. And she had brought the prince right to their doorstep. Ella had to stop this plot. She had to save him. She looked up into the viscount's eyes, his cold calculating eyes. They didn't match his carefree style. This was someone who calculated everything to see what was worth keeping. And if it wasn't, he would destroy it.

He gave her a smile that made her drop her mask. "Or do you rather have information on where your mother was sold as a slave?"

"*What?*" she blurted. Her mother. This was the whole reason she had come. But could she even believe the information was true? Confusion, anger, and fear all crowded her mind. She looked into the viscount's eyes. Still, they were cold, and calculating, even as he spoke words that broke her world.

"Or what about the information on where I placed the rats that were trying to sneak in? I believe their names were Clementine, and a young thing called Harriett."

"All of it, please." He knew her cover. He knew all of her weaknesses. Her friends, her family, and Adrian. What could he possibly want from her? He didn't seem to enjoy tormenting her, so why did he do it? Nothing in her training had prepared her for this.

The viscount watched her in silence, still sitting on the desk. He sighed. "You *will* have to pay for it, dear. I *am* a businessman. And you can only afford one. Make your choice."

"What do you want from me?" This was what it all accumulated to. He allowed her to get this far to get something from her, whatever it was. She could only hope the price was not too big.

"Nothing more than a favor from you. I won't ask you to join in any criminal enterprises, so it shouldn't interfere with your 'Fan Society' creeds. Just a single favor for a single answer. Though you might want to make your choice soon."

"Why?" Ella asked as she watched him hold the papers in front of her, tantalizingly close. Maybe she could simply grab the papers and run. She quickly dismissed that thought. She knew it wouldn't work. He was too relaxed. He would be waiting for her to do such a thing. And since she couldn't get the papers, she would have to make a choice. Could she grant a favor to this man? And if she could, would that mean giving up on her mother?

"If you want to save your prince, you should leave now. I have it on good authority that he is heading back to the square. Or maybe instead, you would like to know where your maids are? I have also placed them near the square. Maybe looters will find them, looters such as the ones that attacked the Mansion House."

"What do you mean?" How did he know? The man who had looted the Mansion House cared little for the people there. And if they were found by a man like him . . . She shuddered. Fear for her friends, fear for the prince, and fear of never finding her mother all fought for control as she tried to decide what to do. She couldn't move, couldn't do anything.

"Take a look." He motioned to the window that he had been looking out when she had come in. Dread filled her as she saw, in the direction of the square, smoke rising from the buildings.

The viscount went back around his desk and turned his chair around so it was facing her. He folded his arms and leaned back. "Make your choice."

Those words were ominous as he sat framed by the flames outside. As Ella had to make a terrible decision.

Chapter Forty-Nine

Adrian rode forward with Drina, the noise and smoke making the horses shift nervously beneath them. Flames of orange and yellow flickered from a few of the buildings on the square. Black smoke billowed out of stone buildings like a deranged teapot, blanketing the sky in ominous clouds. The drastic difference between the square and the street they had left only made the scene that much more horrific.

"Let's go," Drina urged, taking off toward the square. She headed towards a group of the 14th Dragoon standing guard around a building opposite the side of the square that was on fire.

"Wait, Drina." The exhaustion that pulled at his limbs changed to adrenaline as he chased after her. Adrian called out trying to catch up with her before she spoke to the soldiers. Conroy had been speaking all day to members of the 14th Dragoon, and from what he now knew of him that meant talking to them wasn't a good idea.

It was too late. She was already talking to a fox-faced soldier by the time he caught up to her. The man looked from her to Adrian, and pointed to a corner of the square that was not on fire. Did the man look familiar? Was he one of the men who Conroy had talked to? He couldn't tell. The flickering firelight caused shadows to dance across his face. It was difficult to tell if the shadow to cross his face was his expression or just the light.

"This way, cousin." she called as she headed in the direction the soldier had pointed. Adrian looked back at the soldier and had an uneasy feeling that wouldn't go away. He tapped his horse's sides as he hurried to catch up to his cousin. This was becoming an even worse idea as they kept getting closer and closer to the flames.

"What did he say, Drina?" Adrian asked, still covering his face, and trying to inhale as little of the smoke as possible. Concern flooded her eyes at his half-choked question. It looked as if she would stop, but he waved her on.

"The lieutenant said that there is a church over here that those who are in need of care were sent to. We can wait there to talk to Lieutenant-Governor Thomas Brereton, who is in charge of this area once things have calmed down."

They stopped at the opposite corner of the square and were facing the buildings on the outside of the square. Adrian could still hear shouts, though it was far more muted here. The streets were eerie and dark since the buildings blocked the light from the fires.

"This is it," Drina said, looking at the door to the church. The arched door was made of heavy wood. And the windows were high and would be a little over his head when he was not on his horse. The uneasy feeling that persisted only increased as he looked and could see no flicker lights inside the building.

"Are you sure we should be here?" Anxiety dripped from his words as his breaths came in a wheeze.

Drina turned to look at Adrian, taking in his noisy breath and his white fingers that held tightly to his reins. Making her decision, she said, "You don't have to go in with me. Just turn around so I can get down. It is un-lady-like, but it must be done."

Obediently, he turned his horse to look at the opposing side of the street and dismounted. He heard some muffled groaning and the leather rubbing until she landed on the stone streets. He turned to her and said. "I will go with you."

Adrian hurried to open the old church door. He strained to pull the heavy door open, and let Drina in first. Ladies always went first. She lit a lamp that had been sitting near the entrance. Holding it aloft, she went forward. Adrian rushed to her side and stood in front of her.

"Please, let me go first." Adrian nodded. Nodding, she passed the lantern to him.

Raising the light in front of him, Adrian studied their surroundings. It was a much smaller church than he was used to. It still had its high arched ceilings and rows of pews. It had a few ornate decorations that graced its walls, including the royal coat of arms on a stained-glass window.

As he took in their surroundings, Adrian knew something was off. There were no people. The soldier had said that the injured were here, but he couldn't see anyone. He was just about to take Drina and leave, when a mound at the altar shifted.

Adrian jumped, causing the lantern to swing, casting strange moving shadows around the room. He put his arm out to shield his cousin and saw that she had already drawn her gun and was pointing it at the noise. His cousin was far stronger than he had ever been. Bravery gleamed from her eyes as she stared at the bundle at the far end.

Inching closer, Adrian moved towards the mound. As he approached, he made out figures hidden under a tablecloth that must have been purloined from the church. Adrian looked to Drina to make sure she was ready, and he yanked the cloth off.

Two women lay bound and gagged. One that seemed to be his age, perhaps older, had a glazed look on her face. He could see a gash on her head and a pool of blood beneath her on the floor. Drina stowed away her gun and was at the girls' side in an instant. Pulling a cloth from her pocket, she pressed it to the girl's head. And with her other hand, she pulled out the gag.

Seeing that Drina had that well in hand, he turned his attention to the other girl. She was young, and lucky for her, only had a small bump on her head. But judging by the bruise that was already forming, whoever had done this had given her head a good ringing. Adrian began untying her gag, and a nagging thought tugged on the back of his mind. This girl seemed familiar. As the gag fell away, the girl turned around to face him. Suddenly, it hit him. Adrian remembered where he had seen her. This was the girl that had given him instructions at the inn only two days ago. The gag now free, he began undoing her bindings. She may know what Ari was doing.

"I have to get out. I have to let her know," the girl mumbled as he finished releasing her hands. She tried to stand, but wobbled and fell back to the floor.

"Easy now. I will make sure she gets the message, but she is in a delicate situation right now," Adrian whispered in her ear. She blinked, focusing on him, her mouth opening in shock.

"Adrian, we need to get this one out," Drina exclaimed. "She is in bad condition." Adrian turned to her. He could see that she wasn't responding to Drina.

He nodded in acknowledgment and turned to help the young maid to sit comfortably. Once she was situated, he helped his cousin lift the woman. She was a skinny thing, which was lucky, since between the two of them, they just managed to carry her out of the church. They eased her to the ground as his cousin strode to her horse.

"That won't work," Adrian said, bringing his horse near the three steps leading into the church. The less he had to lift her, the better.

Drina looked at the sidesaddle on her horse, then went to Adrian's horse. "This is all very un-lady-like, but it must be done."

Swallowing her pride, she allowed Adrian to help her onto his horse. A woman riding astride could have big implications on a lady's social life. Riding astride would make a woman lose their virginity, or some such idiocy, which made it improper to ride in such a way. But his cousin easily waved away the social implications to help this woman, knowing full well that she would need his saddle to be able to keep herself perched on the horse with the other woman in front of her. Adrian would not have been able to pull the woman up onto his horse while he was astride. Pride blossomed within him as she sat with an easy grace on the horse.

Once Drina was situated, Adrian struggled to get the poor woman on the creature. His breath wheezing like a whistle, he managed to get her on in a somewhat stable position. Strain was already showing on his Drina's face as she held the unconscious woman in her arms.

"Get going. I'll be right behind you with the other. The faster you get her to a doctor, the better." She tightened her jaw and nodded. With a tap of her heels, she started forward as fast as she could without jostling the girl too much.

Seeing her safely out of harm's way, he headed back into the church. The young girl sat slumped on the floor. At least she no longer looked like she was going to tip over. Hurrying over to her, he asked, "Who did this to you?"

She just shook her head. Whether it was to shake out the cobwebs or answer him, he didn't know. He dropped the altar cloth about her shoulders, and helped her to her feet. Whomever had left them there, may come back. If they ran into them, it would likely mean their deaths. With wheezing breath and slow steps, they headed to the door. The girl leaned heavily on him as they walked, but was still moving forward. Her breath kept catching, like she was trying not to heave.

"We will get you out of here. Just hang on," Adrian encouraged, focusing on the girl. It had been a long day, and it had done a number on his already weak body. But as long as he focused on helping her, he could keep putting one foot in front of the other.

When they reached the door, he let her stand on her own. He watched her for a few seconds to make sure she didn't fall. Doing his best to hurry, he opened the door to the deafening shouts outside.

The mob had arrived. And were headed straight for them. He could hear their shouts. "Down with the churches! Down with those who run them!"

Thankfully the hefty door was old and stout. Adrian closed it, blocking out the sound again. Eyes searching franticly, he found an iron bar and used it to barricade the door. He pulled the girl back, and none too soon, as the angry storm of men were soon pounding. The door held and he sighed with relief. But he had relaxed too soon. Something crashed through the window, and landed on a pew and within moments, it was on fire.

I was lucky that a nurse was there. She was a personal
nurse for a gentleman who was visiting Bristol. She
had arrived at the square just in time. I don't know if I
could have held the injured woman any longer. I hope
the poor thing is alright. She did not look good. I shall
pray for her this night.

    Journal of Alexandrina Victoria
    2 September 1831

Chapter Fifty

Make your choice. Those words rang in Ella's head as they echoed her soul with every ring hitting her with a force. Ring. Save her friends that were like a family to her. Ring. Find her missing mother that she had longed to find for years. Ring. Stop a plot that would endanger Adrian, who she cared for and had sworn to protect.

Ring. Ring. Ring. Make. Your. Choice.

Ella was almost completely swallowed by confusion and fear when she remembered a conversation she'd once had with Clementine. Clementine had told her that if Ella hadn't been so emotional, she could have gotten the cat out of the tree. Panic had overtaken her. These people were depending on her. They trusted that she was competent. She could not let fear control her actions. Instead of just touching her fan for comfort, she pulled it out of her sleeve. Flicking it open, she felt the emblem that was embedded within the pattern, so faint you could not tell it was there unless you were looking for it.

The ringing of panic and fear stopped as she thought through her options. First, considering what she knew of his personality, she could take what he said as the truth. He would not lie to her now because he would not get the favor later if the information turned out false. Ella would deal with what the favor was later, since he did promise it would not be criminal in nature.

It all came down to which question she wanted answered the most. She had worked closely with Clementine and Harriett. She knew they were no pushovers and were both well trained. They could get themselves out of most situations. She would have to trust them to escape on their own. Guilt pricked her conscience, but she shoved it down.

Now the big choice: find out about her mother or the plot to kill the prince. The prince would be safe with her. She had trained enough to do that. And yet she didn't know much about the plot. It had originally been a ruse to get the duke to talk to her, but it was true. Could she save Adrian even if she didn't know the details of the plot to kill him?

Then there was her mother. Her own family. This would be her last chance to find out about her mother. Adrian had been helping her so she could find out more information. This would be what he would want her to do. Guilt pricked at her again. Adrian would be fine. He was right outside. After this conversation, she would go right out and make sure he made it safely to the inn. Then she would explain what was going on, and she would keep him close. He would understand her decision. She would protect him.

Her guilt suppressed, she turned to Viscount Edmund. A slow smile came on his face. Still leaning back comfortably in his chair, he asked, "Have you made your decision?"

"Yes. I have." Ella strode to the desk and flicked her fan shut, tapping it on his desk. "In exchange for *one* favor, you will give me information on my mother."

He raised an eyebrow at her words. Leaning forward, he rested his elbows on the desk. Then interlacing his fingers, he rested his chin on them, watching her. "That is an interesting decision, my dear. Are you sure this is the information you want? Final choice?"

Waves of guilt crashed over her again, but with quick efficiency, she shoved it back again. "Yes, final choice."

To show she wouldn't let him get to her, she leaned forward and stared into his blue eyes. They were so dark that it was like looking into the cold recesses of a deep pool, his true emotions hidden far below the calm surface.

How long they watched each other, she didn't know. But he broke the staring contest first. Sitting up, he opened his desk drawer and pulled out a sheet of papers, handing them to her.

Of course, the papers he had been holding in front of her were fake. An intelligent person like him wouldn't hold them out so easily. As she reached to grab them, he spoke to her.

"As a gesture of goodwill, I will give you an extra tidbit of information for free."

Ella just looked at him.

"Your little princeling is no longer where you left him. He was last seen heading to the square," he said, letting go of the papers.

Fear ran through her again as she looked up through the window to the burning square. Griping both the papers and fan tightly, she fled from the room and out the door, feeling his calculating gaze on her far longer than she should have.

Ella sprinted the end of the street where she had left the prince. Adrian was not there. Then, she took off at a run towards the storm of fire and anger hoping she was not too late. And that her choice would not be the worst one she had ever made.

Chapter Fifty-One

Adrian stared into the flames, licking up the sides of the ancient wood. Chest squeezing in fear, he couldn't breathe. Smoke was already filling the room. The heat seared his weak lungs, inflaming them even more. He coughed so hard that he couldn't catch a breath. Fear and strain clouded his thoughts like the smoke around them.

Was this what his life amounted to? He was finally gaining freedom and the first thing he did would get himself killed. Tears dripped from his stinging eyes. What had he accomplished other than putting Ari and others in danger?

Bowing his head in self-pity and gasping for breath, he didn't notice as the altar cloth covered his head. His lung breathed in cleaner air and they relaxed their stranglehold on him. Adrian turned and saw the girl. And within her eyes, a burning desire to live. And he would make sure of that. He would do one princely thing in his life.

In one quick motion, Adrian pulled the cloth off of his head and put it in front of his mouth. He searched for a solution and his gaze fell onto a window. This one was a stained-glass window, and at the top was the royal coat of arms. The door thudded again. Rising to his feet, he pulled the girl up, and they made their way to the back of the room that was situated on the corner of the square. Step by weary step, they made their way away from the pounding door and burning pews.

The girl tripped and they lost their balance, toppling to the floor. But they had made it. They landed at the foot of a small table beneath the window holding two candlesticks. During the fall, he lost his grip on the cloth, and the smoke sent him into a coughing fit. With tremendous effort, he staggered to his feet, heaving the fallen girl to hers as well. The smoke was thickening, making it difficult to see anything through the smoky blackness.

With fumbling fingers, Adrian knocked one candlestick to the ground in his rush to grab the other. Grasping the candlestick, he threw it through the window, shattering the glass bearing the royal crest out onto the street below. It had an instant effect. Smoke rushed out the window, relieving some of the irritation from his lungs. The cool air that had seeped in cleared his thoughts. Adrian rested his head for one moment by the window, as his lungs greedily slurped up less smoky air. The heat behind him pushed him back into motion. They were still not safe. They could not rest. Not here.

Groaning at his aching legs, he pulled himself onto the table. It was small, with just barely enough room to fit two people. He turned to the window. The thick stone sill was level with his eyes, even standing on the table. The arduous task that was before him made him stagger. As he bent down to help the girl up, he nearly toppled over. He managed to keep his footing by quickly grabbing the sill.

Once on the table, the girl started to put the altar cloth over the broken window. Adrian should have thought of that earlier, but the day's events had drained him. Was it even still the same day? Or were they just stuck in an endless cycle of horror?

The young girl was shorter than Adrian, and her head didn't quite reach the edge. She would need his help. But he had just one hand. The other was holding the cloth that was keeping the smoke from his lungs. He would have to drop the cloth to help her.

Taking as deep of a breath as he dared, Adrian dropped the precious cloth. His eyes burned and tears trickled down his blackened face as he reached to help her. Just as he had done with his cousin, he interlaced his fingers to give her a boost. As she slipped her foot into his hands, her skirts brushed his face. Trying not to sneeze, he gritted his teeth and lifting her as much as he could. She floundered. The sill was too wide, making it difficult for her to get a good enough grip to pull herself up. His strength was failing him. With determination and strength he never knew he had, he strained further. Lungs burning with effort and lack of air, as he lifted her an inch higher.

But that was enough. She kicked, getting just enough height to climb onto the ledge. With enough force to knock him over. That small burst of strength failed him, as he toppled off the table to the hard stone floor.

This was it. He had done all he could do. The fall caused him to gasp, pulling the smoke-filled air into his lungs. He struggled to breathe, to move away from the smoke. To grab a cloth. Anything. But he couldn't move. The flames licked closer, eating pew after pew. Sparks crackled out of the fire's maw, burning his face. Fog clouded his mind as he tried once more to tell his limbs to move. But they resisted just as his lungs did as they fought to get enough air to breathe.

Then there was no struggle. His coughing fit calmed to a quiet wheezy breath as he lay on the still cool floor. The back of the pews shined in the light of the fire. Adrian could only lay there and stare into the burning brilliance before him as it consumed all in its path.

Chapter Fifty-Two

Fear made it feel like she had been running forever and yet no time at all. During the flight, she had tucked the papers in her skirts, but she kept her fan ready. She didn't know what sort of danger would be ahead. Skirts flapped against her legs as her feet pounded on the stone streets as she ran. Anxiety made her feet fly faster as she admonished herself; she was supposed to be by Adrian's side, but she had brought him into danger and had left him to fend for himself. It would have been better for him if she had never gotten close to him.

She vowed that after she saved him and made sure he was safe, she would never let him get involved again. The unspoken word '*if*' hung in her mind like a bad smell. It hovered around her as she hurried ever closer to the square.

When she made it to the square and rounded the corner, her heart pounded in fear at the horror that lay before her. The beautifully cut lawn of the park in the center of the square, which would have been peaceful during the day, now held masses of people running around angrily. Others were outside the park shouting, goading them on, while others merely cried. This scene was backdropped by several burning buildings and the acrid stench of smoke.

She had arrived at the square, but now what? Ella had no idea where Adrian would be. Searching the square, she hoped that she would be able to find him. It was difficult to tell who anyone was in all the chaos.

Ella turned to the soldiers where it was there she found Harriett. The young girl was favoring her left leg. Her hair was no longer in a bun, her coarse brown hair tumbled about her shoulders. Black streaked, her face looked like those who had been in a factory. She was limping backwards away from a soldier who held a sword in front of him. No one had noticed what he was doing in the confusion around them. As Ella watched, Harriett tripped on the uneven cobblestone street falling hard to the ground.

Running forward to slam her fan against the wrist that was holding his sword. Unlike the looters in the Mansion House, the soldier moved his hand out of the way at the last second. He turned to face Ella instead, his sharp features making him look like a devil in the night. He swung his sword at Ella.

With a quick flick of her fan, she deflected it before the blade could hit her.

"You silly fan girl. You will regret attacking me today." His voice was quiet yet seemed to cut through the noise, making it easy to hear him.

Anger burned within her. She did not have time for this. Adrian was waiting for her. Whomever he was, she needed to take him down fast. But she had to be wary of his reach. The length of his weapon was much longer than hers, and one mistake could mean death. She had to get this man riled in hopes that he would make a mistake.

"Surprised that a silly girl with a fan could parry your blade?"

The fox-faced soldier only smiled. "I always wanted a clash with the fan girls. This is going to be fun."

Squashing her confusion, Ella took a quick look around to see if there was anyone paying any attention to them. The other soldiers were focusing on the citizens and not on them. Then her eyes caught movement as the soldier lunged. She saw it just in time to sidestep as the sword clipped her side, screeching metal on metal as her steel corset held. If she had taken a direct hit, she would have died. Focus. If she lost this fight now, there would be no one left to save Adrian. She would not let him down. She had gotten him in this mess. She had to get Adrian out of it. And this soldier was in her way.

"Didn't they teach you to pay attention to your opponent?" the man teased, his dark eyes glittering in the firelight. He was enjoying this.

"Who are you?" Ella demanded. There were far too many people who knew more information than she. If she could distract him, perhaps she could get away.

He grinned a wicked grin and laughed. "You can call me Fox. And you are?"

Ella refused to answer. The name he gave her was more like a code name. She would have to find out later who he was. Seeing that she wouldn't answer, the soldier struck again. Dancing away, she avoided the sharp blade, its tip cutting into her skirt as she turned. As he finished his swing, she stepped back in closer and struck his helm with the hilt of her fan.

The wily Fox stepped back before she could attack him again. His smile grew as he circled around her. Testing her, he jabbed her again. Ella kicked his wrist to block it, but didn't amount to much since he hadn't committed fully to the attack. A high-pitched scream echoed in the night from behind them, driving Ella to action. She flicked her fan open, slicing along his face. He howled in pain as her mother's fan cut into his skin. The fan held a nasty surprise for anyone who got close enough to see. Hidden beneath the delicate lace were blades of her own adorning the tip of the metal ribs. The fan proved that just because something was beautiful didn't mean it couldn't be deadly as well.

Covering his face, he now backed away, wary of her. Ella stepped forward, and the soldier lunged for her. She barely managed to use the fan to block, and the blade skittered across the open fan. Then he rolled past her, using the momentum of his thrust, and was back on his feet again. And now he was behind her. As she spun around, his blade had already made its way to her neck. She had rushed things, and now she was paying for it. Ella clenched her teeth in anger as a drop of blood dripped down his blade.

"It was fun playing with you," Fox said. "But I think the time for games is over. I do wish we had more time to play." Blood dripped down his nose, and an amused smile was still on his face.

Ella looked at him, then smiled politely back. "I think not."

He had no time for confusion before Harriett smashed him over the head with a broken chair.

Looking down at his prone body, Ella said, "Didn't your teachers ever tell you to pay attention to your surroundings?"

Ella turned back to Harriett; she was already developing a purple bruise across her face. She also had small scratches on her hands and glass fragments stuck to her skirt and sleeve. Limping forward, she grasped Ella's arms, nearly collapsing. "My lady, the prince, he is still in there. Please help him. He saved my life."

The adrenaline that had pushed her through the fight changed to panic as she asked, "Where is he?"

Gasping for breath, Harriett pointed to the opposite corner where smoke was pouring out of a broken window.

Ella nodded and gestured to Fox. "You stay here and keep an eye on him. Don't let him escape."

Then in a flurry, she ran toward Adrian.

I do not know who this "Fox" soldier was. If he even was a soldier. He was skilled and was unsurprised by my skills. He was dangerous. It was later discovered that he was the one who kidnapped both my assistant and Ghost in the crowds. It is unknown how he was able to pick them out of the crowd. He must have been watching us more carefully than we knew. He disappeared during the commotion. I do not blame my Ghost; she was injured, and Fox was clever. Though, I worry about who he was working for.

Lady Arabella Cooper;
Code name: Cinders
Excerpt from report 162

Chapter Fifty-Three

Adrian's eyes flickered open. He thought he heard his name cutting through the darkness. Was that Ari he heard? He had left her behind. She would be angry that he got himself into this situation. He needed to let her know where he was. He needed to move. And yet his body refused to respond. He was just too tired.

His eyes fluttered shut.

Ella called Adrian's name through the broken window, but he was either too injured to speak or he couldn't hear her. She looked up at the broken window, but it was too high for her to reach. She would have to try the front door. The door that currently had a mob of angry rioters crowding around it.

Going through the door was not an option. If a bunch of angry rioters couldn't break through, she certainly would not be able to. She started skirting the edges of the crowd to see if there was another place she could use to enter. A hand from the mob reached out to grab her. Fear and fury had put her instincts on high alert. She grabbed the man's hand and pulled him closer to her. As she did so, she held the edge of her fan, still red with Fox's blood from his neck. Fear blossomed in his eyes as he lifted his chin away from the deadly weapon. He opened his hands in supplication, blubbering that he was sorry. She shoved him away, irritation bleeding into her emotions, as yet again she was halted in her mission to save Adrian.

Enough was enough. She shoved her way through the crowd, whacking elbows and heads with her heavy fan until she made it to the other side. What she saw was disheartening. The flames could be seen flickering from one of the broken windows, and the others were covered in smoke. Except for the one on the end. But even if she could get inside, that would mean making her way through the flames to get to him. It wasn't even a choice. If they were both going to survive this thought, she needed preparations. She couldn't just run in there without preparing or they would both die. Ella could only hope that he could hang on a little longer.

Running to the home next door, she barged through the couple who were gawking at the riot outside their home. She made it easily into the house. Stunned as they were, they allowed her through without stopping her. On her way through the house, she grabbed a tablecloth as she headed for the kitchens. Luckily, this house was in the wealthier part of town and had indoor plumbing. Turning on the tap, she soaked the tablecloth. Adrenaline pumped through her veins as she rushed back out the door.

This had to work. There were no other choices left. The couple eyed her with fear as she passed them on her way out.

"What are you guys doing out here anyway? You are going to get hurt if you stay here. Go to a friend's house unless you want to be here when the fire leaves that building and catches your house next."

The man with a large girth tried to bluster back at her until his willowy wife took him by the arm. They grabbed their coats and left.

Sighing in relief, Ella scooped up a rock that had been dropped by one of the rioters and threw it through the window closest to the house she had just left. The sound of glass was hard to hear over the yelling rioters. Covering herself with the tablecloth, she tied it in front. She climbed the three steps into the home, then using the door knocker to pull herself up, she climbed onto the railing. This was going to hurt. Ella took three breaths to calm her nerves, tucked her fan back into her sleeve, and with all the strength she could muster, jumped for the window ledge.

Her bare fingers scrambled for purchase on the wide stone ledge. Fingers slipped as blood dripped from her fingers cut on the broken glass. Determination and pure stubbornness made her refuse to let go. Adrian was counting on her. She would not let him die on her. She couldn't, not until she could actually tell him how she felt.

Clenching tighter to the glass-strewn ledge, she pulled herself onto the ledge. Ella's hand stung as sweat and blood mixed together, but she had made it onto the ledge. Coughing into her sleeve, Ella stared into the room. Smoke billowed out the now broken window. She pulled the cloth over her mouth and jumped into the burning room. When she looked through the burning pews, it now became a question of whether she could find him.

Adrian's head throbbed. Was that Ari he heard? Or was that thumping coming from his head? Was someone crying? Words pierced through the fog in his mind. It was Ari, but how could she be here? Was he already dead? The fog of unconsiousness tried to blanket him again. It was so hard to think. It hurt to breathe. Maybe he should stop breathing just so the pain would stop.

But the voice was so incessant. Ari, the girl he had fallen in love with, was calling for him. He had to let her know that he was here. She had tried so hard to protect him. He couldn't die now.

He opened his bleary eyes once again. Something glittered in his view. Adrian blinked to clear his vision, but it stayed. His eyes finally focused on it. It was the candlestick that he knocked to the floor. The flames were reflected in its shiny metal, bringing things into focus. It had fallen just by his fingers. Could he reach it? It glittered right in front of him, so close yet just out of reach.

He just had to move his hand. His finger twitched. He felt himself sinking again back into the oblivion. He couldn't fail. If he did, then Ari would be sad. The searing pain of heat brought him back when an ember landed on his face. Pain made his eyes water. And with a grunt, Adrian moved his hand and grasped the heated metal.

Adrian tried to scream, but his lungs refused to obey. He held on to the burning metal, refused to fall unconscious. He heard Ari cry out again. Desperation was in her voice. She would stay here looking for him. Of all the things she had spoken about, she always was trying to protect him. Ari would not leave him in here. And after everything, he still loved her.

The thought of her drew power from somewhere deep within him. And with that strength, he began hitting the candlestick against the floor repeatedly. The mysterious strength had left him began to wane and his vision once again started to blacken. As it started to fade, he saw Ari. Head covered in a veil of white, her arms outstretched like the wings of the Fey. Ari ran towards him through the flames.

Chapter Fifty-Four

The sound of flames crackling and roaring was the only thing Ella could hear in the burning church. She called Adrian's name again, and again. Fear stabbed her through the heart as she prayed she wasn't too late and called yet again. She would stay here and atone for her mistake of leaving his side. A burning pew broke and flames exploded outward. Could anyone still be alive in these flames? Tears dripped down her face as she searched through the room, hoping to see any sign of life.

Then she heard it. A clang of metal against stone. It rang through the church like bells. Covering her face with the wet tablecloth, she ran down the aisle towards the sound, heedless of the flames around her. There he was, crumpled on the floor, clutching a golden candlestick. She knelt by his side to check to see if those rings were the final death kneels of a dying man or a cry for help. Cradling his head, Ella leaned down to listen. Her heart was pounding in her chest so loudly it made it difficult to hear. His breathing was so weak that the only thing she could hear was a quiet rasp of garbled air. She had to get him out of here. Covering him in the tablecloth, Ella looked up to where Adrian had saved Harriett. The broken window.

Crouched down beside him, she grabbed his arms and pulled him toward the table. He was far lighter than she had expected. She had never thought of him that way before. He had always seemed bigger, so full of life when she spoke to him. Adrian's eyes always twinkled with light whenever he teased her. She could not let that light go out. Heaving to her feet, she set him on the table and leaned him against the wall. Looking into his face, she saw a burn on his cheek. With a gentle hand, she reached out to touch his forehead, which was covered with sweat and soot. He shivered at her touch. His face was hot beneath her wet fingers.

A crash of another pew collapsing warned her of how little time they had. Coughing from the smoke, she steadied her nerves. Then she stepped onto the table. The table was small and she would barely have enough space to crouch down and balance on the corners to lift him to the window sill. Stradling his still form, she lifted. Legs spasming from the effort, she managed to heave him up to her shoulder. Still crouched, she shifted him into position and slowly stood. She had only made it a few inches until she could move no more.

Adrian shifted and moaned, his shallow breath rasping in her ear. Looking down, Ella could see that her skirt was caught on the corner of the table. Frustration at her situation flooded her veins. She couldn't move to pull the skirt off the corner, and, already, the exertion of holding Adrian was wearing on her.

Trembling from the awkward half crouch, she shifted her position as she stood as high as she could. Sweat dripped down her face. Ella could feel Adrian's face against hers, and it was burning up. The muscles in her leg spasmed. Time was running out, but she had only managed to get him halfway up. The crash of another pew collapsing and an ember landing by her foot reminded her she had no more time. Struggling with all her strength, she stood, tearing the skirt.

The skirt which held her precious documents about her mother.

Ella could only watch in horror as the papers slipped from the torn skirts and fluttered onto the floor below. Out of reach.

Tears of frustration ran down her face. It was right there. But she had to save Adrian. She had to. There was no other choice. Ella cried out as the last hope of finding her mother fizzled out. She couldn't get them.

Her choice had been made when she learned that Adrian was in danger. Ella had fallen in love with him, and the only way to retrieve those papers would have been to leave him behind. Not again. Never.

She turned away and faced her exit. A river of tears ran down her face as she heaved Adrian up to the windowsill. Laying unmoving in a clumsy position, Ella hurriedly hoisted herself up beside him. There was no room to maneuver on the ledge. Its only saving grace was that it was a wide stone ledge, making it easier to keep Adrian from falling off. Then she looked down and laughed, exhaustion twisting it to madness.

The ground was too far for her to safely drop him, and it was too far for her to reach him if she went first. Ella turned one final time to the church, her papers now a burning pyre, and cried. Clutching him against her chest, she cried for her failure of being unable to save him. She cried for the loss of the papers that held information about her mother. She cried for herself, as once again, she was like a little girl, going to save the cat, only to be trapped in the tree herself. The angry noises of the mob, louder now that they weren't blocked by the thick stone walls, only enhanced her misery.

"I am so sorry, Adrian. So, sorry." Her tears must have woken him. His dazed eyes focused on her. He smiled then was still.

"Adrian. Please, no. You can't die on me. Adrian!" Any hope that she would be able to save him had started to fade.

Then she heard a knock.

Blinking, Ella looked down. Below the window was a manservant. The man was knocking on the wall with a broken stick, trying to get her attention.

"Pass him to me!" the man urged when she looked at him. He seemed familiar, and he was Adrian's only hope. Giving him a quick kiss on the forehead, she passed Adrian down as hope flickered to life within her.

And so, the third knock came. The knock that
rekindled my hope that Adrian would survive. If I
hadn't heard that knock, who knows if it would have
turned out like this? Would I still have had hope?
Would there have been any chance to save the prince?
All I know is that knock saved me, leaving me with
hope.

Lady Arabella Cooper;
Code name: Cinders
Excerpt from report 172

Part III

Pinney has been acquitted. This has caused much debate because no one has taken credit for the attack. Lieutenant-Governor Thomas Brereton was to have been called forward as a witness, but was found dead in his cell before trial. Is there more going on with this story than what meets the eye? Was he killed for the information he had, or did he commit suicide? More information will be forthcoming.

More news as we try to see if we can get another reform bill through the courts. Will anything be different since the riots?

Newspaper clipping from February 1832
Unable to see byline or newspaper title.

Chapter Fifty-Five

November 1831 Academy

The whole carriage ride to the academy was nauseating, and it wasn't just due to the bumpy ride. She was a failure. Ella was going back to get her scolding from Madame Briar. After her disaster at Bristol, she wouldn't be surprised if they kicked her out of the Fan Society entirely or shipped her off, so she couldn't say anything. Her heart grappled with that thought. She would never see Adrian again.

Sorrow and grief pressed against her like a physical weight. After what she had done to him, he might never want to speak to her again, anyway. If he ever woke up, that is. One of the Fan Society's medics was next to him at all times. This was the only reason she left his side, because she was called to speak to Madame Briar. There was still a plot to kill Adrian, and she didn't know how or when it would happen. She didn't know who was going to instigate it. And she had failed to even learn of it until recently.

Then there was Clementine. Clementine had been badly injured when she was attacked. She was lucky that she got to a nurse in time. Harriet fared better than Clementine, though the landing as she made her escape made it so she would have a small limp for a few weeks.

And the final failure was that she had risked everyone's life for information that she had lost. And they would pay for it the rest of their lives. She would face her punishment because she deserved whatever came.

She arrived at the academy dressed as her cover of being a ward of the countess. Her floral dress was cinched at the waist, and dangling from her wrist was a fan. Ella could not bear to hold her mother's fan. Its stained lace was a constant reminder of the burning pages and that fateful night in Bristol. It was a mark of her failure. Through the open carriage door, Ella looked at the gray building of the academy, its imposing stone features shaming her by its very presence. A footman stood by the carriage door, waiting to help her. She took his hand and stepped out to face her fate.

The long walk to the headmistress's office echoed her steps, reminding her every step of the way that she could not make it as a member of the Fan Society. As she arrived at the door, she took a deep breath to steady her nerves. Then she stepped in as Madame Briar told her to enter. She did, watching her teacher for anything that would indicate what her fate might be. Ella could have been staring at a statue for all Madame Briar's expressions told her. They headed through the secret passageways with Ella followed meekly behind.

Then she was back again. Back to the room that started her mission. She had been so eager then, to be a part of what her mother had been part of. Now here she was at the end of the most important mission she could have ever received, and it only ended in shame.

She sat across from Madame Briar, waiting for judgment. Her mentor steepled her fingers in front of her, deep in thought. The silence continued as it waged havoc on her emotions until her teacher finally spoke.

"What am I to do with you, Ella?" Madame Briar questioned. Ella stiffened, trying her best not to cower into her chair. Instead, she bowed her head.

Madame Briar sighed, retrieving a stack of papers next to her. With each sentence, she shifted to another page. "Of all the missions to test me with, you decided this one would be the best? You put the prince in danger by telling him you were spying. Then you promised that he could help you with finding your mother. Something I expressly told you not to do. Thankfully, you didn't tell him about the Society. But because of this desire to help you, he ended up in a burning building in the middle of a riot. You put your fellow Society members in danger, not only physically, but their covers could have been blown wasting years of work. Some are permanently injured due to your actions. All of this happened because you went against my orders about finding your mother. The information that you then promptly lost." She put the papers aside and stared down her nose at Ella. "What would I tell your mother?"

Tears streamed down her face. Ella couldn't answer. She knew that Madame Briar was right. She had done all of those things. And she could not refute them. Ella could only keep her head bowed and catch the tears that dripped into her hands.

"I should send you out of the country for what you have done, so you could not do any more damage to the Society. The prince would have been in more danger if not for the fact that we already knew about the plot to kill the prince and already set into motion plans to circumvent it."

Relief that Adrian was being looked after was little consolation. The plot to kill the prince would not succeed, and her folly would not hurt him. . . again. Then a thought crossed her mind, and Ella looked up. "Why didn't you tell me about the plot?"

"Because we had to find evidence, and your mission was to marry the prince. There was a lot riding on that. Once you had achieved marriage, then we would have proceeded to give you more information when you were securely in place. Now that this is impossible, we will have to change plans."

Ella looked directly into Madame Briar's eyes and could see emotions creeping back into them.

The headmistress pulled out another sheet of paper. "I should send you away, but I received a report on your behalf convincing me otherwise. You should thank Clementine when you see her."

Clementine, who was always sticking up for Ella, even now after all she had done. Ella's mouth fell open slightly. "What is going to happen to me?"

She raised her eyebrow. "For now, probation. While we wait to see what happens with the prince, you will be in a supporting role. Since the Bristol riots prove that there is a credible threat to the royal family, we need all hands to help get things changed. And if you do that, I have a mission that you will need to take care of. Prove yourself to be the woman I know you are. Show me that these failures are not all you are capable of. Now, I want an actual report that tells me *everything*. I only have some of what was done, and I need it *all* to make an assessment of you."

"You're not going to kick me out?" Ella asked, still in shock that she wasn't going to be exiled.

"Not yet. Though, any more incidents like this and I will. Am I understood?"

"Yes, Madame." Ella wanted to say more. She knew that Madame Briar was hiding something from her, but she didn't dare ask. Madame Briar was being lenient on her for some reason.

After everything that Ella had done, she deserved worse. It was no surprise that Madame Briar didn't share her intentions.

Madame Briar nodded, then motioned for the door. "Olivia will catch you up on everything. Speak to her about what you will be working on."

Unable to believe what had just happened, Ella headed to the door, then stopped. "What about the viscount and Fox?"

Madame Briar looked up from a report. "Right now, we don't have enough information. I have people looking into both of them."

"We know about the viscount."

"Yes, and the promise he had extracted from you is worrying, as well as his knowledge of the Fan Society. It seems as if he has known about us for a long time and has chosen to do nothing about it. He has always kept within his bounds. I doubt we have to worry about him giving away our secrets for the moment. This riot seems to have more secrets than it appears. For now, we will do as we have always done and keep watch, but this time with a more careful eye."

Ella was going to continue out the door, but the guilt pushed out one final question. "Why am I not being punished?"

Madame Briar gave a faraway look and answered in a melancholy tone, "I once made a horrible mistake because I believed that I was in the right and now its consequences are bearing fruit. There is an even greater danger out there than you know, and I have a feeling that we will need you to weather the coming storm. And I know that you *will* pay the price of your choice. Even if you don't see the price just yet. And it will be far greater than any punishment that I could give you."

Nodding, not understanding Madame Briar's response, but accepting it, Ella continued out the door. There was a lot to think about in all that had happened, but her thoughts kept turning back to the prince. She might be able to see the prince again, but should she?

And would he even want to see her?

. . . message has been sent to the duchess's daughter. She seems open to the idea. She is far cleverer than was originally given credit for. In hopes that she will give us information, all we can do now is wait for . . .

Lady Luella Jones;
Codenamed: Warrior
Excerpt from a report, most of the
message lost due to age

Chapter Fifty-Six

January 1832 Clarence House

Adrian could hear murmuring voices bled through the darkness of sleep. After nearly dying several times in the days after the riot, his body had been so weak that he couldn't even lift his head. He was back to the nightmare of his childhood, the times when he was constantly on the edge of living and dying. But this time, he had managed to help two girls. Admittedly, it wasn't the most perfect attempt, but he had managed to accomplish something. He saved someone's life. And now he understood what he needed to do.

Opening his eyes, he could see Abigail and Mathew deep in conversation. They both seemed upset. Mathew brushed a lock of Abigail's hair that had fallen from her bun, tucking it into place, calming her down. That was new. During his time in bed, Adrian had seen them grow close, but he didn't know how close. Now the love and affection in their eyes could not be denied.

"When are you two going to get married?" Adrian asked in a rasp before breaking into a coughing fit. Breathing in the smoke had caused permanent damage to his already weak lungs. The doctor suspected that he would always have hoarseness in his voice and a chronic cough.

Abigail was instantly by his side, offering him something to drink. When he managed to catch his breath again, he sipped at the liquid. Its cool wetness refreshed his irritated throat.

"Thank you, Abigail," Adrian muttered. She nodded, then busied herself with helping him into a more comfortable position, pointedly ignoring Mathew's sideways glances. Mathew stood stiffly, shuffling side to side as his gaze slid to Abigail, then, catching Adrian's gaze, he looked away in an instant. Adrian couldn't help but smile at his friends' awkward attempts to ignore each other.

Adrian rasped. "If you two would like to get married, I give you my permission. Though, only if I get to be there."

Abigail and Mathew looked at each other, then Abigail bowed her head and broke the silence. "Your Highness, we had hoped to keep it from interfering with your health. We wouldn't presume to do anything until you are well."

Adrian laughed, or attempted to, as his laugh turned into a wheeze. He only just managed to keep it from becoming another coughing fit. Happiness blossomed within him at the thought of his friends finding joy. "You two have looked after me since I was a child. You deserve happiness. You are good for each other. Though when did all of this start happening?" Before the whole debacle in Bristol, Adrian only knew that Mathew had a one-sided crush on Abigail. But it seemed a lot had happened while he had slept.

Abigail and Mathew looked at each other. Mathew's cheeks turning red beneath his freckles. He cleared his throat and started, "Remember when we had that disagreement before we left for Bristol?"

Adrian nodded.

Mathew cleared his throat and continued. "I was worried about you, but you weren't talking to me. So, I went to Abigail to see if she knew anything, since, other than me, she knows you the most."

Adrian furrowed his brows and motioned for him to continue. Things were starting to come together.

"After you failed to return from the Mansion House, we went with several guards to look for you," Mathew said, a pained expression on his face. "We ended up at the headquarters. That was where they had set up triage and Abigail could help with the injured while searching for you among them. Just in case . . . As Abigail helped with the injured, she came across a maid. Her name was Minnie; Lady Arabella's maid. She told Abigail that there was another maid who needed help. We had not realized that you had managed to help the one she had mentioned escape at that time. Since the soldiers were dealing with the riot, Abigail called me to help. I hurried across the square and found you stuck on the church windowsill with Lady Arabella."

Adrian's eyes widened. "So, she was there? I thought I had imagined her."

Now things were lining up. Ari must have worried when he wasn't where she had left him and had gone to find him. The young housemaid must have found Ella after he had gotten her out. Relief spread through him at how things had managed to turn out. He turned to look at Mathew. Mathew had his worried face on. The one where he was trying to hide how bad it had become.

"How close was I?" Adrian asked.

Adrian sensed that he was going to give him a cheery, but less than honest, answer. Adrian stopped him with a raised eyebrow. Mathew bowed his head and, holding back how worried he had been, said, "It was close. You almost didn't make it. If we had not been nearby, you would have already been dead."

"Thank goodness you were, then. I assume that the two of you got close as you waited on me these past few months?" Adrian gave a breathy laugh at Mathew's blush and Abigail's nod. "You are just like a romance novel, but I'm happy for you."

Abigail smiled. "I think it would be better to discuss this after you are better."

With a smile, Adrian nodded in agreement.

"Your Highness?" Mathew spoke up. "I hesitate to mention this, but there is a guest here to see you. She apologizes that she did not send word ahead of her arrival, but she was worried that she would be refused. If you are not feeling your best, we can wait. Lady . . ."

At the first mention of a guest, Adrian's thoughts immediately fell to Ari, and he barely heard the rest of what Mathew said. He had been hoping to see her. After seeing his friend's adoration for each other, Adrian's own heart ached to see Ari. She had risked her life to save his. He had to see her. "Allow her in."

Standing, Mathew went to receive the guest. Abigail kept her set next to Adrian, keeping an eye on her patient. The guest Mathew brought in was not who he was expecting. His heart fell when he didn't see Ari, but his cousin Drina enter his room. Adrian motioned her forward, trying to not let his face show his disappointment. Drina looked from Adrian to the servants, making it obvious that she wished to speak with him alone as she did her greeting.

Adrian motioned for Mathew and Abigail to leave, and Mathew looked at him with concern. He knew that Mathew was worried about being kept in the dark again. Adrian learned his lesson. He would no longer leave them in the dark. They had proven themselves.

"I will talk to you after I speak to her first," Adrian told Mathew. Mathew hesitated, searching his face, then bowed and left. Abigail sat stubbornly in her chair. He was her patient. Adrian would be fine for a while, and he doubted that Drina would speak with her in the room.

"You can wait just outside the door in case anything goes wrong. I am feeling much better. Please, Abigail?"

She nodded reluctantly and left him to talk to his cousin alone. They had a lot to discuss.

After everyone had exited, Drina bowed her head. Her expressions had gone back to the proper lady that most people knew. But Adrian could see the spark in her brilliant blue eyes that others would miss. "I apologize for having to appear before you like this. I would not have violated protocol without a good reason."

Adrian smiled and motioned to the chair that Abigail had just vacated. "After surviving Bristol together, I will allow for the inconvenience."

With a genuine smile, she shook her head, remaining standing. She held his gaze. Adrian could only imagine what she saw: hair choppy from where it had burned, a skinny body ravaged from fevers, and a permanent wheeze emanating from his throat. Though instead of giving him a look of pity, she nodded, as if checking to make sure he was alive, and everything else was inconsequential.

"First, I would like to apologize for the behavior of my family. After everything they have done to you. I have no right to ask this, but would you be willing to allow me to take care of them?" Drina asked.

Watching Drina, he could see the determination from her straight back and eyes that locked on his. This was not the girl who had cowered from her family a few months ago. But he wasn't sure what she was referring to. "What do you mean 'take care of your family'? Do you think you are able to go against your own family? Do you even know what they were involved in?"

A single tear leaked from her eye as she kept her gaze locked on his. "They tried to kill you."

That information should have been more of a shock to him, but after everything that had happened, he wasn't surprised. Though he was surprised that she spoke so forwardly of it, considering what she was speaking of was treason.

"What do you have to say for yourself?"

Drina got down on her knees on the floor before him, making him embarrassed, and cried, "I know that is treason, but my mother is only being controlled by Conroy. I will make sure she will never make an attempt again or I understand that my life would be in forfeit."

"Considering that if she made the attempt again, I would be dead already," Adrian said, making an attempt at a joke. Drina kept her face bent to the ground as she continued her kneeling. Sighing, Adrian considered what she said. She truly was asking a great boon from him. Adrian couldn't know when another attempt on his life was to be made. And considering familial ties, he shouldn't even trust her. But after everything he did, no longer was this the girl who did everything she could to please her mother. No, this is a girl who would be queen. Adrian knew what he needed to do.

"Please get up. It would do no good for the next Queen Regnant to be on the floor."

Surprise filled her features, allowing her youth to shine through. "Your Highness?"

Adrian smiled as he told her his intentions, and she could only stand there in shock.

Chapter Fifty-Seven

1832 Clarence House

Ella thought facing Madame Briar would be the tensest meeting she would have to face. She was wrong. After spending a few weeks hiding inside the walls of the academy doing menial work, she received a summons from the prince. Ella had almost forgotten that she had promised to tell him everything. She had hoped he would have forgotten as well.

After reading Ella's complete report, Madame Briar had given her permission to tell him the basics of the Fan Society. Which made it all the more terrifying to speak to him. Previously, she could hide behind the Society's secrecy. But he had proven himself to be capable of handling their big secret, and he could now be a Friend of the Society.

Now she would have to face his questions, as well as her failure to protect him. Waiting before his door was like waiting for a death sentence. Ella was dressed in a dark green day dress. It was as close to black she could get without it being considered in mourning. And it was simple but for the black ribbon around her waist. She expected this would be the death of their relationship. This would be when she found out what he thought of her. All she should ask for was for forgiveness for all of her failures. Her heart ached at the thought that he would never want to see her again after this. She held back a tear as she waited for the well-deserved anger from Adrian.

The door opened, revealing Mathew, the one who had helped her with Adrian at the window ledge. She smiled in acknowledgment as he let her in. Adrian was propped up in bed. His radiant smile and the fact that he was sitting up released the tears she had been holding back.

"Are you okay?" he asked. He looked ready to get out of bed to go to her. Not wanting him to strain himself, she hurried over to stop him.

"Yes, Your Highness. I'm just glad to see you are looking better."

She looked down at his sickly pallor and stick-thin arms. He looked back at her, a question in his eyes. "Are you sure we are looking at the same thing?"

Ella couldn't help but laugh.

"Didn't I tell you not to call me 'Your Highness', but to call me Adrian?" he teased.

She could only blush. After the rush of emotion seeing him in person, talking and laughing, even if he told her to never see him again, she would be fine. All of the stress and tension she had been carrying around after the incident had been released. Adrian was alive. But even the rush of joy could not help the stabbing guilt she felt with every wheeze he breathed. He may have survived, but it had taken its toll.

She teased him back. "Of course, Your Highness. I will follow every order you give."

Instead of replying in a playful tone, however, he said, "It is time for you to tell me what exactly is going on."

She nodded, and at the motion of his hand, sat on the chair that was beside his bed. "First, my name is Arabella Cooper, but most of my family called me Ella."

"Your mother's name was Nora Cooper?" Adrian asked. For some reason, that name rang a bell in his memory, but after talking to Ari for several hours and in his weakened state, it was difficult to dredge up the memory that was needed. It was important, but he would have to find out another day.

Adrian gave into a massive yawn, and Ella gave a small bow to end the exchange. "I believe it is time for me to go, Adrian."

Desire and necessity warred with each other. He knew that his body couldn't take much more today, and so he nodded in acknowledgment. "I expect to hear more of this later."

The smile she gave him lit up the room as Mathew escorted her out. As that was happening, Abigail came in to check in on him. "I'll call the doctor to make sure you didn't strain yourself."

Adrian accepted her request, even though he hated when the doctor came in. It always reminded him of nearly dying, but if he didn't allow the doctor to visit, Abigail would only worry. Already his eyes were starting to droop as Abigail started to shut his door. That glimmer of something he had felt during his conversation with Ella forced his eyes open. He had something he needed to do before he slept. "While you are out, can you get Mathew for me? There is something I need to do."

She raised her eyebrow, showing her disapproval and concern with that one expression.

"I promise that it will not take long. Five minutes at most. Please, Abigail." Adrian begged.

"Yes, Your Highness."

It didn't take long for Mathew to return, as he was already on his way back.

"Mathew," Adrian said. "I need you to send a message to Lady Euphemia. There is something I need to speak to her about."

Drina gave me some information that needs to get to Ari, or I guess Arabella. Ella had made sure that I knew the truth of her family's circumstances, but only in a letter that I was required to burn. She has avoided any letter of mine. The only ones she couldn't avoid were the ones with the royal seal on them, but all return comments needed to be cryptic because of the sensitive nature of the topic. I need to see Ella. With this information, I hope she will be willing to come and speak to me.

    Diary of Crown Prince Adrian
    January 1832

Chapter Fifty-Eight

21 April 1832, Apsley House

The hall boy led the young gentleman through the house. His curious eyes kept glancing back at him, then, remembering his duty, he looked straight ahead. The boy's sleeve had a spot of jam from when he filched a pastry from the kitchen. The pastry that was almost hidden in his pocket. Ella held back a chuckle as she stayed in character as the young gentleman she was pretending to be.

Dressed in the corset that changed her shape to look more like a gentleman's figure, Ella wore a waistcoat over the top. Her mousy brown hair was tucked under a wig with much shorter hair and she wore a top hat. Ella disliked dressing up as a man. The wig was itchy, and there were fewer spaces to hide weaponry. Though, remembering her dunk in the river, the ensemble was less heavy than her skirts.

Sighing, Ella focused back on the task at hand. After that debacle at Bristol, and the prince, the Fan Society had decided that this would be her test. The Fan Society had put her back on active duty for this one mission. Seeing as how she had been the last person to contact the Duke of Wellington, she had been chosen to speak to him again. It was a test, and if she failed, who knew what the Fan Society would do with her?

The cheeky hall boy had directed her to the duke's office. Brushing at her jacket, Ella steeled her nerves.

While the duke had guessed that she was a girl in their previous encounter, it was decided that it would be better to keep her true identity a mystery. It was time to play her part. The Society had already sent him a message so he would know she would be coming, and so when the knock sounded on the door, she was immediately let in. The curly-topped hall boy gave her one last curious look before closing the door behind her.

Sitting on a small couch that seemed to be dwarfed by his size was the broad-shouldered duke. When she entered, he raised an eyebrow at her outfit but made no mention of it until he motioned for her to sit.

"Here we are again. Mister . . ." He left the question hanging, knowing it would have been proper for her to introduce herself. She smiled instead, letting his question hang unanswered. He inclined his head in acknowledgment and continued. "I believe I told you something about the prince, though I have yet to hear of his good health."

Guilt laced through her at that pointed comment. "Due to circumstances, he will not be returning to the public eye for quite some time."

He eyed her, mulling over her response. While he was thinking, there was a knock on the door, and a maid entered. The matronly woman pulled a tray from her cart and set out the tea. With military efficiency, she was soon done, and she slipped from the room as if she was never there.

Ella took a sip of her tea. "This is well made. My thanks."

The Duke acknowledged her with a nod and took a sip of his own tea. After a satisfying sip, he set the cup down and asked pointedly. "Why have you come here?"

Ella could feel the weight of his gaze. Though his voice was calm, she had a feeling that if she didn't answer the question to his satisfaction, this conversation would be a failure. Putting on her polite smile, she replied, "I was wondering if you have an interest in politics."

The Duke raised his brow at her, took another sip of his tea, and asked, "Why would an old man like me be interested in politics?"

Ella looked at his straight back and how his teacup seemed to be engulfed in his big hands. It was comedic that anyone viewed him as harmless. Taking one more sip to formulate an answer, she finally replied, "You are a man with very strong ideals. And you are not afraid to promote them, even if it means going against the grain. Sometimes that dedication has paid off, and other times . . ." she shrugged, leaving the unsaid words hanging in the air. Ella needed to keep him interested.

Watching her, the duke replied, "I don't know if you have noticed, but since my ill-begotten duel, I have not been in favor. Not to mention the vote of no confidence when I was voted for Prime Minister. The pull you are looking for may have to be found elsewhere."

Ella laughed outright, waving a dismissive hand. "That duel was a few years ago. No one cares about it anymore. And the Prime Minister position? That has to do with your policy of no reform. As you can see, over a hundred people were killed during the riots. This is an issue that people feel strongly about. People also felt quite strongly about the Catholic emancipation. And we all have seen where that has landed us," she said, reminding him of when he was able to push through a law that was heavily opposed. Ella could see that he was warming to her line of thinking. He only needed one more push, and she knew what would appeal to him.

"Would you be willing to take a gamble, Lord Wellington?" Ella asked.

He set his cup down and leaned forward. "What do you have in mind?"

Smiling inside, Ella knew she had caught his interest. Now she needed him to accept her terms. She set her tea down. "Have you ever thought about creating your own political party?"

We are calling this the days of May. The people are calling for action. They want the reform bill. Will the nobility allow their powers to be checked? Many people are getting active on the subject, including the Duke of Wellington, a war hero. The people, however, wouldn't even listen to him. They are even refusing to put their money into the banks. What will the crown do? How much longer are they going to allow this to continue? Or will there be another incident like the one in Bristol? We will find out during the next court date on . . .

Newspaper clipping from 7 May 1832
Unable to see byline or newspaper title.

Chapter Fifty-Nine

17 May 1832, Clarence House

Adrian had planned enough. After talking to Drina that day, they began meeting together regularly. They meticulously planned what he was going to say to his father. The only thing left now was to actually speak to him. Adrian was nervous, as his plans to talk to his father had never once gone well. But previously, he was acting like a whiney child. But today was different. He had faced the truth. Now it was time to help his father face it as well.

Adrian had wanted to wait to speak to the king until he could properly stand to talk to him, but due to the unrest and the decisions of the court recently, they had to take a risk and speak to him earlier than planned. Adrian needed all of his strength to speak to his father, and allowed himself to be wheeled down the corridor to his Father's office. Mathew spoke to Phillip, who went on to announce Adrian.

"Your Majesty, your son wishes to speak to you."

"Enter," the king boomed through the door.

Mathew helped Adrian to his feet and pulled the chair out of sight into the hallway. Before opening the door, Mathew whispered in Adrian's ear. "Good luck, young sir."

Nervousness made his breath short and his fingers curl. Adrian should be able to do this. He had survived a riot, as well as nearly being burned alive. He should be able to speak to his own father. Now, if only he could believe that his father was capable of changing his opinion.

Nodding to Mathew, Mathew opened the door so he could face his father.

The king was sitting at his desk, looking through the papers that the steward had delivered to him. As Adrian entered, his face beamed and he motioned for him to come in. "You still look horrible, son. Please sit."

Adrian shook his head and walked with a determined pace up to the desk. "No, thank you. I would rather stand. There is something that I need to talk to you about."

King William stacked his papers absentmindedly as he spoke to his son. "I'm glad that you are doing better, but maybe you should take things slowly. You had a rough time of it. Sit. It is better for you. I'm glad you are feeling well enough to come, but I worry that coming out this far can damage your health, especially since the fire."

Adrian held back his sigh. This was what his father did. He talked over everyone and paid no attention to what the people around him wanted, thinking that he knew best. But Adrian was not going to be like he was a year ago. Things had changed. He wasn't going to whine for his father's attention, nor was he going to yell at him. But he was not going to let his father ignore what he was going to say. With a firm voice, he interjected. "No, Father, we need to talk."

The king continued shuffling his papers. "Can it not wait until you are feeling better? I don't know why you went to Bristol, and I'm disappointed that the guards did not protect you. They have been disciplined. You don't have to worry about them."

"No, Father. We need to speak of the reform act."

It was as if the king had been struck by lightning. He paused his movement. "I have already told you that you don't need to worry about that. Concerning yourself with politics will destroy your body. Just let yourself recover."

Adrian's old frustration bubbled through him, that he was being sheltered so much. It was like going through the world blindfolded while being held hostage in a gilded cage. No, he was not a porcelain doll to be placed protectively in a China cabinet and never let out. This would not happen again.

"Father, I will *never* be healthy. That is why I need to speak to you."

Adrian's father truly looked at him for the first time. "What does your health have to do with the reform? You know nothing of politics."

"Only because you would never allow my teachers to teach me about it. All for fear that I would be overtaxed and cause my sickness to return. But I know, Father. I know what's going on. I was in the riots, and have heard the screams of the people. Have you?" Adrian asked.

The king's face turned red. "The people don't know how to rule themselves. That is why there is the nobility. We are meant to rule them. It's the duty of our birth."

In the past, when his father was in this mood, Adrian would normally just argue back. And his father would shut him down. When that happened, the conversation they needed to have would never take place. Today, Adrian was different. He had changed. And just as he had changed, so could his father change his own mind. Adrian just needed to show him.

"The French thought the same as well, Father. Look what happened to them. Remember the French Revolution?" Adrian asked. That stopped the king cold. Adrian continued before his father could interrupt, "Now is the time for change. The people are changing, and if we don't change with them, we will be swept away. The reform will not cause the nobility to fall to ruin. It will only allow it so that the people's voices will be heard. Is that so wrong?"

The red in his father's face had disappeared as quickly as it had come. Tension held Adrian still as his father looked him in the eyes.

"Do you really want to do this? These people were the ones who nearly killed you."

"They just want to be heard. Just as I wish to." The frustration of being told what was best for you without being heard was something Adrian understood all too well.

His father smiled. "You have changed so much. Maybe you should start taking over some of your princely duties."

Feeling a rush of accomplishment, Adrian couldn't stop a grin from growing. His father had finally acknowledged him. After everything, his father listened to him. But yet again, he would have to go against his father's wishes.

"That is the other thing I wish to speak about," Adrian said, reluctant to destroy the happiness he felt. "I wish to abdicate the throne."

"*What?*" his father boomed, standing and pounding his fist on the table. "You don't understand what will happen if you abdicate. I have kept you in the position you have been in to protect you. After everything I went through to keep you safe, the answer is no."

Adrian waited until his father's outburst subsided. They stared at each other, silent except for Adrian's whistling breath. Adrian wasn't angry at his father's outburst, nor was he cowering. He merely waited until his father sat back down. Then, unruffled, Adrian continued. "You are correct in saying that I know nothing of politics. I also have ill health. I also know that if I abdicate, people will still try to use me for their own means. That is why I propose a solution."

His father raised an eyebrow but didn't comment.

Taking that as agreement to speak, Adrian went on. "I propose that you should support my cousin Alexandria as queen. Before you say anything, yes, I do agree that her mother is a problem. But Drina knows this and will keep her from causing too much trouble. I saw Drina during the riot, Father. She was brave and intelligent. She was willing to do what needed to get done within her capabilities."

The king sat back, rubbing his face. "That could work. I do like Drina despite hating that wretch of a mother. But then it comes back to the problem that people will still try to take advantage of you."

This was the part Adrian had been leading up to. Knowing that he would never be the prince was what the people needed, this was what he needed to do. But if the people knew he was of royal blood, they would try to turn him into a puppet. He would not allow that to happen. Adrian thought long and hard about what he wanted, and he had a solution.

"Fake my death. People already believe that I would drop dead at any moment. Give me a new name, and I will pretend to be someone else. The people never really saw me. And after being away for the last few months, most have forgotten me anyway. You can support Drina when she comes of age, and no one can use me against her."

His father's face was stern, and Adrian could almost hear his jaw clenching. Looking back into Adrian's eyes, the king sighed. "Are you sure this is what you want?"

Relief spread through Adrian. His father would honor his request.

Adrian nodded. "Yes, it is."

"We will have to think this through a bit more thoroughly, but this is the first time I have seen you like this."

"Actually, there is one more thing I want to ask you about."

Letting out a belly laugh, his father said, "Oh? There's more?"

Smiling, Adrian spoke to him about helping Ari.

Chapter Sixty

June 1832, Clarence House

Ella had received a message from Adrian to attend a meeting with the king. Confused at what the king could want from her, but unable to refuse, she made her way to Clarence House. What she had arrived to was not what she had been expecting. Instead of an interrogation of her actions that she thought would happen, she was instead brought into the private office of the king and was told to stand to the side. After a few moments of curiously waiting, her stepfamily arrived. It was then that Ella found out that she had been called in for the hearing of her stepfamily. Left to view the proceedings from the side of the room, Ella could only watch as the king recited what Lady Victoria and her stepdaughters had been brought in for.

Ella didn't know what to feel as she watched her stepmother and stepsister Audrey kneeling on the ground, dressed in their finest. Their dumfounded looks made her want to laugh, but it would have been improper, so she kept her smile hidden behind her fan. Euphemia flicked her eyes towards Ella, then gritted her teeth and stared at the ground. This was a rather odd proceeding, considering she was allowed to be here. Another thing that was odd was that the prince was strangely absent. She had thought he was doing better, but she hadn't seen him. Ella's heart fell as she continued to watch the proceedings.

The king brought forth evidence of Lady Victoria using too much money and skimping on her taxes. "What do you have to say for yourself?"

"Your Majesty," her stepmother pled. "Since the death of my husband, I have had a hard time finding help with the finances. If anything is wrong, I would be happy to pay. Things have been difficult for a woman taking care of her daughters. I'm so sorry this is all very odd."

Lady Victoria did a beautiful job looking pitiful as she spouted half-truths and lies. Ella was confused about where this was all going. Normally, there wouldn't even need to be a hearing for this type of crime. And Ella still didn't know why she had been called to be present.

"This proceeding has been kept confidential because I didn't think you would want it publicized . . . for the sake of your daughter," the king said with a raise of his brow.

"I always think of my daughters, your majesty. It greatly pleases me that you would keep this out of the public's eyes for their sake. But pardon me for my impropriety. I would not have wanted to take so much time out of your busy day. Would not a letter have been sufficient?"

King William, who had kept his expression controlled the entire proceeded, now pinned Lady Victoria in her place with a burning stare. "A letter would have sufficed if that was the only thing that had been wrong." He held out his hand to Phillip, who handed him another report. The king read out loud every way that they mistreated Ella. A report that sounded like it had been written in Euphemia's own hand. Ella was starting to get a better understanding of why she had been called here.

The king continued. "Considering the only reason I allowed you to keep your title was due to my friendship with Baron Cooper and for respect to all that he had done for the crown. I allowed you to keep the title to help take care of his daughter. Is this what you call taking care of her?"

The innocent smile Ella's stepmother had kept on her face faltered. "Your Majesty, I was only trying to teach the girl about hard work and. . ." Her arrogant stepmother, seeing the king's expression, stopped mid-sentence and bowed her head, though Ella could see her hands go white from gripping her dress.

Audrey pipped in. "But what about me marrying the prince?"

Ella had to stifle her laughter when Lady Victoria elbowed her daughter, hissing, "Be quiet, you stupid girl."

"But I didn't do anything other than what you told me. I did nothing wrong." Audrey stated.

Lady Victoria turned to the king and apologized profusely.

Looking at the king, Ella could see a gleam in his eye as he looked on the proceedings. "Shut your daughter's mouth or your punishment will be greater."

His heavy gaze silenced them more thoroughly than his words.

"Now, then. At the behest of someone I care about, this has been kept private. After everything that has been going on with the unrest, it would be best that this not be announced. But for the crimes you have committed, the title and lands that were so graciously bestowed upon you will be relinquished."

At each of his words, her stepmother's face got paler until she was as white as a sheet. Audrey looked around in a daze, confused. But Euphemia appeared unconcerned by what was unfolding before her.

But the king had not finished. "The lands will be held for Lady Cooper until she bears an heir."

Shock ran through Ella. Emotions tumbling over themselves, each wanting to be in the forefront of her mind. Her father's title would be kept in her family's line. It would no longer be in the hands of her horrid stepmother. Then questions of who had done this for her popped through her head. Did the prince do this for her? Why? What was she going to do now?

"But she has been sentenced as a slave for trying to push my sister down the stairs. She would be unable to obtain the lands." Audrey stated, folding her arms and shrugging.

The king silenced her with a look, and spoke. "I already know what has become of that child, and she, indeed, will be the inheritor of the title and lands." The king had had enough of her stepfamily and waved them away. "You shall leave."

Audrey and Lady Victoria could only sit in silence as the guards dragged them away. Euphemia showed her noble side as she stood, and with her head held high, walked out without resistance, with only one final look at Ella as she left.

Ella waited to be dismissed, but instead, everyone else in the room was dismissed. The king motioned her closer. Ella did as was commanded. Keeping her head bowed, stood before him. She gave him the appropriate curtsey. "Your Majesty."

She waited for him to answer, but Ella only felt the pressure of his eyes on her. His presence was so big it filled the room, that it made the silence suffocating.

"Lady Cooper, I hear you have gained my son's heart." the king said, breaking the silence.

"I beg your pardon, Your Majesty?" Her heart fluttered at the mention of Adrian. He said that Adrian loved her? After everything, she still couldn't believe it. She had to refrain from using her fan to hide her blush as she tried to put things together.

His belly laughter filled the room. "You should come in, my son."

A door on the side of the room opened to reveal Adrian. He was doing much better than the time she last saw him. His too skinny arms had filled out, and he was walking toward her. But the thing that didn't change was the kindness in his eyes as he neared. Giving her a bow, he said, "My lady."

His words still held a whistle in them, proving that he was not at his best, and would never be. But she could only ask, "Did you do this, Your Highness?"

Adrian only smiled as King William spoke, a grin still splitting the king's face. "Come, sit. We have much to talk about."

The king clapped his hands as a servant entered and placed chairs for them, Adrian's chair next to hers, which was odd, but she wouldn't complain. She could only hold some semblance of decorum as she tried to avoid Adrian's gaze, knowing full well if she looked at him, she would not stop blushing. Adrian had no such compulsion. She could feel his gaze throughout the conversation as the king explained his son's desires.

As the king explained what Adrian wanted to do, she had to refrain from letting her jaw drop. Wanting to fake his death and renounce his claim to the throne?

"What do you think?" the king asked her, as she was still gathering her thoughts.

"Your Majesty, it would be improper for me to give my thoughts on something of this magnitude. I would be incapable of going against the wishes of the throne, but I do wonder what is going to happen with His Highness."

The king laughed at her words. "You speak eloquently, just as a wife should. I can see why my son likes you. Though this is being done rather inappropriately, but considering the circumstances, this is as much as I can do. Would you be willing to marry my son? Of course, that would mean that you would not be marrying a prince, and you would have to keep his identity a secret. But having a wife to care for his needs would make my heart feel at ease."

Shock at those words filled her, and she turned to Adrian. His smile was so charming, and as she thought about it, his words had merit. And wasn't her original mission to marry Adrian? He wasn't a prince. But with Princess Alexandria in line for the throne, there was no need to marry the prince. And since she would be in the know about the prince's situation, if Ella marries the prince, she would have a connection to the next in line. As Clementine would say, your mission can give you happiness, too.

"If Your Majesty would accept one such as me, I would be honored to accept this proposal." As she said this, her heart felt light, and now that the worries that had kept her from Adrian were no longer weighing her down, she felt as if she could accept his feelings. It was impossible to keep a blush and a smile from her face, and Adrian reacted in kind.

The king rested in his chair with a knowing smile, then, clapping his hands on the table, summoned the servants in. "We will be discussing the specifics later, but for now, it was a pleasure to meet you, Lady Arabella."

Ignoring societal rules, he swept away from the room, giving her and Adrian time alone. Some servants entered the room, making it so some things could not be said. But Adrian stood and held his hand out to help her up. "My fiancé, I hope this helps you."

Keeping a pleasant smile on her face, she made sure not to react to the paper he slid into her hand. "I'm sure it will, my lord."

Hiding the paper, she allowed herself to be escorted by her new fiancé.

Chapter Sixty-One

June 1832, The Academy

In the hidden office at the academy, Ella stood before Madame Briar. After reporting what had transpired, as well as relaying the message that she had received from Adrian, she waited in anticipation. Adrian's information gave her hope. But for now, Ella could only look at the Fan Society symbol that was engraved on the wall as she stood in anticipation. Holding back a sigh, she could only hope the headmistress would read faster.

Madame Briar didn't give anything away as she read over what the prince had given her. Ella was starting to think that she liked giving no reactions so that her students would be trained to deal with tension.

Finally, Madame Briar sat up in her chair, eyeing Ella with consideration. "What do you think of this information?"

"Considering the source of information, I believe that this information is correct. Can we get her back?" Ella asked her last question, almost a plea. The prince had given her information on her mother. Drina had found out some information on Conroy and shared it with the prince. In it were some pages of slaves that he owned. One of them was her mother. At the sight of her mother's name, the hope that she would find her blossomed anew.

Giving her a warm smile, Madame Briar said, "Yes, my dear. I think we can." Before Ella could jump in, she held out a warning finger. "But it will take some planning. We can't just send someone over there to break her out. With the reform now being passed, we can use this momentum and push for better anti-slavery laws. That way, it keeps anything we do out of the limelight, understand? We will send her word as soon as possible. Your mother is strong. If she has lasted this long, she can last a little bit longer. I will have your word that you will follow my orders on this."

Her happiness fell as she understood Madame Briar's words. But after everything that had happened because she failed to do as ordered, she knew not to push it. Ella nodded. "I promise."

"Now, on a happier note, how do you feel about the prince?"

It only took a moment for Ella to react to the change of conversation. Madame Briar was known for it, and Ella answered with no reservation. "The prince is very kind-hearted. He has no prejudices, nor concerns for class. He was naive when I first met him but has grown considerably. He was also able to handle shocking information rather well and is willing to learn. And he forgave me."

Giving her a polite smile, Madame Briar spoke again "I must have misspoken. Do you have feelings for him?"

In an instant, her cheeks were aflame. Though the stone room was muggy, Ella could not blame the heat on her cheeks on the weather. Knowing she couldn't hide it, she nodded.

"Did you know your mother told me the same things about your father when I asked her that same question?"

Shaking her head, she drank in the information of her parents. Ella had known that marrying her father was her mother's mission.

And from her memories, she had known that they loved each other, but to have her say what Ella had been hoping made her feel closer.

Pulling open a drawer, Madame Briar pulled out a narrow box and handed it to her. Ella opened it and gasped in surprise. It was her mother's fan that she had left behind in the riot. It was no longer stained from its ordeal in Bristol, but was now a pristine white. With a gentle hand, Ella lifted it out of the box, and rubbed her thumb across its embroidered Fan Society symbol. Looking up to Madame Briar, Ella asked, "How?"

"You really should thank Clementine. She trusted that everything would turn out for the best and sent it to me. She told me that the mission would happen, and so it has. She also said that you are a better than the person I thought you were, and she had proven herself right. You have gone above what was expected of you. You have passed your test and have become a full member of the Society." Madame Briar then passed her a ring bearing the symbol of the Fan Society.

"Even with all of my mistakes. She even was in danger because of me." Ella said, not reaching for the ring.

"Clementine said she was happy that you trusted her to do her job and disappointed that she had failed you. Now that you know you made a mistake, do better." Madame Briar continued to hold out the ring.

Ella held out her hand as Madame Briar slipped it on. The weight of what had just happened felt inadequate for the tiny room. But before she could continue to admire her ring, Madame interrupted her ogling. "Now, it is time to get to work. With the help of your people, we need to look into the cause of the riots, as well as keep an eye on Viscount Edmund. Also, we need to find the organization that this Fox character comes from. Are you ready?"

Holding her fan, and feeling the weight of the ring, Ella looked into Madame Briar's face and replied, "I'm ready."

Year 2000, Academy

The archeologist sat amidst the papers covered by dust and hidden for years behind a wall. He made sure his gloves were securely on his hands and his hair was tucked under a hat. It would be bad if his hair or other oils from his skin got on these delicate pages. Taking his time, he flipped through the papers before packing them away to keep it from crumbling more. As the man sifted through, the more his excitement grew. To think that this had been hidden for hundreds of years, only to be recovered by the renovation of this old building. Upon the latest finding, he found a strange marking of a dagger and serpents intertwining them.

One of the police officers stepped to the opening in the wall and stopped to look at the engraved fan in a circle of eyes on the wall. She had been the one to liaison with the museum for the security of the artifacts.

"This is one of the greatest finds in history, if what I'm reading is correct. This goes against what we currently know about in history. And all of the information in this time was controlled by a secret society," the archeologist said excitedly, being careful not to touch anything while he was emotional. It would be bad to destroy his discovery in his excitement. He placed the final paper in the box. An emblem with twin snakes and a dagger stabbed through them was on the top paper.

With great care, he picked up the box that he had packed with papers and books and passed it to the gloved officer. The officer was well versed in handling artifacts and had helped him on more than one occasion.

"Will you help bring this to the car so it can be shipped to the museum? I can't wait till they see this! Be very careful so they are stored out of the sunlight."

The police officer nodded, and the man went back to packing more boxes of artifacts. She headed down the stone steps to the car parked in front, then gently set the box in the back of a van. She next took off her gloves and tucked them in her belt as she wiped her brow in the afternoon sun. The light glinted off her ring. A ring that had a circle of eyes with an open fan in the center.

About the Author

Dasha Tryon Wallace

Dasha Tryon Wallace is a mother of a very active son. With her husband, they live in the middle of nowhere with their dog in a small town. She loves practicing martial arts, which may have had an influence in the fighting style in the book.

Dasha is an avid reader and librarians have had a hard time keeping her well-stocked with new material. Her friends at school always wondered why she was reading more than one book at a time and how she could tell where she was at in each book.

With so many interests, she is more than capable of engaging in conversation with everyone, much to the dismay of her untalkative husband. This is the second book she has written, and she has plans for many more. You can find out more about her and her upcoming books at www.dashawallace.com.

www.ingramcontent.com/pod-product-compliance
Lightning Source LLC
Chambersburg PA
CBHW032145190726
48290CB00005BB/1421